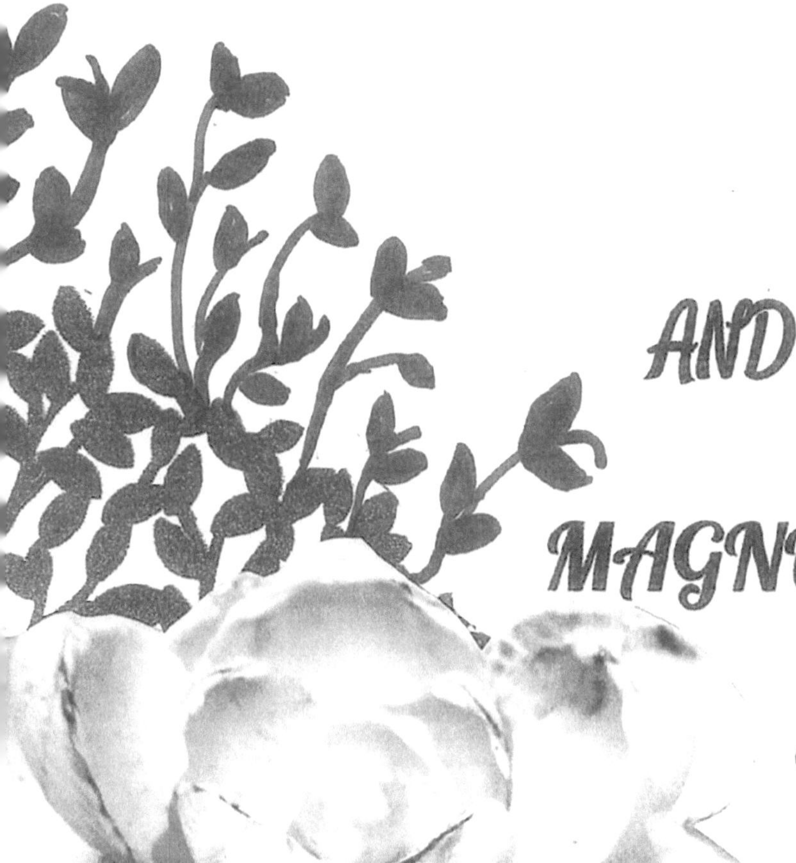

AND THE MAGNOLIAS WERE IN BLOOM

TELA DAWSON

Kravitz and Sons LLC
204 E Arlington Blvd. Suite B
Greenville, NC 27858

Published by Kravitz and Sons LLC.

ISBN: 979-8-89639-388-7 (sc)
ISBN: 979-8-89639-387-0 (e)

AND THE MAGNOLIAS WERE IN BLOOM

TELA DAWSON

KS

Kravitz & Sons
PUBLISHING, MARKETING AND ADVERTISING

To families everywhere

To all who love life even when tough times come—
you take it in stride and decide to forge forward
Victories are forever, no matter how long it takes
We will win!

Then leave memories for a lifetime to come and
share dreams that will always bring life
and love and a legacy of family

To family, I salute you

FOREWORD

I love to eat. This book is like a bowl of ice cream or a candy bar. You just can't put it down.

One page and then another.

It is sweet to the imagination. History comes alive, full of emotions. It is pure adventure and depicts the importance of family.

It contains lessons for real people, how to get through tough times, and the trials and victories in everyday life.

It is a must read. A gem.

Such a great story, it should be made into a movie.

I search for oil and drill oil wells. In my opinion, this story is a discovery that will make a billion barrels of oil.

Success.

Gary James

Table of Contents

CHAPTER 1

River Bend

THE CHILDREN GATHERED around their great-grandmother. Abigaile Amelie Hurley was matriarch and owner of the River Bend Plantation.

She walked slowly because of her age.

She told stories for many years of how River Bend came to be.

She would start out with a prayer. She asked God to help her to remember all the special times of her youth. Truth and accuracy were her desire.

Grandma would begin her stories with the words, 'And the magnolias were in bloom," referring to the time she met Mr. Hurley, our grandfather.

This is her story.

*****

I was a very young girl when Mr. Hurley came to my parents' house. I saw him. He was my dream, my hope, my love. I was only thirteen, and all grown up in my mind.

He said hello, and my knees buckled. I felt a surge of electricity enter my body. I almost fell. From that moment, I knew he would be mine.

He was twenty-three, so he would have to wait until I turned sixteen. A mere ten years older. I just knew he was the one.

He would ask for my hand in just three years. It was going to be my dream, and it would come true.

Dear ones, my daddy asked Mr. Hurley to join us regularly for dinner.

My heart raced each time he rode up to our house. It was small and simple, next to our dry goods store. He did business with my daddy, but I knew he wanted to see me. It was a gift to me every time he came. I sat next to him every time he visited us.

Weeks and months passed, and I had another birthday. I was fourteen now. I had only two more birthdays to go, and my Mr. Hurley could seek me as his soon-to-be wife. I so hoped he felt the same, but he never encouraged me.

Dinners and desserts. The plans to sit beside my dream continued.

*****

"Children, my sweet children, listen to me. Never give up hope, for without hope your heart will grow sick," Abigaile, our dear great-grandmother repeated. "Never give up." And then she continued her story.

"I had two more birthdays, and the beauty of my Southern youth shone, signs of a beautiful magnolia in full bloom. I was pretty with eyes of green and hair of gold. A peachy glow was on my face, and I faced once again my Mr. Hurley."

"How did he know to wait for you, Grandma?"

"I really don't know, but it could only be the hand of God that could blossom a love as deep as your grandpa and I had. I still remembered my heart was filled with excitement. Would this be the time I was waiting for? My sixteenth birthday was a treasure to behold. Family and friends brought gifts that filled our small entry table and overflowed to the chairs that graced our town house. But I did not see my Mr. Hurley. Was he coming? My heart sank, and the day was over. I cried all night and asked God why. But no answer. All my years of waiting were lost, I thought.

I fell asleep, and the morning sun peeked through my glass curtains. My heart was broken.

Well, I would have to go on. All my hopes and dreams were lost, or so I thought.

And then it happened. I heard a horse whinny, and the sound of hooves upon the brick road in front of our store. I was quick to jump up and peer out of my bedroom window.

Children, it was my Mr. Hurley, your great-grandfather.

He was trying to be respectful of my youth and my party, but he said he could wait no longer. We had a special bond that he never had with any other. He said I was his from the beginning, and he told my daddy of his love for me from the moment he saw me. He asked for my hand.

I was delighted, and my daddy gave him my hand in marriage.

Before my next birthday, I was Mrs. Abner Darnell Hurley. We were so in love. Your grandfather was so special.

We lived above my parents' store, and my Abner began his quest for his dream.

He wanted to build me his dream land and a beautiful house for his true love and his hoped-for family.

Grandpa Hurley worked very hard. We both did. I tended my daddy's store, and together we built River Bend. Acre by acre, we added to our dream. In time, it reached over two thousand acres. Hard work and love. That is how we did it.

Your great-uncles were born, and life was good. Then it happened; war between our states had divided families and friends. We arranged our lives to help those in need.

Children, remember to bless all who are in need. Someone needs a hat, offer them yours.

Abigaile Amelie was a person who desired to help, no matter who it was. But war took a toll on her outlook. And now Abigaile Amelie Hurley had left a story of life and love and family. A story of the land and the treasures that it can produce.

Our young country had been through so many ups and downs, she said.

Our country's youth had seen new frontiers to conquer. Savage attacks of man against man, different colors and creeds, and fights over land ownership. There were new inventions in communication and transportation, not that of horses but of wheels. Brighter, shinier wheels, she continued. When the war came to Georgia, our River Bend Plantation was under attack. As it was with almost all the Southern states.

Men would arrive and demand food for them and their horses.

We tried to help, but more was asked of us than we were comfortable giving.

After they left River Bend, we gathered our ruby and cobalt crystals and hid them beneath the floorboards of the great dining room and the ballroom where parties took place.

In those days, when the weather was too warm outside, we retreated inside, where the great windows were opened, and the tall ceilings carried the heat away.

Our home had crimson velvet drapes with glass curtains that framed each of the walk-through windows. It was a beautiful, inviting place that called all of us to enjoy.

Now after we hid our stemware, we took our Silver and China and divided them into four stacks. All the sterling silver flatware in one stack and sterling silver trays (large and small) in another. Our hand-painted China was wrapped in cotton, and that made up another stack.

How many more stacks? Dear ones, there was only one more stack! What was in that stack?

Jewelry was in the fourth stack. All my wedding jewels and those of my grandmother, my namesake.

We carried them out and placed them, stack by stack, into deep holes dug at each corner of the River Bend house, twenty paces from each corner, and we placed these things of value carefully down these four-foot holes. We covered them and put leaves on top to make it appear like the other parts of the grounds.

We lived with much less and longed for the days of war to be over. Four years had passed.

And then the sun came up, and the war of the States was over. Our boys were coming home, our friends and family members.

There was one thing that we all wanted to remember and forget at the same time. War— civil war—was a poison pill we all had to swallow.

The years have passed when brother fought against brother, and the lands burned with hate and disappointment.

It was 1868 and a time that revealed a country healed. Brothers existed side by side. No more North, no more South. We were united again, harmony among states and families.

A new generation of Northerners and Southerners were born. Time, children, is almost over, Abigaile would say.

From Texas to Kentucky, the fields were ready for new crops, and old and new towns ready for new businesses and unity among the families of old. Blessings to share.

The stories of our grandparents were remembered by young gentlemen and young ladies, passed on to the next children of gentler times. Family history was in the making once again.

And history was in the making no matter who you were. The stories of River Bend Plantation were history: stories of love, loss, and victories.

The story of love never stopped. For down the road from River Bend Plantation, there was another plantation, not nearly as large, but also noted for the fine crops it grew. Cotton was its main harvest, and indigo was a second crop that seemed to produce about the same dollar in about half the space. Indigo yielded a blue dye used in fine chinaware and fabrics to produce the rich hues of summer. Intense to soft, its colors were like that of morning glories and the finest sapphires from Kashmir, India. It ranged from corn flower to rich royal blue. It was a crop that grew quickly, making it very profitable, and could be harvested each month.

At Willow Oaks Plantation, the tales of how it came to be were just as impressive as those of River Bend Plantation. A young man with dreams of wealth, land, and family. A new family with whom one day he might share his dreams. Children; perhaps a beautiful young girl who would turn every young man's head and rival the beauty of a finished piece of jewelry, with pearls and fine diamonds, that work Manship of his maker. And a boy or two to carry on that name, his legacy, the Butler name. This young love waited for years, and Mr. Butlers hopes and dreams of family seemed to elude him.

But like a plant that must germinate and show itself to the sun, it takes time to develop.

So, it was for Mr. Aaron Jeffery Poe Butler. With hard work and money earned, his dream began to take shape. But no love yet.

His first of many forty-acre plots of ground were his.

His daddy would always tell him that "hard work and a lot of determination can only bring success." Mr. Butler was sure that God would not leave him alone and barren of family. So onward and upward. His hard work continued. A gathering of young men and Southern ladies hap penned each Sunday after church, a picnic on church grounds and an afternoon tea for the beaus and debutants. They practiced all the manners and polite conversations taught them by their elders. It was there at one of the spring picnics where Mr. Aaron Jeffery Poe Butler met a beauty he could not describe. Her beauty was mesmerizing. Hair of gold and blue eyes, petite in size and a smile that made her face shine like the sun.

His heart stopped, and he could not gather the nerve to just say hello.

Each Sunday passed by, and the picnics invited all eligible men and young belles to join in.

The picnics of summer were coming to a close. Mr. Aaron Jeffery Poe Butler had gathered his composure and decided this would be the day. The day where his admiration and desire would meet.

He took a deep breath and approached his beauty. It seemed like a hundred miles until he reached her. She began to walk toward Mr. Buffer. You see, she had also been too shy to say hello to him.

New respect and a deep love had begun to grow from the first time they shared a picnic basket.

Miss Delilah Grace Willingham had met him halfway, and their eyes met.

She was overcome with pure fear. Never in her life had she been so forward. But the fear left her the moment he smiled. He offered his hand to her, and they strolled down a long pathway lined with magnolia trees and weeping willows.

Mr. Butler was so taken in by the beauty of Miss Delilah that he failed to see the trees.

The same trees that graced his land, his Willow Oaks.

As the cool breeze crossed their path, the polite con versation turned to the topic of hopes and dreams. His hopes. His dreams. It was from that moment Miss Delilah fell in love.

A man with vision and dreams and a love for God. She saw a man committed to his belief in hard work and the blessing of God. Her heart melted, and history was in the making. Months had passed, and wedding bells were ringing.

Wedding, China, crystal, and silver—lots of silver—were bestowed upon this gentle young couple, all the finery that a Southern couple would need to entertain small intimate groups or large crowds.

Mr. Butler and Miss Delilah were joined in holy matrimony on Christmas Day, a celebration of the birth of Jesus and the new birth of love between the two.

Mr. Butlers dream had many parts, and his new bride was just the beginning.

Willow Oaks was beginning to blossom with new life. Soon their love gave birth to that Southern little belle he had prayed for. She had piercing blue eyes and golden hair that shone like the sun, just like her momma.

His heart was full. He had never known such happiness. Her love and a child had changed his whole world. God had answered his prayers.

This man, Mr. Butler, was respected by so many. Younger gentlemen tried to emulate him, and older men of great accomplishments admired this man of God who was, it seemed, successful at everything he touched.

A new wind was blowing through a state that was almost a hundred years old. Planters and plantation owners were not in short supply. The fields were covered with rich, dark soil, and water flowed through all the lands.

It was a land rich in minerals that enhanced their crops with beauty unsurpassed.

Magnolia trees seemed to perfume the air, and great sturdy oaks shaded their streams. Weeping willows were everywhere along the creeks and roadsides, wherever water was standing after the rains.

It was a countryside where beauty bloomed and dreams came true—dreams of ownership, lands, and a beautiful family to share in the history that was in the making.

Mr. Butler was a man of character and vision. These were the traits a new city was looking for.

Meetings with men of all ages and plans for statehood started this way. The question-and-answer sessions were helping these men of destination formulate a plan. What plan? I didn't know, but the challenge intrigued him.

They wanted me to be the mayor of a new town that would bear my name.

I never believed in myself, but others did. I accepted the challenge, and my name became a town men flocked to with dreams and hopes for a new life. A life of victories and hopes for new love.

This new city had all the markings of Southern gentility: a library, school, and lumberyard, a blacksmith and stables, and a dry goods store that featured the nearby plantation's tobacco and indigo dye, the dye that all the ladies used in their hand-painted China. The store also stocked cottonseed and hand-forged tools, new lines of fabric shipped from

Europe, and a few guns—the 1846 Colt Walker, the pocket revolvers, and the Kentucky rifle.

All the important items of the day.

Mr. Buder was blessed again and again with the admiration of the townsfolk, and Miss Delilah was to bless her love with one more child, a child who was a carbon copy of his daddy. Flaming red hair and brown eyes, a sturdy little body and ruddy complexion.

As a new daddy, the buttons on his jackets were popping off. One gorgeous little girl and now a son. God has blessed me.

My town is growing, and my family also. My plantation is producing quality products, and our prayers are truly being answered.

For ten years, Mr. Butler and his family enjoyed the fruits of their hard work.

And then Georgia was plagued by the war. The Civil War. The war of brother against brother. It was a stink that covered our land. The land we worked so hard for.

Young men of different ages were caught up in a cause, the cause of the South, where a life with certain amenities were being threatened.

Household help and workers in the field were running away for a freedom they thought they didn't have.

But like River Bend Plantation, Willow Oaks cared for their people. They were treated with respect and given a place to live and all the food they wanted. Unlike some of their neighbors.

Unlike the consensus of opinion, Mr. Butler and Mr. Hurley believed in the Bible, and it said to love all.

And the proof was in the pudding. Almost all their helpers stayed and kept these places that would one day tell a story of love for all who lived there.

And so, it was the war came to an end. But it would take years before the fields would live again.

But it didn't discourage our Mr. Buder or Mr. Hurley. It simply made them more determined.

The holes that hid the plantation's treasure were uncovered. Silver and China found its way back into the Butler pantries, and the jewelry that once graced our grand mother's body came out of hiding. The leaded glassware was carefully brought up from the floorboards where they had lain in wait for five years.

Parts of the walk-through windows needed replacement, and the rugs that covered the cypress floors were not fit for use. Dirt, dust, and blood were signs left from the trauma our South had endured.

But now, from Texas to Kentucky, the fields were ready for new crops, and the towns opened for the peoples of the North and South to develop new family ties and stories that would become a history all could be proud of. Something and someone to bless and not tear down. The North and the South would rise again.

Stories, family stories, handed down from generation to generation.

Young gentlemen and young ladies could and would regularly gather their elders and hear the tales of former ways of life, love, and war.

The story was always the same, but they were not able to comprehend how one day, in their fixture, they would be enlightening the children on the details of their life, their love, and how God was there in all the trials and troubles of their lives.

And the generations of Butlers and Hurleys continued. But to everyone's surprise, the two families never met. Their beloved lands were never joined to make one very large, wealthy plantation.

There were always sons born to the owners of Willow Oaks and River Bend plantations. The beautiful Southern belles were courted by other gentlemen from different plantation owners.

Ergo the plantations retained family ownership. The daughters became ladies of different plantations, and the Southern way continued.

Families built new homes, and life for the next generation was good.

But the memories of war and lost loved ones were not easy to forget.

Pictures of lost family members and lands were, it seemed, a constant reminder of the pains of the South. But it was unheard of for generations to consider that their loss was mirrored in the North as well.

So many bumps in the road for both the North and the South.

Millions of wounded soldiers and plantation workers were homeless and hungry, and lawlessness abounded. Homes were burned. Fields lay in ruin, and the crops had no workers, no one to plant and no one to harvest.

The prewar social order was virtually lost.

With no money to pay for skilled labor, the art of sharecropping and tenant farming became the new norm.

Mr. Butler had developed a dry goods store prior to the war and found it could prosper again by selling needed items to the sharecroppers.

But his store went against the norm. Goods were available to all at a no-interest cost, something that was looked upon by others as an unwise practice.

But Mr. Butler was a man of God, and he loved his fellow man and offered the same deal to all.

He always said God would take care of all his needs, no matter what they were.

He seemed to be the square peg that his fellow countrymen were trying to round off. But he stood his ground.

It was Gods way or the highway. He would not rear range his moral code for dollar increases.

For the years that followed the war and the generations to come, this family never ran out of food or was at a loss for anything. God had honored and promoted this man His way.

So much time had passed before the Civil War, and now the next decades began.

Great-grandparents, grandparents, parents, and children have all inherited a past, a past of family heroes and those members of questionable character.

But those who weathered the bumps in the road of life left a legacy, a legacy of honor, a legacy of victories due to hard work and love that transcended the pages of time, not just love of family but a love of God and His commands.

CHAPTER 2
A New Chance

THIS COUNTRY HAD healed its wounds. The conflict of brother against brother was no more.

The North and South seemed to be reunited as one. A United States. It was a new generation, where the war of the states was no more, and we were all excited about the new opportunities that were unfolding before us.

Harmony was our byword. We had been reborn as a nation. Our money had taken on a new motto. "In God We Trust." This was an open acknowledgment of our blessings. But it wasn't until 1955 that our paper money carried that message.

The weather was warm, and as was the norm, we all retreated under the tall ceilings of our homes, our River Bend home, where the war of the states had left us as we were at the beginning.

Our needs were many, but they always seemed to be met.

Great-Grandma Abigaile would gather her grandchildren together and begin her stories once again.

She would always pray and seek requests from her grandbabies. "Tell us everything, Grandma!"

Requests were received, and Miss Abigaile began.

"It was my fourteenth birthday"

"Yes, Grandma, tell us more."

Her wrinkled face was smiling now, and she began, "I was fourteen, and your Grandpa Hurley was joining our family for dinner."

I was a young girl with hopes and dreams. And Mr. Hurley was my new dream. He was so handsome, flaming red hair and broad shoulders. He looked like a big red headed Adonis, a Greek god to my eyes.

He was twenty-four, and I was fourteen. My eyes glazed over, and I was blinded by love.

All he had to do was wait for me until I was sixteen. The years passed by so slowly, but my love grew with each visit. My prince charming was waiting for me! I was hoping that he cared for me like I cared for him. Yet he never uttered a word, not a word, until my sixteenth birthday. He asked my daddy for my hand in marriage. I was living my dream. My Mr. Hurley would be mine.

"Yes, Grandma, go on."

"Time to stop and give me a rest. I will tell you more tomorrow."

Tomorrow could not come quickly enough. It was a story that we had heard many times before, but she always seemed to divulge a little more of history with each story time.

"Grandpa Hurley and I were inseparable. We loved each other, very much. We worked hard, and River Bend was ours. And in time, it will be y all's. Grandpa said I was his from the first time he saw me. He was such a gentleman. Southern charm and real handsome. His red hair was curly and hung down to his broad shoulders. He was mine!"

The children heard her repeat her story over and over. What was wrong? Grandma fell to the floor; we were unable to revive her. The doctor was called, and we were waiting what seemed like hours. But the crisis was over. Grandma had not eaten and had fainted as a result. From that moment, forward, we had snacks for Grandma at every story time.

Life was fast-forwarding, and the young ones who sat by Abigaile were growing up, growing up with hopes of their true loves finding them. Two boys and one girl. They were next in line to take over River Bend after their par ents were no more. Grandmas' namesake, Abigaile Grace, was being taught the finer things in being the new face of Southern gentility and Southern royalty.

They would surely find the place in history that would bless the generations to come, just like their great-grand mother had found her Mr. Hurley.

And story time continued. Grandma Abigaile was a true pro at this adventure through time.

The children were silent as their great-grandmother entered the great hall. The glass curtains were blowing in the soft breezes of summer. The magnolias were in bloom, and the sweet fragrance of the outdoors filled the room.

A prayer, and she began, "Children"—but the sound of hurried excitement carried down the stairs. Grandmother stopped, and the announcement came forth. "It is time." The children were unaware of the meaning of these words, but Abigaile knew exactly what it meant.

She was going to welcome a new Hurley into this world. Tears of joy ran down her fair face and puddled into her silk and Chantilly lace hanky. She had lived another day to welcome her new grandchild into her home, River Bend. A place where her love, Mr. Hurley, had welcomed their own.

Tears of pain came with the joy. Grandma Abigaile had been alone now without Mr. Hurley for almost fifteen years. But tears didn't stop this fine lady long before she dismissed her grandchildren and headed upstairs.

The pains of childbirth were soon over, and a new Little Miss Hurley was born. Her name was Abigaile Grace, a sign of respect for ancestry and love that had bloomed here in this home. A blessing from above.

As Miss Abigaile lost her newborn looks, you could truly see that the name she was given at birth was God directed. She had golden hair and eyes of green that could match the finest emerald in Great-Grandmothers jewel box. She was the mirror image of her namesake, a small Southern beauty.

Laughter filled the house while time seemed at moments to stand still.

Great-Grandmother was preparing for story time with her beautiful grandchildren. She would put on her big belle skirts and floppy hat and always tuck her silk hanky into her waistband. She proceeded down the carved stairway. She would always make story time a memory of yesteryear, because a picture was worth a thousand words.

As she descended the stairs, she gave thanks to God for the amazing life He had let her live.

Buckets of tears had fallen in her life, from birth to a new hope and a dream. Soon she was looking back at her own life: the moments with her parents, her beloved, and her children and theirs were likened to a sky full of fireworks. These memories were so dear. But even in death, life goes on, and stories of yesterday's trials and victories live on in her memory, all to be unveiled at story time.

Abigaile Amelie had lived and lived and lived some more. And just like she was taught, she never failed to give thanks.

And the stories didn't stop. Grandma was full of life, and her children and their child beheld the Spirit of God in full bloom. Just like all the stories started, the magnolias were blooming, and the air was filled with the sweet fragrance of spring and summer.

As blond curls grew longer on Little Abigaile, Grandma's blondness was no longer visible. The silver shine on her head showed the signs of wisdom. Her peachy skin showed the wrinkles of time. She was beginning to show signs of wisdom and the lines of life. The sunshine of her golden locks had now turned. Just like her wedding silver showed the signs of being used, so did she.

Little Abigaile hung on her every word. It was as if she, Grandma, was renewed with new life when her mirror image came into her world.

Grandma's stories were so alive, as if she was acting out all her life for her grandchildren.

She could feel the joy of her youth return. Her dresses and ribbons still fit her petite frame.

Little Abigaile was a beautiful replica of her grandma. It was like reliving her own youth, she would say, when Little Abigaile was around.

Even though she loved Abigaile so, Grandma never showed favoritism. For each of her other grandchildren were a gift from God and had special and unique qualities that pulled at Grandma's heartstrings. Little Abigaile was the youngest of three! Two boys were born from Abigaile's parents' love.

Grandma gave thanks when each was born. "Gifts from God." Who else could put together these ones of such handsome appearance? Neither had red hair like her Abner Hurley, but they carried the Hurley name, a name of character and strength, with a heritage of peace that carried all the Hurleys before them into a life of service, compassion, and love for their fellow man.

The Hurleys were a family blessed by God Himself. If anyone asked them how they did everything or anything, they would declare, "It was the hand of God."

Great-Grandma Abigaile was the top of the pyramid of blessing, and it all started with her and Mr. Hurley turning their whole lives over to God when they married.

Even during the War of the States, they professed favor and gave God their best.

A story of life, love, loss, and victories. No one could believe one family could be so blessed.

Grandma Abigaile Amelie Hurley would always respond, "When you give God your all, He gives you His all."

Story time was a regular occurrence at River Bend once a week, summer, winter, spring, and fall.

One would not or could not miss this special event. The time was set, and Grandma Abigaile glided down the grand stairway. Her belle skirt and silk ribbons danced in the breeze, and down she came. The children were waiting for her. They were all waiting with expectation of history coming alive.

Grandma Abigaile began, "And the magnolias were in bloom." Summer was coming to an end, and school was about to start.

Grandmas story time would be postponed soon. The weekends would be her new time for her history lessons.

And the magnolias were in bloom. When I was sixteen years old, I was engaged to your Great-Grandfather, Mr. Hurley.

My daddy gave him permission to marry me. A spring outdoor wedding was planned. Right before I turned seventeen, I was Mrs. Abner Hurley.

We worked really hard, and your Great-Grandfather and I lived above the country store. My daddy's store. We saved our wages and began the purchases of land, a few acres at a time. It was the beginning of our River Bend.

It was our dream, and we gathered two thousand acres. We had bottom land close to the river, and farmlands that were lying close up to some of the Rolling Hills.

We called our land River Bend. We planted cotton and indigo.

We had helpers to harvest and plant our lands. Our babies were born on River Bend plantation. We named them Carter Jefferson Beauregard and Edward Harper Oakley.

We had a small house, and after nine years, Mr. Hurley built the house we now live in. On a small hilltop where we could overlook all our lands, the oak trees were scattered.

Willow trees stood along the creek bottoms and rivers edge, and the wild magnolias were everywhere. When spring came, the air was sweet like a fine French perfume. Our house was larger than I wanted, but Mr. Hurley insisted we would need the room. All our bedrooms were above the grand stairway. Three on the left, and three on the right. All our public spaces were downstairs.

Our kitchen was outside in another building.

"Why?" the children asked.

"Dear ones, in the days of old, we had open fires to cook, and we didn't want our house to burn down. You see, one of our neighbors had that happen to them. So we built our kitchen outside the main house. Then a few years ago, we were able to move our kitchen inside. Now we cook meals inside our house."

And Grandma Abigaile continued.

After a few more years passed, the war came to our lands. Our families were divided, and our lives were lost to our neighbors and friends. We tried to lift the spirits of our family with song and prayer, but some only saw hurt and pain. Towns burned, and lives were lost.

But we had promised God when the war began that what we had was His. And He told us that a thousand may fall on our left and a thousand at our right, but it would not come near us.

We took the Bible as our life's instructor.

And, dear ones, we never missed a meal or had our home attacked, even though our neighbors fell by the wayside.

We always tried to love others. Sometimes it was really tough, but we had to be obedient to what God said to do.

Grandma signaled that her story time was over for that day, and she dismissed her little ones, but Grandmas little lady stayed behind.

At first, Little Abigaile started to come toward her Great-Grandmother but then stopped. Amelia didn't notice that tears were falling down little Abigaile's cheeks. The story of the war had touched her deeply. Little Abigaile had turned ten that summer, and the reality of life, loss, and death touched her. "How could people not like other people? Why?" she asked.

Her grandmother had no answer, but she replied, "AU we can do is pray and let God do what He will do. But, Abigaile, we will all have choices to make in our lives. So, before you choose, always pray, and God will help you to make a right decision."

"Even now, Grandma?"

"Yes, my darling, even ow. If someone needs a helping hand, try to be of assistance. Now, darling, we will continue our stories a little later. Grandmother is a little tired."

And up the curved stairway she went.

Thoughts of her Mr. Hurley were awakened again. Tears began to fall down her cheeks. The lines of time were moistened by her tears, and her silk hanky caught the rest. She felt alone, even when so many family members were nearby. But it was only the memories of her lost love that fueled her tears.

Down the hallway, her Abigaile was singing and dancing. She peered out of her door, and a miracle happened. Her tears stopped, and a gentle smile feuded her aged face. Her little darling reminded her of all the love she thought she lost. It was not lost, but reborn in this new generation.

It was her family and a part of her and Mr. Hurley. They were very much alive; she could go on and start each day as if it were her first and maybe her last.

Little Abigaile had made a smile appear from tears. Life was good.

As the matriarch of this family, Great-Grandmother had always tried to instill a godly life and principles and her personal motto, "Help those in need.

Even when our family and home were under attack, we had to remember God was in control, she thought.

War, hunger, and loss could not stay alive. I will leave a story, a heritage, of life, love, and family A story of our land and the treasures that it could produce. Not those of cotton and indigo but jewels of life that will continue throughout all time. One generation of love passed on to the next and the next.

Now that I am approaching my seventy-fifth year, I can recognize small blessings at a much quicker rate than when I was younger. Everything has seemed to take on a much deeper meaning in life.

My darling boys and their family have made me a part of this new generation.

My hair is silver, and my eyes are still green. I look at myself and sometimes fail to see my silver hair and my lines of wisdom and age upon my face. But I still see that young girl I once was. So full of life, of future hopes and dreams. Dreams of a special bear and fairy-tale romance and a family.

And then my small frame reminds me of my true age. It seems as though my height was diminishing a touch. My skirts are dragging across the floors, and my waist has grown a little larger.

But nothing will discourage me. I have my loved ones and my stories of yesteryear. They will live on.

Just as a young girl matures in life, my memory of those times and all my loves have, I thought, reached the peak of my aging life.

But it seems like my life has not reached its end. When my Little Miss Abigaile was born, it ignited a new flame within me. I was almost seventy-nine and still like a spring chicken. A new flame of hope for the future. A true living image of myself and all the hopes of a little girl untouched by the pains of war and loss. And now new life and my stories and new hopes will live on.

Darling Little Abigaile was indeed the picture-perfect image of her Great-Grandmother Abigaile Amelie.

It was the day Little Abigaile turned twelve years old that a birthday party was planned in celebration of this special occasion.

All her classmates were invited to a party like those her Grandma Abigaile had when she was a girl, out on the grounds of River Bend under the great oak and willow trees that shaded the place of her birth.

Children from all over came to enjoy the pony rides and delicious treats that were served.

For the first time, Grandma saw her young granddaughter showing signs of a becoming a young woman.

She was remembering the time she first met Mr. Hurley. She was only fourteen and believed she was a woman, but her daddy assured her she was still a child and had a long way to go before she was mature enough to think about love. But her heart sang each time her Mr. Hurley came around.

Her daddy was a wise man, but she was sure that he was not right about her Mr. Hurley.

Abigaile Amelie was surely growing up. The birthday party was the social event of the

young children's life. The beginnings of cotillions and debutant coming-out parties.

The possible meeting of plantation and plantation. A hope for young love to develop and grow. One day it might, maybe, be the joining of lands and families. But youth had a way, in this new generation, of being fickle. Her hopes would have to be put on hold. At least for a while.

She and Mr. Hurley always wanted to add land to River Bend. But none of her family had any interest in the boys or girls who a joined their beloved River Bend.

Perhaps in time Miss Abigaile might find her true love in one of the next-door plantations.

Rather in one of the young men who were heir to nearby lands.

"I guess Mr. Hurley," Amelia said, "left a want in me that has yet to be fulfilled."

But Grandmas hopes would lay dormant for at least several more years.

No new loves and no new lands, yet.

Little Abigaile was of a new generation where reading, writing, and arithmetic were reaching new heights for all Great-Grandmas grandchildren.

In her time, Amelia would recall, education in the social graces and the finer points of cotton farming were taught.

But now it was taught in a way she was not familiar with. But she commended the furthering of all knowledge, believing it could be helpful.

"You see, when my great-grandmother was alive," Grandma recalled, "things were not so different. I was open to every new thing. My young mind was hungry for something that would make my heart sing. But at that point, young ladies of my time were not encouraged to chase a dream of anything else accept that of Georgia royalty and all the responsibilities that came with it.

"My daddy was a shop owner, as was Mr. Hurley. That was an honored position, one that had its privileges with all landowners. I never believed that I would, one day, landowner. But Mr. Hurley had dreams, and they would become mine. Our River Bend has lasted many years, and I am guessing it will withstand the test of time long after I am gone.

"But until that time comes, I will—no, I must—carry on in my matriarchal duties, as the caretaker and storyteller of River Bend Plantation and its history.

"With grandsons in our family line, I am assured that River Bend would carry the Hurley name for many years to come.

CHAPTER 3
1800s Gone with the Wind

My Mr. HURLEY was a man of hopes and dreams, and for all the years we were one. I learned to hope and dream new ideas, and River Bend and our family allowed this to be a reality for me.

It was the weekend once again, and story time was still an excitement for my young ones.

I had a new story to tell. This time to my little ones.

I put on my green velvet skirt and ivory lace blouse, along with my large straw hat with beautiful green ribbons that matched my skirt and my eyes. I placed my great-grand mother s emeralds and pearls around my neck, placed the earrings on my earlobes, and the matching bracelet around my wrist. I felt as though I was going to my first cotillion. I descended my River Bend stairs and called out to my grandchildren.

"Young ones, it is time."

There was a sound of little feet upon our cypress floors like that of a herd of small elephants. We met in the entry hall, and I was escorted into our great living hall.

This was a place where, for years, I had met my grandchildren.

I sat on a beautiful carved chaise longue where my belled skirt could cover the seat. With my gloves lying across my lap and my lace hanky awaiting the tears that would surely fell once again, I was just about ready to begin.

My grandsons were ready for me to begin, but I was taken aback by the fragrance that filled the room. Those smells seemed to call me back. Back to a different time in my life, when I was young and love was in bloom.

Tears filled my eyes and began to stream down my time-wrinkled face and the laugh lines that curved around my lips.

Then I looked up and noticed I had a concerned audience. "Grandma! Grandma!" It jarred my mind and brought me back to today.

The crimson velvet drapes and lace glass curtains were blowing in the breeze.

As I sat on the chaise longue, I happened to notice that the crimson drapers and my green velvet skirt appeared to resemble the colors of Christmas.

All my Christmases only said how old I was, yet I was hoping for ten or twenty more years. "Now, my darling. The magnolias were in full bloom." This was Grandmas beginnings for her stories.

In my days at school, I found books to read and new places I had never seen or heard about.

When my great-grandmother came over from Europe, she didn't have much. Her parents were hoping for a new life in a new country. But as soon as they arrived, there were many others searching for a new life just like my great-grandmother and her parents were.

They reached out for a new land, and the wagons began to roll. Roll across the planes and hills of this new country.

They didn't have much, but all their belongings were safely tucked away on the covered wagon they had secured.

It was days, weeks, and many months of cold winds and temperatures so hot you could cook bacon and eggs atop the metal pans.

Wild Indians and sickness attacked our wagon train. But my great-grandmother and her parents were very strong. When the wagon train circled up for nighttime, she told me that they would count everyone to see if any had been picked off by the wild red man. They were native to the new land we would call home one day. We would also see strange new animals. We tried to stay together because there is safety in numbers.

Her parents when they lived in the old country were dressmakers and cobblers. They came from a small town called Alsace-Lorraine, in France.

They named my great-grandmother Ottilie Amelie, after a princess, Augusta Sophia Amelie, just like my second name.

"Grandma, did they have pretty fabrics to make clothes with?"

Dear, the fabric remnants that she worked with came from royal clothing. The royal dressmaker would order more fabrics just to make sure they had enough to complete the suits and dresses of the king and queen and the dear princess. They would sell her the leftovers for pennies.

Her momma's name was Katherine Ottilie Koenig. She was the dressmaker to royalty.

So many times, we search for answers of where we came from. We find only a fraction of our history, our past. The origin of our family is in Bavaria. All our names can be traced back to towns and people of distinction. We were never able to trace every member, but one thing for sure, we all originated from one set of ancestral parents.

"Who is that? What are their names?"

Their names were Adam and Eve. From then to now, the magnolias have been in bloom for us.

So, from the beginning, we can trace our family tree, with a few of the branches missing.

But that is not a problem.

We are from royalty, the King of kings, Jesus.

I was named after my great-grandmother. But now my full name is Abigaile Amelie Hurley.

Now, back in the days when the country was being settled, these lands were very rough and rugged and dangerous. We had to become tough as nails to survive. Your family members of old were the perfect example of resiliency. They took a licking and were beat down, but they got up and continued to go forward.

When they decided to come to the Americas, they could only take the bare necessities.

Some of the shipmates that arrived with my great-grand mother's parents got sick and fell to their death in many different ways.

This was the end of their family lines. Their heritage was lost forever. But our family was strong.

Ottilie Amelie lost so many of her friends. It made her very sad. But her parents told her that God had a plan.

We should not cry for the loss, but pray for the strength to continue on the journey He has planned for us.

Of course, to a small child or an adult, this is a hard pill to swallow. But the world continues to go on. They traveled many miles and had many hardships. But God helped them.

They settled in a place called New Orleans, Louisiana. They lived there for fifteen years.

They made dresses and shoes.

My great-grandmother met her love in that place when he came into her daddy's shoe shop to have his boots repaired.

She was only seventeen years old, but old enough to become his wife.

Her momma made her a wedding dress of fine satin and silk It had Chantilly lace that came all the way from Paris, France.

She told me that no one ever could look more beautiful than she did on her wedding day.

They were so happy, and the new lands were open for them to possess. So, they moved to our beloved Georgia. They homesteaded six hundred acres of mountain and valley land. They wanted to raise horses and cattle, the kind of horses we call quarter horses, for racing, and the big beef steers known as Herefords for food.

They were very successful. They had many children, but not all of them survived. Only two boys made it through to adulthoods.

Did they have family? Oh yes! You see, that is how I got here. Family history, dear ones.

Family history. Both these young men moved to the lands we now live in.

Did they have a plantation? No, they ran a dry goods store, and that is how my momma and daddy started their dry goods store.

My daddy learned how to work and take care of all the people that needed his help.

What happened to the horses and cattle? Dear ones, perhaps this might be a story for another day.

*****

Grandma stood up, and her belle skirt swayed front to back. She started to take a step forward, and her young namesake stopped her.

"Grandma, how will I know?"

"Know what, dear one?"

"When will I know, and how will I know, I have met my only love?"

"Dear one, each young man and each young lady have an inner clock. Just like our great clock in the hall. It will chime music in your heart at a special time. At first, it may only be an inner smile that sounds only one note. But if you give it time, your heart will make a melody like that of Frederic Chopin and Ludwig van Beethoven, a composition of notes that work so beautifully together that you can.

RIVER BEND

"They stayed hidden for years until one day Otilie's mom called her in. My great-grandmother was sat down in front of a dressing table with a beautiful beveled mirror. She was told to close her eyes, and her mom placed the emeralds around Otilie's neck She was fifteen years old. She opened her eyes and saw the necklace, bracelet, and the earrings. They matched her eyes. Just like you and me.

"These jewels are truly family jewels that have been passed down now to you that one day you will pass them on to your daughter or granddaughter.

"I will keep these for now until you get married." And Abigaile Amelie showed her a picture of her Mr. Hurley and herself on their wedding day. The emeralds were on her neck. Something old as a tradition. So, darling, these are for you. Maybe on your wedding day, you could wear them. No matter what, these emeralds are yours."

Grandma Abigaile Amelie was complete. She had passed on a legacy.

Little Abigaile had a legacy that she would cherish all her life. Her brothers would have something special from Mr. Hurley.

But Grandma was waiting until they were a bit older to tell them. Great-Grandmother Abigaile was retiring for an afternoon nap.

The summer breezes were flowing around the house, and the crimson velvet curtains were moving to the music of the magnolia trees.

Perhaps if the moment presented itself, another story of the history of River Bend might just reveal itself.

But for now, Great-Grandmother Abigaile heard her feather mattress and pillows calling her name.

In the meantime, Little Abigaile and her brothers played outside. A lively game of hide- and-seek and a ride through the grounds at River Bend, maybe a swim in the river down below.

The children's afternoon was all planned out so Grandmother could rest without any loud noises.

But Grandmother was alive with thoughts of her next story and of the memories of the life, now lost, she had once lived.

Should I tell the children about how men taught other men? How God interceded at all times? Of wars and all the new things, I have seen in my lifetime? So many choices! My eyes are at half mast, and my aging body is beginning to relax into the soft feathers of my bed Thank You, God for quieting my mind. I know you will show me what or if another story of our history might be told.

Little Abigaile was still in dreamland. Her great-grand mother had given her crown jewels, something that her own great-grandmother had given her. Jewels that were once worn by a princess. Jewels that stayed hidden away from everyone.

Even in the stories of war and the holes that hid the Hurley treasures, the emeralds were safe and protected.

This was the age when our country, our Georgia, was fighting for freedom. When land was a rich possession, and new inventions of all sorts were being revealed.

A new frontier with adventurers were abundant, men and women willing to risk all they had, even their family, to grab a piece of this new world.

My grandmother was so blessed, but she incurred many hardships too, thought Grandma.

After the war, she told us of lack and want everywhere, but God always gave them their daily bread.

And then she would say, "Then the sun came up again, and the life we knew before the war began to bloom again. And my emeralds were unearthed. They were set in gold with pearls and diamonds. All that time in the ground, four years, they never lost their luster."

The sun was beginning to sink in the sky, and the dinner bell chimed loudly. Three taps on the large bell always signified it was dinnertime.

Everyone had fifteen minutes to gather their thoughts and toys and head for the grand dining hall, where in years past the North and South joined in prayer to bless their food and pray for peace.

Our country was so young, and we wanted peace.

CHAPTER 4

New Dreams

WE WERE STRONG, we had new dreams. All those arriving from the old country, where we had come from decades ago, were happy. Evening fell upon River Bend Plantation, the memories of old were kept alive, and the hopes for new adventures lived big in the hearts of the young Hurley family.

Great-Grandmother gathered her young together for a short yet colorful bedtime story. This was something that captured the young ones' imagination, year after year.

Even though there are many who don't agree with her, Great-Grandmother Abigaile's recollection is truth. But she knew where truth was, and she was so very sure that those who might refute her stories did not or could not tell because they did not live it.

Eyes and ears all turned to Grandma, and her story began. "The magnolias were in bloom.

And the rain fell upon our cotton and indigo. We planted a new crop.

Tobacco. We had seen it grown in other parts of our lands and felt sure it would be good for our plantation.

"We had to order seeds. Then we had our helpers pre pare a special indoor bed where the seeds could germinate. It sometimes took six to eight weeks for our seedlings to mature enough to plant in the fields. And we learned how to cut and harvest our tobacco. We could get three and maybe four cuttings before the frost."

"Grandma! Did you smoke the tobacco?"

"No, dear ones. It was not ladylike. Just the gentlemen enjoyed our tobacco.

"It was such a great crop for our plantation. We were able to produce, dry, and sell our harvest. It took four to eight weeks to dry. We loaded our tobacco leaves on carts and wagons. Then we put our crop on the trains, and it was shipped everywhere the rails could go.

"Our railroads go to many more places today.

"We had as our cash crops, tobacco, cotton, and indigo.

"The plantation down the way from us grew the same things as we did, and rice. That plantation's name was Willow Oaks.

"It is a pretty place, but only half the size of River Bend. The family that lived there was called Butler."

Little Abigaile raised her hand and said there was a boy at her school with that same name.

Maybe he lived at Willow Oaks.

"Darling, light of life, when school begins again, you can ask him."

"Okay, Grandma, I will do that. Grandma, did you have parties and have that family over?" "No, darling, not that I can recall. I do not know why, but we can plan a party next fall and invite your classmate. Mr. Butler, maybe he lives at Willow Oaks and can attend.

"Well, it is time for bed. Tomorrow is another day. Perhaps after church and dinner, we can revisit our story of River Bend. Sweet dreams, my dear ones."

Grandma Abigaile was tired, but her mind continued to reel on about her River Bend, and her love, Mr. Hurley.

As she was preparing for bed, she noticed the sweet smell of the magnolia trees. She crawled into her feather-filled mattress and covered her petite body with a quilt she had made when she and Mr. Hurley first married.

It cradled around her frame like those memories of her parents and her true love, Mr. Hurley.

How she missed him. The soft touch and the warmth of his body next to hers.

Tears began, and the sounds of sadness entered the hallways.

All ran to her bedside only to find a smile and a prayer on her lips. "All is well," she said, and off to sleep they all went.

Dreams of yesteryears rocked her to sleep. A new day would open to all who lived in the large columned house— not just a house but a home, a home where all generations lived in harmony with history and new futures joining together as one family.

The sun beckoned to all at River Bend to awake, arise from slumber. A new day has come, and new adventures are at hand.

Soon you would hear the patter of feet on the cypress floors.

Signs of family were everywhere. Children laughing and adults whispering words of love.

A family went to sleep as one and joined the new day the same.

Eggs, biscuits, and gravy, and for some, Grandma Abigaile s homemade strawberry preserves were served up in the great dining hall.

Fine China, stemware, and silver were used at every meal. It was a grandma thing.

"Enjoy what you have when you have it," Grandma would say, with memories of wartime when they buried their treasures.

All enjoyed breakfast, and off they went upstairs to dress for church.

In their Sunday best, they entered their little church. Friends were greeted, and hugs were passed out among older gentlemen and ladies. Some had known each other for fifty-plus years.

The preacher was long-winded but had a good message. He said, "Use what God gives you now, don't hide it under a basket."

It seemed like Grandma Abigaile had the preacher message that Sunday. But all in all, it was a good word and so true, and she practiced it every moment every day.

It seemed like God was telling everyone to grow where you are planted and shine for all to see. Use all the treasures every day and enjoy all the blessings that are in front of you. Share your good fortune and thank God for everything every day.

Dinner on the grounds. Picnic style. Sandwiches and peach cobbler, and sweet Georgia ice tea after church.

And story time was just around the corner.

Grandma Abigaile was preparing. Her belle skirt and ribbons were laid out across the feather bed, and her princess emerald and pearls lay atop her dressing table along with her floppy hat.

Just a little longer, and her dear ones would gather in expectation of the continuing stories of River Bend.

Grandma Abigaile dressed in her costume of yester years, and down the curved stairway she descended, down into her great hall where the crimson velvet drapes flanked each of the walk-through windows.

She sat on her chaise longue, and her belled skirt draped over the arm of the hand-carved chaise.

She glanced down at her stocking feet and heard a sound like a herd of antelopes being chased by a pride of lions.

All her dear ones came running when story time was due. None could miss this history lesson of River Bend.

Even the boys who were full of itchy breeches were still and silent during Grandma Abigaile s accounts of their parents and those times at River Bend.

For the boys would one day inherit and run the plantation called River Bend. It was enough for two brothers to handle and then some.

All was quiet and still. All eyes and ears were on Grandma Abigaile. She began.

"And the magnolias were in bloom." *Help me, Lord, to recall with accuracy the details of our life before these dear ones were here.*

"Oh yes! The trains were reaching new places, and our crops went to many more cities and the nearby states.

"Tobacco was a fashionable thing. After mealtime, all the gentlemen would gather in the gentlemen's parlor. They might talk about horses or crops while almost all would light up a pipe or the long cigars that were made up of our tobacco.

"The ladies would gather in the ladies' parlor, and the piano would call to one. A melody would sound out. A book of sonnets, that is poems, would be shared with all. A sewing basket might be opened, and beautiful pearl but tons would show themselves. Ribbons and velvet and silk squares offered an opportunity to become a beautiful bed cover. All the ladies could quilt and play piano. There were some who could paint a picture that you could touch and feel the life in it, from trees and flowers to the likeness of a family member. Our ladies were taught from a very early age all the social graces and were educated in the arts.

"Here in this great room, the pictures you see were all painted by some of your relatives. None were as talented as Monet, but you can judge for yourself. All your studies will show your hidden talents in time to come.

"Over the course of time, our family grew in number, and the blessings of God were very evident.

"We never went hungry. We tried to help all. Those who had less we treated all the same, our friends who had more and those who had less."

Our time for stories had come to an end that day. Grandma was expecting an old friend for afternoon tea.

Her costume and jewels were retired to the chifforobe in Grandmas room.

The large bell outside the oversized entry door chimed, and Grandmas friend Miss Matilda entered. She was small and slim in stature. It looked like a strong wind could blow her over. But she was strong as an ox and gentle like a lamb in all her ways. A lady like many of the ladies of the old South, she was near Grandmas age, and when they met, they talked about their loves and losses. Tears would fall into their lace hankies, and sips of tea cooled their parched lips.

The hours seemed to melt away like ice on a hot summer's day. Laughter would sound out, and these two aged Southern ladies would hug and hug some more, and Miss Matilda would retreat to her horse-drawn buggy. She was ready to part ways and dream again about the next time Abigaile Amelie Hurley would reunite to recall and remember the days of old, as well as the times when their loves were alive and held them.

The sun was retreating, and the mist of the evening settled upon River Bend. A cool Southern breeze entered through the large walk-through windows, and the sweet smell of the magnolia tree lingered into every corner of this great home.

A time for refreshing the soul and body. Time to pray and thank God for another day to live and love.

Miss Matilda's horse would be given a command and a tug on her reins, and off they would go to Miss Matilda's carriage house. The horse's name was Sally Louise, and she wanted that square of hay waiting for her at home. It was like Sally Louise could think. A song that was popular back then went like this: "Over the river and through the woods."

Grandma Abigaile and Miss Matilda touched each other's heart.

They could feel the joy and pain each had experienced. Without words, their hearts could join and laugh and share joy whenever they were together.

The sun set and called all to rest. For the new day that was approaching would soon unfold new challenges and new beginnings to the chapters in Grandma Abigaile s life.

Sweet dreams for all were the wish in River Bend.

The sweet smell of the magnolia trees lingered, and Mrs. Abigaile Hurley fell fast asleep. The day with sweet Miss Matilda satisfied her and fulfilled a need like no other family and friends, and recollections of yesteryear filled her heart. Now dreams of her love, Mr. Hurley, could come.

As the sun peeked over the horizon. The cock let out his morning song. Cock-a-doodle-do called out to all at River Bend to awake from their slumber.

The pitter-patter of bare feet on the cypress floors sounded like a herd of hundred-pound turtles. The wide hallways joined the bedrooms left and right. It brought the stairway into central focus, where guests could see the majesty.

A dream stairway curved around an entry hall. Once you entered, your eyes were paralyzed by the elegant curve and hand-carved handrail.

But these were the thoughts of those who visited River Bend. To the Hurley family, it was simply the norm. It was nothing special; it was all they had known. But everyone else was all wide- eyed and speechless. Even the young ones from other plantations were all struck. This was a show of craftsmanship that seemed to have died out or was not approachable because of cost, even though other places around the county were all established at similar times. The planters and their wives seemed to be happy with less elegance and a simpler and much smaller cottage-style home, only five to six thousand square feet, half the size of River Bend.

Monday morning was here, and the summer was only half over. Many more days for picnics and fun dining in the grand dining room.

Breakfast and dinner were enjoyed by all, and Grandma Abigaile was about to prepare for her afternoon story time.

She dressed in her old Southern costume, the large belle skirt and ribbons and one very floppy straw hat. And to top off her attire, one very beautiful emerald and pearl necklace, earrings, and a bracelet that would cover her wrist and part of her gloved hand. These jewels were those passed down to her from her great-grandmother Ottilie Amelie, who got them from her mother, who had received them from a princess.

How these jewels had survived all these years and were still in their original beautiful gold setting was truly a wonder.

So, with humility comes a great harvest. The harvest of true love for each other and the harvest of memories passed on to the new and next generations to come.

This was a promise that lived big in the mind and heart of Great-Grandmother Abigaile Amelie Hurley.

As she gracefully glided down the curved staircase, the herd of turtles she had heard early that morning rode the handrail down to the bottom story. They had passed Grandma Abigaile so quickly that it seemed like a blur. But the race was on.

Excited about story time, they raced each other to the great ballroom where the carved chaise longue awaited Grandmas presence.

Early afternoon and the heat of summer was blooming; even the crimson drapes felt warm to the touch.

Grandma Abigaile Amelie entered the grand ballroom, and the children hurried to help her to her story chaise longue.

"Sit, my dear ones, and Grandma Abigaile will begin.

I am not sure what I am to tell you today, but if you help me to remember our last stories, I am sure we can pick up from there.

"Oh, yes. The paintings here in this room were all painted by your relatives.

"And the magnolias were in bloom. Help me, Lord, to recall.

"If you look really hard, you can see how these family members all look somewhat alike. You see the hair and eyes are liken to yours. These are family traits that are part of your biological makeup. Some of you have blond hair and green eyes, like me. And some of your blue eyes and brown hair. But none of you have Mr. Hurleys red hair. But if you have children one day, they could have

Mr. Hurleys flaming red hair. It is the genes that you are carrying inside you.

"Now, when we harvested our indigo crop, we would always retrieve several bushels so that our family's ladies would have enough blue pigment to paint our fine China. The oil paints that were used in their artwork and all the eyes and clothing painted in blue are from our indigo plants.

"We were able to harvest this crop many times a year. So, there was always enough to make our blue color. Boys, do you want to try your hand at painting?"

"No, Grandma! More stories please!"

"All right, dear ones. Do you recall at the top of the stairs, the last step? When my Mr. Hurley was building this home, he carved our names on the kickplate and dated it. When you go up again to your rooms, take time and look at it. Our love has survived all these years. When you take a wife, you can carve your names next to ours. It will also stand the test of time, and you can tell your family of our history. Little Abigaile."

"Yes, Grandma."

"Remember these stories of our family, and you will become the next storyteller of River

Bend and the Hurley family.

"Now, dear ones, when your great-uncles were very young, they had a horse race down to the river's edge and back to the house. The horses collided, they fell Off into a thorn bush, and both broke their right arms. That was the beginning of many accidents Grandma had to tend to. Y'all have to be careful."

"Okay."

"Dear ones, I think I might take a short nap before supper. Help me up!"

"Yes, ma'am."

Up the stairs they went, and Grandma entered her room.

The belled skirt took its place inside the chifforobe, and the emerald and pearls returned to the velvet box that had protected them for so many years. Her hat lay at the end of the bed, and the daybed was ready for Grandma.

Dreams of the war tormented her, and she awakened with tears rolling down her face. Even though it had been so many years since the war began and so many since it ended, the memories of that time were as vivid as the days it happened.

Grandma was always so happy, it was hurting her heart to relive those times of brother against brother for twenty-five years. Miss Matilda and Grandma had this same memory. Perhaps that was what bonded them together.

But their visits were always filled with hope and the love of their family. More happy than sad.

Supper was served in the great dining room. The family joined together for evening prayers, and the soft Southern breezes called the silver moon to shine. The stars were so numerous that it reminded them all of the woodpecker's tree holes everywhere. The moon shone through the night sky and made the heavens look like diamonds.

Grandma Abigaile was tired, but her memory kept bringing her back to wartime. Her little mind was reliving the times of war and how God had delivered them from all and always gave them food to eat and a family that was united and hopeful. Grandma Abigaile would relive and then live for the new in life. Each of these times made her more determined to thank God more and more for His love. Her prayers never stopped, and she knew victory over the torment would be hers.

The feather bed was calling Grandma Abigaile Amelie.

The summer night, once again, was filled with the fragrance of the tall green magnolia tree blooms. Huge white flowers covered the trees, and one might think that winter snow had fallen. But it was just our summer magnolias showing their beauty. A true gift from God. Beauty and the sweet fragrance of our Georgia summers.

Sleep came easily, and the hope to dream of Mr. Hurley was Grandma Abigaile's prayer.

The moon was a huge glowing ball of light. The stars were twinkling, and the night sky was all aglow. Crickets were sounding their voices in unison, and the frogs made a melody that a symphony could not duplicate.

That sound was like a lullaby that a young mother might hum for her sweet new little bundle of joy.

Peace fell on the Hurley household, and River Bend was preparing to receive a new day.

The night mist was covering the willows, and the moss dripped with moisture from the sky.

A summer rain helped cool the night and heal the lands, helping new life to grow.

The morning was awakened by the gleaming light of the sunrise. River Bend was welcoming the new day.

Grandma Abigaile was waiting for the herd of turtles to invade the hallways. But it was silent. No one was awake yet. This gave Grandma a chance to pray. "Help me, Lord. Give me a new outlook on life so that I might show others Your love."

The herd of turtles ran, and River Bend was awakened.

Grits were cooking and bacon frying. There was the call for breakfast, and all joined in the great dining hall. Fine China and silver graced the long table, and cobalt-colored glasses held fresh milk. It was set this way every day since the war. "Use what you have and enjoy Gods blessings; do not hide them under a basket" was Grandmas Abigaile's reminder of when she had had less many years ago.

The boys hurried outside, and Little Abigaile was waiting for her grandma to leave the table. "Grandma," Little Abigaile called, "can I try on the emeralds?

"Yes, light of my life, let's go upstairs and see how they look on you this morning." Grandma took her time, but Little Abigaile flew past her like a tornado.

The velvet jewelry box came out of a special hiding place, and Grandma placed the princess emeralds around her granddaughters neck the room stood still. No words were spoken. A smile as big as Georgia was evident all across Little Abigaile's face. Grandma had one too. Both were in another world. The jewels were a show of generations passed. A gift that had lived on for years. Even though Mr. Hurley had bestowed on his wife many other jewels, these had a family history. They had traveled many miles and many years to land around a young girl's neckline.

Little Abigaile took a deep breath and stood up. She twirled around and began to dance. The emeralds seemed to put her feet in motion. She wiggled and giggled and danced all around. Grandma joined in. Another deep breath, and both came back into reality.

"These are so pretty, Grandma. Thank you, Grandma. Maybe I could come in and try the princess emeralds just one more time soon!"

"Yes, light of my life."

The herd of turtles was back. "Grandma, Grandma, is it time?"

"Soon, my dear ones. Be patient. Soon. The journey down the past will be very soon.

Lunch first."

"Yummy."

"Stick around, dear ones."

The table was set, and the new peanut butter sandwiches were on the menu. This was another way for the peanut crops to be used in the South.

"Now, dear ones, prepare yourselves. Story time is coming. Gather around in the grand ballroom, and I shall tell you some more of the history of River Bend, the Hurley family, and our beloved Georgia."

Grandma went upstairs and adorned herself in story telling attire. First came the belled skirt with ribbons, and next the famed floppy hat. Last but not least, the princess emeralds.

The outfit was coming alive. The story of yesteryear and its history could be seen. Down the stairs, and story time began.

"And the magnolias were in bloom." Help me, God.

"Dear ones, the tasty dinner you just partook in was not always around.

"In the South there were many crops that the sun made grow. Cotton, indigo, tobacco, and the root crop called pea nuts. At first, we started growing peanuts for our animals. It was an excellent food source that had health benefits for our animals. It helped them grow strong muscle structure. When the peanuts were pressed, they yielded an oil. The boil weevil threatened our cotton crops. Peanuts were planted, and our cash crops were saved. This food source was given to really old people as a good extra source of protein. The crushed peanut could be placed on the tongue when the old people couldn't chew meat anymore. This food for people was introduced at the 1904 world's fair. We use our peanut oil for frying, and I want you to think how we might use peanuts another way. let's go to the kitchen, and tomorrow we will make a treat with peanuts. "Next, after our cooking lesson we will have to taste our treats before supper. But do not tell your mom or dad. Now we will stop and tomorrow begin again. Go play!"

Grandma stopped a little early and was preparing for another visit from Miss Matilda. It was her birthday. She was turning eighty-five. Every time Miss Matilda came, it was close to suppertime. Grandma was so excited, her costume was put away once again, and the princess emeralds were placed in their hiding place.

You could hear the buggy approaching. The wheels were pushing the pebbles aside and bouncing on the underside of her buggy. Sally Louise was taking Miss Matilda to Grandmothers house again, only this time she would stay overnight in her home away from home. Hay cubes were waiting, and Miss Matilda could hardly slow her down.

Animals could sense kindness and treats that were there for them. But then if anyone offered you a goodie each time you came, you might be expecting it always. Animals have a big memory, and Sally Louise was amazing. She stopped in front of River Bend. Miss Matilda stepped out, and one of Grandmas dear ones took Sally Louise back to her home away from home.

Grandma giggled, and these two silver-haired ladies grabbed each other as if they were long-lost cousins. A long hug and tears began. It was as if their hearts were talking. But no words had been uttered.

They were happy to be together again. The family at River Bend were all much younger.

They were like twin sisters, the same small frame and silver hair. Their age didn't matter. Their memories were almost identical. Their upbringing, marriage, children, the war, their homes, and the loss of their one and only true love.

There was a big birthday supper and a cake so large that Miss Matilda could carry some home to enjoy on Fridays to come. Presents filled the table. They acted like a beautiful centerpiece, all wrapped in blue to match the hand-painted blue China and the cobalt-blue lead crystal, some homemade and filled with berry wine and roasted duck a l'orange. Miss Matilda's favorite sweet iced tea and cake were served on the veranda.

The lightning bugs were alive with a glowing twinkle. The summers were known for their beautiful night skies and lightning bugs aglow up in the trees. It was like everything was celebrating Miss Matilda's birthday.

All retired for the evening when Grandma Abigaile Amelie gave Miss Matilda her gift. Matilda held the present close, and tears ran down her cheeks. She stopped and opened her gift, and more tears fell. She took it out of the blue velvet box and peered at her reflection. It was the most beautiful sterling silver hand mirror with matching brush and comb. Miss Matilda had broken hers several months earlier. Tears were freely flowing down Matilda's cheeks again. She felt fragile and young. The mirror showed a picture of a small little petite silver-haired lady. There was the saying "you are only as old as you feel." Right now, she felt really old. Maybe eighty-six.

The crickets were singing, the lightning bugs were glowing, and old friends hugged and retired for the evening.

Even though only six years separated them in age, it did not seem to matter. It was the lives they shared that kept them as close as salt and pepper. One without the other just didn't make sense. Miss Matilda had shared Abigaile Amelia's hopes and dreams, and she Matilda's.

Birthday breakfast and strong hot tea was enjoyed. Sally Louise was being readied for her trip home.

More hugs were exchanged, and off Miss Matilda went. Miss Matilda had her family close, but it seemed like she and Abigaile Amelie were closer.

Grandma Abigaile Amelie was renewed and looked to the new day with huge expectations. What, she knew not. Just new. Perhaps a tall iced tea on the veranda and a short stroll on the grounds of River Bend. She had lived so many years at River Bend; she never wanted to venture away. She had everything there that made her happy. And besides, that is where her Mr. Hurley lay waiting for her to join him. But she knew her time was not over; she had many more history lessons to tell her dear ones.

Grandma's two boys were tending to all the needs of River Bend, and Little Abigail s daddy was there too. With two thousand acres of cotton, tobacco, and indigo, there were harvests every three months, and summer was one of the busiest times of the year.

Summer was half over, and the children, Grandmas dear ones, were using their summer to hunt squirrels, fish, and play hide-and-seek.

In a big house like River Bend, there were hundreds of places to hide. But there were no clothes closets, only chifforobes, because the taxes on property were charged on this number of rooms, and closets, no matter how large or small, were counted as another room. So, the children would hide under tables and beds and sometimes in the covers of an unmade bed. They could play this way for hours.

However, Little Abigaile was being taught the social graces while the boy hunted squirrels.

Etiquette and quilt making were also taught.

By the time Little Abigaile was ready to marry, she would be totally prepared to manage and create a home for her and her new husband. But that wouldn't be for a few more years. She was just twelve, so that would not be for a while. Even though her great-grandma had married at age seventeen, times had changed. Boys and girls were furthering their education. The boys would one day run River Bend, and Little Abigaile would meet and marry and move away to a new place where she might become the matriarch of a new family. But for now, fun was on the summer agenda.

As for Little Abigaile, she was already dreaming of her handsome prince she would meet one day. She liked dark hair and blue or green eyes. She wanted someone who was like her daddy. Big and strong and could ride a horse as fast as the wind.

Little Abigaile was an avid reader. Some of her favorite books were Little House in the Big Woods and Swallowable, she would read them over and over again. She tried to get her brothers to read a book, but they just wanted to fish and shoot squirrels. Boys, she guessed! It was a common thread that all boys shared.

The summer was moving right along. Meals at the big table for all the Hurleys. Hunting and fishing for the boys, and etiquette and painting lessons for little Abigaile. Grandma Abigaile continued historical stories of the Hurley family and of River Bend.

No one could tell the hurts of the heart that lay within Grandma Abigaile. Every once in a while, an unexplained tear would fall down from her emerald-green eyes that she would catch in her lace hankie. They would start and stop and start again. But being of great Southern royalty, she, Grandma, would retreat as quickly as possible to hide her happiness or sad moments. Her life was a love story of life.

Pain and love shadowed her life daily no matter the cause.

Could there be more to Grandma Abigaile's tears? She was not sharing! Just one little thing. She wanted to live to be a hundred. This seemed to be a tall order for this petite lady. But she was in prayer, always asking God for new strength and bright eyes. She was seventy-nine and was hoping for a big Southern-style dinner on the grounds of River Bend. She only had twenty- one more birthdays to pass before her party, and a hundred candles would light up the night. Her dinner table would be outside on the grounds of River Bend under one of the great oaks, and the linens of her time would dress the table. Beautiful ruby-colored China and stemware would cover the mahogany table, and all grandmas silver would be brought outside. A table set for royalty.

Georgian royalty. Mrs. Abner Darwell Hurley, perhaps more little Hurleys, would be born. But by that time, her darling little Abigaile might be married. So many things could happen in twenty- one years. Only time would tell.

Grandma Abigaile hid these dreams from everyone except her dear friend Miss Matilda.

Miss Matilda had lots of grandchildren, but they were all far away. Miss Matilda's husband had been a blacksmith, so there was no reason or land for her family to take over. Just a shop where her husband did blacksmithing and a small home, he had built for her and their children, two girls and two boys.

Miss Matilda was a strong feisty little lady who could push a plow, rein a horse in, and dig a hole as good and faster than any man.

It seemed like rough and ready meets soft and elegant. But the heart knows a perfect match. And that was just what Miss Matilda and Grandma Abigaile Amelie were. A perfect match. Both petites, with a memory uniting them in a friendship and sisterhood that blood kin just didn't have. Just twenty-one years for Grandma to wait, and only fifteen years for Miss Matilda, for them both to reach a hundred years old.

CHAPTER 5

Birthday Parties

GRANDA WAS GOING to plan each of her next twenty-one birthdays. All the Hurley family and all Georgia royalty would be on the guest list.

But for now, she would have to settle for planning the other Hurley birthday parties.

Just a few more weeks of summer, and the school year would be in session. But until then, just like Grandmas birthday parties, dinner on the grounds, fishing, hunting, and China painting. But most of all, Grandmas story times. Every day, midafternoon, from now till school, Grandma was going to share with her dear ones. History upon history. Her life and those of family friends and River Bend.

When the evenings came to River Bend, the setting sun left a streak of sun-drenched clouds glowing with shades of orange, peach, purple, and reds like some of the Monet paintings that graced the entry hall. The shades of summer for all Georgia to enjoy.

Nighttime came with lightning bugs, dancing, and frogs sounding their songs of night. A typical night in the beloved Georgia that Grandma loved.

Sleep was easy that night for all in the Hurley home. Even Grandma didn't fight for sleep. Her mind was at peace. Her day had been busy, but not unlike any of the other days when God had given her sweet sleep. As soon as her head hit the feather pillow, she had dreams of Mr.

Hurley, her love, and her years when River Bend were in its beginnings.

And then the herd of turtles rang out the morning. All the Hurleys and especially Grandma Abigail were all aglow with the thoughts of this new day.

All descended the great curved staircase, and a beautiful breakfast called out to them. Somehow it smelled like heaven. Cinnamon rolls and yeast, cured sugar ham, hot tea, and fresh peaches and strawberries, all placed on silver trays like every other day, but it seemed like the beginnings of a party day. But nothing had been planned. So what was this all about? Was there news of something new, or was this the end of something old? Nobody knew. Yet there seemed like electricity was passing out excitement in all the Hurley clan.

Only time would reveal the story.

Nothing new yet. And Grandma Abigaile Amelie was almost ready for her story time. The big belled skirt came out, and the ribbon almost finished the outfit. There were two things missing. One floppy hat and the princess emeralds. The little blue velvet box came out of hiding. Opening the blue velvet box brought tears to Grandma Abigaile Amelies green eyes. She remembered when she first put these on. She was still a child, age twelve, but she felt like a grown-up.

These were given to her by her great-grandmother. She remembered her grandmothers' tears. She told Abigaile Amelie that she was the keeper of history. Not just the princess emeralds but the keeper of family history. And she was to relate these moments in time to all those who would go after her.

She caught her tears in her lace hanky, and down the stair she came.

She had forgotten her princess emeralds, so back up the stairs she went. The emeralds lay on her dressing table waiting to be placed around Grandmas neck.

It was as if Grandma could hear her history calling, but it was just the princess emeralds calling, wear me.

They were placed around her, neck and back down the stairs she went, ready for her dear ones to gather and help her into her chaise longue where her belled skirt could drape over the back. She was ready to begin.

With her dear ones ready to hear another history story, Grandma Abigaile Amelie said, "Dear ones..."

But wait, there was a big commotion in the entry hall. Was this the expected news all were waiting for? No! It was just two of the dogs running and slipping on the floors and being propelled into each and every piece of furniture.

The boys had left the door open, and their playmates, the dogs, thought that was an invitation to come on in. With animals captured, story time could commence.

All were gathered again and seated in expectation of what Grandma Abigaile would share.

"Dear ones, are you ready?"

"Yes, yes, yes!" they all replied. "Please, Grandma, begin."

"Good, dear ones. The magnolias were in bloom, just like they are now." Then came the prayer for recall. Grandmas' dear ones were sitting on the edge of their seats, and the history of family and River Bend began.

"When I was a little itty-bitty girl, I saw a whole lot of new things. In my younger days, we saw the inventions of the safety pins, the typewriter, the sewing machine, and the things we use right here at River Bend. All these were new inventions here in our country between 1840 and 1845. These were just a few. I will tell you about more of these modern marvels in a bit."

Oh no, not again. The dogs got in and were searching for their playmates. Grandma had to stop again. Two times, and story time was over for the day.

Supper on the grounds, and ice tea on the veranda. Lightning bugs and starlight collided. The electric lights lit up the house, and the stars and lightning bugs danced against the night sky. It was snow on the magnolia trees, and dream time was approaching fast. No winter, just white blooms and sweet fragrance everywhere.

Grandma Abigaile Amelie was ready for sweet dreams of Mr. Hurley. The rest of the family was not quite ready, so Grandma retired alone.

Summer was at an end, and school was starting. Little Abigaile was super ready for reading, writing, and numbers, her first day of seventh grade, new studies, and a few new classmates. For soon she might find out if that boy named Butler was the one who lived next door at Willow Oaks.

As she looked around the classroom and the playground, she didn't see the boy. Well, she didn't think again about it. Days and weeks went by and still she couldn't find that boy, but in late December there was a school Christmas party. Grades 1—12 were invited.

This was a school party. Plain, simple. Hardly any dec
orations, and most of them were handmade. They were
pretty, but they didn't even come close to the parties that
Grandma Abigaile Amelie had a hand in. Her decorations
were hand-blown glass, China dolls, and silk cords braided
together in shades of gold, red, and green. This braided
cord draped around the grand tree that stood twelve feet
tall and took up an eight-foot space in between the two
walk-through windows beside the crimson drapes. It was
a gorgeous sight to behold.

But for now, the Christmas party at school would be
the best and most memorable because there he was. The
boy whom Little Abigaile had been searching for since the
beginning of the school year. He was tall, with raven-black
hair and eyes that were like the sky on one of Georgia's
summer days. Piercing blue eyes that took Little Abigaile's
breath and her speech away. This boy was not in her class.
Where had he been all this time? He was in the ninth grade.

An older man. She was smitten. She almost fell with
what her Grandma Abigaile called the vapors. She was a
little scared at age twelve, and not a one took note of her
embarrassing moment.

The school Christmas party was almost over before
Little Abigaile could gather enough nerve to approach this
handsome hunk. He was so tall, she had to bend her head
back to speak to him. Little Abigaile was just five feet tall,
and this heartthrob was at least a foot taller than she.

"Is your name Butler?" "How did you know?"

"I just guessed," she said. "You see, I am Abigaile Hurley,
and I live next door to you at River Bend. Where have you
been this year? I have not seen you in school."

"My family lost some of our helpers, so I had to stay home and help."

"Oh!"

The world was standing still for what seemed to be hours when Mr. Buder said, "See you." Litde Abigaile was, for the first time ever, feeling all grown-up.

"Oh gee. I forgot to ask his name. His first name." His name would have to wait. But she could finally report to her Great-Grandma Abigaile Amelie that the party they had discussed earlier that summer was surely on.

The holidays were filled with visitors from all around. It was a must-see for all Georgia royalty. A display of Venetian glass, French silk, and hand-painted ornaments in the shape of teardrops, large and small to drip elegance all around this stately Christmas tree.

Presents large and small were placed at the base of this enormous green spruce. Wrapped in colors of pink, purple, and red with a hand-engraved silver ornament atop each package, a special ornament that could be collected and saved for each family member, no matter where they might live. At River Bend or elsewhere, each family member had a smaller Christmas tree in their own bedroom where these memories of past Christmases came alive. A memory of birth to the present were visible to enjoy.

Grandma Abigaile Amelie was running out of room on her tree but was willing to get a larger tree next year to help her next twenty-one ornaments. Because she was surely planning on reaching a hundred before she would give way to the thought of getting older or be ready to be planted next to Mr. Hurley at River Bend. Many more hopes and dreams and weekly visits with her dear friend, Miss Matilda.

Christmas was over, and a new year was rounding the bend.

Miss Matilda arrived and brought over a gift for her dear friend, a box she had brought back from Paris filled with new dishes. These were hand carried by Miss Matilda for her friend of many years, dishes that had emerald-green bands wrapped around an ivory base with a pearlized look about it.

It was a gift of love. Miss Matilda had met her four children and their families all in Paris to marvel at the iconic Eiffel Tower. They had missed the World Fair in 1889, but the beauty of such a structure would be there forever. That was a story of a lifetime Miss Matilda would cherish forever.

Small moments of their time were always a reminder of family for Miss Matilda, but the huge China service for twelve in emerald green called out, take me home. This was no mistake. Miss Matilda brought out her pocketbook, and it was done.

Something for her dearest friend.

When Grandma Abigaile opened the box, she couldn't see what was inside. It was filled with shredded straw and paper that hid the green surprise.

The look of awe and amazement changed Grandmas face. Her green eyes seem to fight up. Light up like the Christmas tree. Emerald green and gold China peeked out, and emerald- colored eyes filled with tears. A match that said, *made for each other.*

But Miss Matilda had no idea that Grandma Abigaile had something special, very special, for her as well.

Hugs exchanged and thank-you would have to be silenced. Grandma Abigaile was retrieving Miss Matilda's gift. Grandma didn't need help like Miss Matilda. She clutched the small box close to her bosom. It was not wrapped in anything but velvet. A golden ribbon tied the box tight, and a small bow called out, *Untie Me.*

Later in the century, there would be a saying that diamonds are a girl's best friend. It had not been coined yet, and the rage of the elegant ladies of the South was pearls. Gorgeous all- natural opera-length pearls.

Miss Matilda untied the golden bow. Her heart was racing. What could this be? The velvet box was holding a surprise. No more waiting. The box was opened.

Miss Matilda was so overwhelmed that the vapors enveloped her. She had never seen anything so beautiful in her jewelry box. She definitely could find the space. As she came to, she placed the perfect pearls around her neck. Now was the time for hugs, and more hugs.

Both of these ladies received a huge surprise. Neither one of these Southern belles ever believed they could be surprised anymore because they were able to get anything they wanted for themselves! But the hearts of two petite Southern belles had been joined like those of a husband and wife. Friendship and memories of their love and children brought these petite gray- haired ladies together. Just like salt and pepper, the perfect seasoning that would make old and new live right.

They parted ways, and life at River Bend began again.

The nights were chilly, and a light snow was falling, not like the snowy look of the summer magnolias but a snowflake-filled sky dropping individual unique and beautiful flakes of pure white.

The white blanket that lay on the grounds resembled growing cotton. But the sun came out, and the short delay was just that, a momentary slowing down that only set back the growing process a few weeks.

But in the meantime, tobacco leaves were hanging in the barns drying, and the indigo was curing as well.

School began again, and Little Abigaile could hardly wait, hoping to see Mr. Butler again. She picked out her best dress in her chifforobe and tied back her long ponytail with a beautiful ribbon that matched her chosen attire.

But all her preparation met with disappointment. No Mr. Butler. The way home was a time of tears. Her handsome Mr. Butler was nowhere to be found. *I would have to be a big girl and pray for my emotions to not control me.* But it was a tall order, thought Little Miss Abigaile.

Little Abigaile was maturing in her little body slowly, but her heart was in full bloom. She was disappointed, but then tomorrow was bound to show up. Her hope could not be crushed.

Another chance would offer our Little Abigaile another day to dream and perhaps a love that might last as long as Great-Grandma Abigaile Amelie and Mr. Hurleys did.

Little Abigaile s Mr. Buder would wait for her too.

Easter was here at River Bend, and Little Abigail s Mr. Buder had eluded her.

He had not been at school for months. *Please, Lord, let him be okay.*

It was in between one of the harvests, and there he was, Little Abigaile's tall, raven-haired, blue-eyed hunk. Mr. Buder. Little Abigaile was not going to wait. As soon as she saw him, she sashayed right on over and asked him a question. "What is your name? Where do you live? Are you an only child? How old are you, and what is your favorite color and food?" He was bombarded with inquiry, but it didn't shake his confidence. He began to answer.

"My name is Harrison Darcy Buder. I live at Willow Oaks Plantation. I have two brothers. I am fifteen years old. My favorite color is blue because it matches my eyes. My favorite food is sugar-cured ham and watermelon. Any more questions?"

Miss Abigaile blushed beet red and sprinted away at record speed.

Questions asked and answered at record-breaking speed. Little Abigaile was mortified.

She had been so aggressive and forward, hence her speed and retreat far away.

But there was one more thing she had learned, and this time it was about herself. She was not happy being Little Abigaile anymore. She was now and forevermore wanting to be addressed as Miss Abigaile. And she was going to announce her revelation to her Great-Grandmother Abigaile Amelie first, then to the rest of her family. Grandma was very important, so she received this news first because she was Miss Abigaile s biggest fan. And, after all, her namesake.

How might Grandma take the news? Miss Abigaile was sure that her revelation would be accepted because, just like her grandma, she had fallen hard and in love with an older man. Grandma Abigaile really understood the heart. Miss Abigaile was young, but God seemed to be enlightening her young green eyes and pure heart with clarity for the future. Or at least that was Miss Abigaile s hope.

As Miss Abigaile arrived home, she searched high and low but couldn't find her grandma.

Miss Abigaile's face fell like a soufle. Yes, all could wait maybe, but not for too long.

Grandma Abigaile Amelie had gone to see her dear friend Miss Matilda early that day.

They were celebrating life and love and loss one more time.

Miss Matilda had her perfect pearls on as they both enjoyed high tea, and Abigaile Amelie wore her princess emeralds: they both agreed that life was too short to not enjoy all the gifts God had given them, even if man was the giver here on earth.

The weekend was approaching. On the ride home, Grandma was thinking what she would share with her dear ones for story time.

Home at last, and Miss Abigaile ran to welcome her namesake. "Grandma, Grandma! I have wonderful and exciting news."

"Hold on, let me step down and wash off the dust."

"Grandma, hurry, I am bursting." Miss Abigaile was beet red and ready to explode. "Guess what? I am just like you."

"Slow down, child. What do you mean?"

Miss Abigaile repeated herself. "I am just like you. I have fallen in love with an older man just like you did."

"What!"

"Grandma, do you remember last summer when you were telling us about Willow Oaks?"

"Yes, dear."

"Well, I met him. He is twelve inches taller than me. He has blue eyes like the sky and raven-black hair. He is fifteen years old. He lives at Willow Oaks. He has two brothers, and some of their workers ran out, and he had to help with the harvest part of this school year. Isn't he wonderful?"

"Slow down, child. What is his name?"

"Oh, Grandma! It is a grand rich melody of a name. It is Harrison Darcy Butler. Isn't it beautiful? I am almost thirteen now, and he could wait for me like Mr. Hurley did for you."

"Child, when did you decide he was your love?"

"When I first saw him. He won my heart. It was like electricity, Grandma. I almost threw up."

Grandma couldn't see her Little Abigaile growing up so fast.

"Oh! And one more thing. I want to be called Miss Abigaile, not Little Abigaile. I am growing up and in love. I need to have a grown-up lady name. Miss Abigaile is how I want to be called from now on."

"Okay, Miss Abigaile it will be."

Summer was almost here, and Grandmas story times would be frequent. Almost every day.

School was closing for the year, and a party was planned. They had brought in a Ferris wheel, and a cotton candy machine was spinning sugar into cloudlike pillows of goodness. They had candy apples and stuffed teddy bears as a prize for the ring toss. It was just like a county fair. And Mr. Butler was there with his raven-black hair waving in the wind. Miss Abigaile took every chance to be close to Mr. Butler. Being a young Southern gentleman, he chatted with Miss Abigaile and tried to seem like he was interested in what she was talking about. But someone called his name, and off he went. Miss Abigaile was left with half a sentence still on her lips. *What did I do wrong? He just left.*

But this didn't dampen her spirit too much. Her heart still stood still. That her love would come back was her hope. But even if he didn't, she still kept her heart ablaze with the memory of their time together.

The heat of summer was here. The big walk-through windows stayed open. The tall ceilings caught the heat of summer. The breezes blew through the live oaks and willow trees. But the most magnificent sight and smell of summer was the tall, majestic magnolia trees. The heavenly fragrance drifted throughout River Bend. The bedrooms upstairs carried the flavor of summer. The bedding was laid back each day to allow the sweet smell to penetrate and lull the sleepy nights away.

By this time, Miss Abigaile was ready for her birthday to come around. But she didn't want the party she had had for her twelfth year. No, she and Great-Grandma Abigaile Amelie needed to celebrate together. Grandma was turning eighty, and Miss Abigaile was going to be a teenager. Milestones for both.

A big birthday cake with lots of chocolate icing. Seven layers tall. You see, chocolate was a sweet passion they both shared. Since 1900, when Hershey bars came out, Grandma had been snacking on them, and her Little Abigaile was just the same. Chocolate and her name. They shared both.

Two peas in a pod. Blond hair once upon a time for Grandma and gorgeous green eyes for both.

The plan for their birthday celebration was unique. They both loved exotic animals, and the Ringling Brothers and Barnum and Bailey circus had come to their town. Hoping to be seated in the first row, they stopped a moment and prayed. *God, help us get front-row seats. Amen.* They were escorted in and seated right down front-row center. They glanced at each other and smiled and looked up as if to thank God.

The lights were dimmed, and the ringmaster entered the great ring. Quiet, quiet. A hush fell in the tent. "I have an announcement before we begin. We have a birthday duo. Abigaile and Abigaile." The two Abigail's stood up, and a round of applause sounded. They were given whistles, and each sounded the show to begin.

It was a special moment both could share over and over again. The wild-animal trainer came out, and the tigers were led into the ring on long leashes. The roars sent fear into each Abigaile. So close to the exotic was a rare treat, and a scary thing all at the same time. Lions, tigers, and bears. All danced for the two Abigayle's. Cotton candy and chocolate milkshakes helped to calm the nerves of Abigaile and Abigaile.

Grandma Abigaile Amelie and Miss Abigaile had reached the hills of fear and chocolate and came out winners.

Back home at River Bend, the night was calling. Tomorrow would come again, and laughter would live in the hearts of two so close in spirit that Miss Abigaile could almost speak forth some of her grandmothers' thoughts before she voiced them.

Miss Abigaile's brothers were sounding the break of morning, and the herd of turtles hurried down to see what treat there would be for breakfast. Growing boys, all they could think of was hunting, fishing, and food. And lots of it. They would finish one meal and be searching for more to fill the emptiness that seemed never to be filled.

The smell of freshly baked bread, bacon, and fresh strawberry preserves filled the house. Now, who wouldn't come running? All descended the great staircase and gathered in the great dining hall where green China from Miss Matilda adorned the long mahogany table. New green goblets held milk for the children and an iced tea for the adults. Fresh orange juice and a side of grits were also offered alongside coffee.

A prayer of thanks for the bounty, and all dug in.

The summer harvest was about to begin when Abigaile remembered what her Mr. Butler had done during part of the school year. Maybe he was doing the same thing as during River Bend's harvest.

For now, her brothers were too young to help, but as they progressed in age, they would be taught about the tobacco, cotton, and indigo plants and what it would take to create a cash crop that would supply the needs of River Bend and the Hurley family. But, for now, just being a kid and having fun was their job.

However, for Miss Abigaile, she found herself wanting to learn and participate in more grown-up activities. She took her role as an upcoming lady very seriously. She gave it her all. It was almost as if she would be expecting to be graded on her abilities by her mother and her namesake, Great-Grandmother Abigaile Amelie, but neither one had a single concern as to her abilities, because she had been instructed in the art of being "Lady of the House" since she was a very young girl.

The summer day peaked at an early time, and nights were longer. Breezes and the smell of freshly cut grass and magnolia blossoms seemed to fill the halls with sweet love of summer vacations.

The first weeks of summer had gone, and Grandma was ready to resume her history lessons of family and River Bend.

Gathering her dear ones and preparing for her after noon delight was fabulous, and her story times were an excitement that she looked forward to.

The grand living room was all set up with the grand carved chaise longue waiting for Grandma Abigaile and her belled skirt to take a seat.

After dinner, a brief moment was taken, and then Grandma Abigaile ascended this great stairway and entered her bedroom.

She hadn't put on her Southern belle costume for several months. Story time had taken a back seat to the school year and homework.

The babies had grown up, and the Little Abigaile was now Miss Abigaile and a teenager.

The boys were fourteen and fifteen years old, and the outdoors was still a big call. It was really hard for two red blooded Southern boys to be still for anything, but when it came to Great- Grandmother Abigaile Amelies history stories, it was obvious they were calm and respectful of her and could hardly wait to take in all that the Hurley family and River bend was.

All gathered, and the Hurley family history was ready to begin.

Great-Grandmother Abigaile Amelie took her place on the beautiful carved chaise longue, and the room stood still. A hush fell on the Hurley children, and story time began.

"And the magnolias were in bloom." A prayer where all joined in, and Grandma began.

*****

Our horse-and-buggy days may have come to an end. My dear friend of many years, Miss Matilda, had to put poor Sally Louise down. She was sick and never recovered.

Miss Matilda saw a new-fangled invention. It was called an automobile. She told me it was the wave of the future. She got one, so the next time she comes, it will be in no buggy but her new car. She had named her "Nellie."

This is not just the invention of the future. In my life time, I have seen so many new things.

For the girls of all ages, the sewing machine, safety pins, cotton candy, and candy corn for us all. For all the bugs that fly around, the flyswatter. Candled apples, curtain rods, fortune cookies, supermarkets, flash lamps, and the amazing mousetrap. Zippers, bottle caps, pinking shears, and the jukebox, but I think that the washing machine and the refrigerator are top on my list so far.

You see, before all the invention we use today, it was much harder to keep food fresh and keep our clothes sparkly clean. We had cellars and stone-covered storage houses. The ground and rock kept the foods somewhat cool, and the smokehouse was where our cured meats would hang until we were ready to enjoy them.

I grew up in the dark ages, as you call it, and life was so much more trying and difficult.

But Mr. Hurley was willing to do anything and everything better for me and his boys.

Now, let's continue. Traffic lights were started, stop signs, and that fabulous Ferris wheel and the fabulous teddy bear named after President Theodore Roosevelt. A lot of new things in this new country.

We used to cook in a separate little room outside the big house. One time many years ago, one of the cooks accidently set that room on fire, so for many years we cooked outside in a separate little house until we made special arrangements to protect our cooking stoves and no more fires could burn anything down.

When Mr. Hurley and I were starting River Bend, we planted our first cotton crop.

When the cotton was mature and ready for harvest, we all got out in the fields with our helpers and picked our cotton. We wore heavy gloves because the cotton bolls were so very sharp. We picked cotton from early in the morning until dark. It was very hard work.

As our plantation grew, we needed more and more helpers, and as your uncles were born, I was not as able to help like I had done at the beginning.

The one thing that I learned was that our helpers needed to be respected and treated like we wanted to be treated. So, every day, I cooked a very nice dinner and snacks so they could be able to function. You see, children, if you want to be loved, you show love. If you want to be treated well, you treat others the same way.

The Bible tells us to love one another as you love yourself.

What goes around comes around, and the most import ant thing is to never think you are better than anyone else.

We, the women of this United States, got our first opportunity to vote. A music style called jazz was born. Louis Armstrong was a Black man who made this jazz music popular, and baseball s Babe Ruth was a man who could hit a baseball way out of the field. It was called a home run. This is a game known as our American game. It is a lot like stickball.

The wine and alcohol that were made in our barns were then known to be illegal, so we are not supposed to make it anymore.

So many things have changed since I was a young girl, but the one thing that will never change is my love for you, my dear ones.

CHAPTER 6
Grandma's Love

"MY LOVE WILL always be with you, no matter where you go or what you do. No matter

how old you get, you will remember my hugs and the stories of River Bend.

"My dear ones, it is time to prepare for a nap and then supper. Boys, go play, and Miss Abigaile, could you help me place the princess emeralds away in their velvet box and into their secret hiding place?"

Grandma Abigaile and Miss Abigaile ascended the great curved stairway together.

Grandma had a tear in her eyes. She was remembering her great-grandmother. She could surely feel her hugs and love envelop her. A memory of that love passed down like all the stories she was relating to her dear ones.

It was so true. Love is something that never goes out of style and is something you just don't forget, a warm feeling of worth and a gift that all people are to each other.

Great-Grandmother Abigaile Amelie was ready for an afternoon refresher, but her little mind was not willing to settle down. Her thoughts were alive with memories of her great-grandmother, how, when she was a young girl, like Miss Abigaile is now, there was an evening ritual that she and her great-grandmother went through.

With nightgowns on, they would join in the bedroom and take the seat at Great- Grandmother Ottilie Amelies dresser. The sterling silver dresser set was taken out of the dresser drawer. The mirror and brush had an embossed flower, like that of a magnolia, atop each piece. It was gorgeous.

Abigaile Amelie would stand behind her great-grand mother, and the heavy brush would be admired, and then the bun that was in the back of her grandmother's head was unpinned, and the braids were undone. Fingers pressed into the braids, the ribbons of hair would be loosed, a shake of the head, and the ritual would begin.

Abigaile Amelie would stand close, and the brush would meet the long gray hair. One brushstroke and a step to the dresser and a big step back. Back and forth for stroke after stroke, a hundred to be exact.

This was a memory that Abigaile Amelie and Miss Abigaile could now share. Grandma handed Miss Abigaile the brush, and the beginnings of new memories were set in motion.

The daybed was calling, close to the four-poster bed that Great-Grandmother Abigaile Amelie retired in each day since she and Mr. Hurley built River Bend. A mattress that had been sewn together and stuffed with down feathers from chicken and ducks, it has seen better days, but to Abigaile Amelie it was perfect. It hugged her like Mr. Hurley was there. Even though he had been gone for quite some time, she could still feel his warmth each time she slipped into bed. A hug of love like no other allowed her to have sweet sleep and dreams of her lost love, Mr. Hurley. Grandma Abigaile Amelie was all aglow after her rest, and supper on the ground was planned. A roast goose with trufle sauce and fresh green beans from the garden. Mashed potatoes with trufle gravy and peach cobbler and whipped cream atop each scoop of cobbler.

Iced sweet tea, and a cubed watermelon salad.

Truly a Southern delight. More conversations on the porch, and the lightning bugs lit up the night.

The sweet smell of magnolias and wisteria and sweet peach honeysuckle filled the air. While the magnolias were filling the upstairs with perfume, the wisteria and peach honeysuckle filled the downstairs and the porches with the smells of sweet spring and a new rebirth for a new year. They considered spring and summer a new year because all was new. Animals would birth their babies, and the earth would bring forth the seeds of late winter. A show of new birth in the lands peaked out, and new sprouts emerged.

Nighttime sleep was calling. But Great-Grandma Abigaile Amelie wanted to introduce her

Miss Abigaile to the remembrance of the special time she had with her great-grandmother.

So, she called out for her Miss Abigaile to join her. With nightgowns on, Great-Grandma invited Miss Abigaile to grab the sterling dresser set out of the drawer and began to tell Miss Abigaile of her special time with her Great Grandmother Ottilie Amelie.

As she began to tell her Miss Abigaile the story of her special time, Miss Abigaile stood behind Abigaile Amelie and started to brush the long silver hair of her great-grand mother. Miss Abigaile took one step forward and one back over and over again.

Tears began to fall. Grandma could hardly believe it was the same thing, the same way she and her grandmother had done, so many years before, a hundred strokes counted.

The summer night called, and a golden memory flooded her mind, and tears poured forth emotions of love. Tears fell again.

The dresser set was the source of her tears. She was reminded of when she first received her beautiful set. It was her tenth wedding anniversary to Mr. Hurley. When the two boys were very young, Mr. Hurley had plucked a magnolia blossom from one of River Bend trees and carried it to a local craftsman, one who worked in wood. The wood worker was the best in Southern Georgia. Mr. Hurley had told Abigaile Amelie this story many times at her request. He had taken the wood carving of the magnolia blossoms large and small to a silversmith. He took the detailed wood carving and poured molten silver over them to bring forth a three-dimensional picture of River Bend's magnolia trees.

A beveled mirror was placed inside the exception ally large hand mirror, and an ivory comb that had been hand carved from an elephant's tusk. The stiff bristles of the brush were retrieved from a wild boar and some of the horses that lived on River Bend. All made for the true love of Mr. Hurleys life. Abigaile Amelie carried this story in her heart to share with Miss Abigaile when she handed over her set on Miss Abigaile's wedding day. Miss Abigaile was already thirteen, so it might not be that long.

It was almost Thanksgiving, and Mr. Butler showed up again at school. Miss Abigaile was so excited she could hardly catch her breath.

During the summer, Miss Abigaile had turned from a childish figure to one of a maturing young woman.

Would Mr. Butler notice, or would her growth spurt go unnoticed? Only time would tell.

And then it happened. He turned, and his eyes lit up. Or at least that was Miss Abigaile's view. He turned and said hello. Her heart melted. Her Mr. Butler had noticed her. She could hardly wait to tell her great-grandmother, but for now, the school day was not over.

Back home again, and Miss Abigaile came running. "He spoke to me, Grandma! Mr. Harrison Darcy Butler spoke to me. He is so handsome. Grandma, I am going to marry him one day." A surprising declaration, but Grandma could only recall her own declaration for her Mr. Hurley. It was indeed many, many years ago, but a love declaration never dies.

"I understand, my darling," said Grandma. "Perhaps tomorrow, before Thanksgiving holiday is here, you might ask him over for a piece of pie. You know, my Miss Abigaile, men love to eat, and they are best when they are not hungry."

The hope of another encounter was lost. Miss Abigaile did not see him again.

It would not be until the school Christmas party that her hopes would be fulfilled.

This time was magical. An uncommon snowfall left everything in a blanket of white. The magnolia trees had lost all their blooms of summer, but the snow made them appear like they were in full spring bloom. The air was cold and crisp, and the smell was that of fresh laundry hanging on the clotheslines.

The school would close for the holiday, but not before the students could present a gift to each other or their teacher. Miss Abigaile got the surprise of her life. Mr. Butler approached her. He had one last gift in his hands. He had passed out some to friends and a gift for his teacher, but there was one left. The gift he had for a young girl who took his fancy.

A box, small in size, was wrapped with red paper and a green silk ribbon.

He had saved this one to the last. He wanted to save more time with Miss Abigaile before he would have to go home.

"Here, Miss Abigaile, this is for you. My mother said every young Southern girl would like them."

Abigaile received her gift from Mr. Butler and asked if she could open it. "Yes, sure, you bet, why not. It's yours, go ahead." He was tongue-tied, but Miss Abigaile got the message.

She unwrapped the small box and folded back white delicate tissue paper. She was stunned. Inside the box underneath the transparent tissue paper was a folded lace trimmed hankie with the initial A on it. Just one hankie, beautiful, regal, worthy of words of thanks, but none came out of Abigaile's mouth. She blinked and smiled and lunged forward and gave her Mr. Butler a long hug and a quick peck on his check She felt like a true princess. Her prince had noticed her and presented her with a token. A token of love, Miss Abigaile was hoping, but only time could dis close the matter of this gift.

She had nothing for him, but his gift from her was how she received his.

Abigaile felt her heart come alive.

This would be the best Christmas she had ever known.

They parted ways, and both experienced a new joy they had never known. Mr. Butler had turned sixteen, and Miss Abigaile was now thirteen.

Grandma saw the smile that crossed Miss Abigaile's face. From ear to ear. A glow that shone brighter than the fresh-fallen snow.

The boys ran past Grandma Abigaile. Grandma Abigaile walked briskly toward her namesake. She could tell something of great importance must have taken place.

With her gifts all in her book bag, she was holding one to her small bosom. Grandma was all so curious. But before Grandma Abigaile could ask, Miss Abigaile unleashed the news.

"He talked to me. My Mr. Butler talked to me. And look, Grandma, he gave me a gift. It is so beautiful. I will keep it forever. I think he loves me. Oh, Grandma, this is the best Christmas ever!"

"Child, can I see?"

"Sorry, Grandma. Look, it has my initial on it. He is so handsome and gorgeous, and I love him. Oh, and I couldn't help myself. I hugged him. I also gave him a little kiss on his cheek, was that okay?"

"Sure, darling. Just contain your excitement next time to a thank-you. Now Christmas can begin."

"I got my first gift from my love, Mr. Harrison Darcy Buder," Abigaile exclaimed.

This was a memory she would cherish. This was a feeling that she never felt before. Her books of mystery and intrigue never took her to places where this new feeling took her.

Over the holiday, River Bend was dressed in red, green, gold, and a new color, cobalt blue, and a pale shade of pink. The new color combination was displayed in every room of the house; even the kitchen held a new pale-pink set of dishes made of pressed glass. Depression glass. Clean and delicate patterns of bows and flowers circled the dinnerware.

The annual River Bend Christmas party welcomed old and new friends. Gifts were given and received.

The snow was still hiding in the shadows, and the cold air hovered. Horse and buggies came and went, and one new automobile arrived right up front.

The house at River Bend had come alive with the sounds of music and caroling. Christmas had arrived. But for Miss Abigaile, it began that day of the school Christmas party and her gift from Mr. Butler. She had never known such joy. But she would have to wait until school began again to catch a glimpse of her love.

The night arrived early, and the Hurley household was ready for a long winters nap. But for Grandma Abigaile and Miss Abigaile, the bed did not call yet.

The silver dresser set was placed on top of Grandmas dresser, and the call to Miss Abigaile was sounded. "Come here, my dear one. Miss Abigaile knew the call would be for her Great-Grandmother Abigaile Amelie to share a memory that would be there forever. Perhaps a story for the new storyteller, or Miss Abigaile, to share with her granddaughter one day.

The two Abigaile's smiled laughed and shared a tear together. And the great feather bed summoned Grandma.

Two days before Christmas, and all were busy wrap ping and preparing food for the big Christmas banquet.

Grandma Abigaile had ordered all her silver ornaments and took time to wrap each one specially. The paper and ribbon had to fit each person's personality. Elegant to fun cowboy wrapping for her boys. Grandma placed each hand wrapped ornament on top of each person's pillow, along with an envelope filled with fifty crisp dollar bills for each adult and twenty silver dollars for her dear young ones.

This was her way of saying I love you. Downstairs, there were piles of presents all circling the grand tree. It looked like a village lived there. So many gifts wrapped in shades of blue, pale pink, red, green, and gold, but standing front and center there was a hand-painted China nativity, standing three feet tall.

No one could ever not say that Jesus was not the rea son for the season because the nativity was placed in front of the blessings that surrounded the tree.

It was a nativity that had been brought back with family members who had visited the beginnings of this unique and blessed clan, a place where the Hurley family had their European start, and the princess emeralds were received and then passed down.

The Christmas banquet was enjoyed by all. Leftovers were served with potatoes, veggies, soups, and desserts. There was not one morsel wasted.

It was just about New Year's Eve, and Miss Matilda drove up to the front door of River Bend. It was her regular visit where Abigaile Amelie and she would exchange belated Christmas gifts and relive their memories. With smiles and tears, they never felt empty of life when it was time to go home.

This year was no exception. Smiles and stories of the last few months. Last year, Miss Matilda had traveled to Paris to meet all her children and their children. This year, she would tell Abigaile Amelie of the joys and horror stories that took place at her home as they all came a- calling. They stayed for two weeks. A little long for Matilda, but God helped her follow through with all their plans.

Miss Matilda had traveled to a far-off continent before Thanksgiving and brought out of her purse a small box. It was smaller than her coin purse and fit perfectly in the palm of her hand. She presented it to Abigaile Amelie and said Merry Christmas.

These two had been exchanging tokens of love for many years. Abigaile Amelies eyes grew large, like saucers. Inside the box was a ring that covered her finger knuckle to knuckle. It sparkled with a fire of many different colors.

There were pinks, blues, greens, yellows, and a streak of red that seemed to light the whole stone.

"I got this on my trip to Australia. There is a mine there where opals like this are available to buy. While I was there, the other mine was a diamond mine. So, I just got the two together, and before I left, your ring was ready to come back to Georgia." The yellow gold picked up the flashes of golden color, and the diamonds seemed to light up the other colors. "Since we both wear the same-size ring, it was very easy to get it right."

Abigaile Amelie was glowing like her new ring. She put it on. Miss Matilda was right. It fit like a glove.

Hugs and thank-you' s, and then Abigaile retrieved her gift for Miss Matilda.

The box Abigaile brought out was also small but elongated in size. About as long as her hand from tip to wrist. Abigaile had not wrapped her box either. Just a beautiful velvet box that matched the box she gave Miss Matilda last year.

Similar responses by both friends. Eyes wide open, and the gloved hand opened her Christmas gift. She said, "It matches my long pearl necklace." Abigaile had planned this since last Christmas. A three-strand bracelet with a clasp covered with diamonds and small seed pearls.

Both ladies had given lasting treasures that their family could also enjoy long after both were gone.

And the most amazing sight was that each was wearing their crown jewels. Abigaile was wearing her princess emeralds, and Matilda adorned her neck with the perfect pearls she had received last year, from Abigaile Amelie.

Both were pictures of age, grace, and jeweled perfection. Hugs and more hugs were given and received.

New Year's Day and one more week before school would resume.

A few more story times were planned for Grandmother Abigaile Amelies dear ones.

Nighttime was fast approaching. Miss Matilda drove her automobile back to her cottage, and supper was served at River Bend. Finally, all the banquet leftovers were gone, and a steak meal was served up. Mashed potatoes, fried okra, and a new dish. Shrimp with garlic and butter, bubbly hot and scrumptious. A new favorite at River Bend.

Nighttime, and hair brushing with Grandma was on the agenda.

The snow was melting, and the shadows were still holding some of the winters first snow.

The morning came, and the herd of turtles bounded up and down the wide hallways of River Bend.

Breakfast called to all, and the menu was full of their favorites. Freshly baked cinnamon rolls, sugar-cured bacon, eggs, and a side of canned peaches.

You could smell the "come and get it" in the air.

A warm cozy fire was taking the winter chill off the air, and sweaters were draped on the backs of the mahogany chairs.

The table was set with ruby-red everything, and the silver flatware that had been saved from the days of war graced the table.

A blessing for their bounty, and the family Hurley finished off the piles of food. The boys had two hollow legs, and it took twice as much to fill them up.

Grandma Abigaile Amelie announced there would be a story time today. The children were excited. They almost clapped and shouted, "Yeah," but they knew it was not befitting of a young gentleman and certainly not at the table, so quietly, they said, "Great-Grandma, looking forward to."

Breakfast was over, and play time inside and out was the job for two noisy growing boys, but Miss Abigaile had her heart on daydreaming and reading one of her novels.

Miss Abigaile was growing up. Her response to Grandmas announcement was one of a proper young Southern lady, quiet with a big smile. Ready, willing, and able to be the up-and-coming keeper of stories and history, keeper of the Hurley family.

She was a quick study, with all eyes and ears collecting a great amount of information, to be recalled at another point in time.

Miss Abigaile had been dubbed the keeper of stories by Grandma just months before.

Inside, play was suggested. Checkers and backgammon were the boys' favorite. Two boys, two players, they played for pennies and candy.

Dinner was served, and it was almost story time.

Grandma Abigaile Amelie was excited. She was going to share about a cousin three degrees removed, who was going to come to Georgia. He wasn't a Hurley. He was going to be welcomed at River Bend when he arrived.

But first she would have to prepare herself. Ascending the great curved stair was beginning to be a little harder than usual.

This was a concern at first. Grandma forgot the winter played havoc with her joints, but this only occurred during the winter months.

So, she progressed. Her very special preparations for her dear ones' story time were her costume.

The same belled skirt, but this time Grandma adorned her hat and belt with green and black velvet ribbon. As she hadn't changed her ribbons in years, these new ribbons seemed to bring a new elegance to Grandma's Southern dress. One of rich color and a soft texture that were a true complement to the princess emeralds and pearls.

Miss Abigaile assisted her grandma and took the princess emeralds from their double secret hiding place. She carefully removed the generation jewels from their resting place and rubbed them softly over and over and over again. She placed them around Grandma's neck and placed the pearl and emerald bracelet around Grandma's delicate wrist. Then the pair of earrings were clipped on to her small earlobes, a perfect picture of a Southern lady, and the gifts from a royal princess, emeralds and pearls.

Story time was almost here, and Grandma Abigaile Amelie was filled to the brim with excitement.

"Dear ones, dear ones." They all stopped what they were doing and hurried to the great hall.

They always sat in the same place. It was as if they had assigned seating. No matter the reason, the boys and Miss Abigaile were ready. Ready to hear another real story of families past and that of River Bend.

The boys seemed to absorb all and everything like sponges, but it was Grandma's Miss Abigaile who could relate these stories verbatim, almost like she had taken notes or had a photographic memory. She was the perfect person to entrust all grandma's stories to.

Many times, it made others wonder if these memories were exact or embellished, but to most it was at least 50 percent true, or more, or maybe less, but the stories were a timeline of history past. But in this case, the whole truth of these recollections was very true. A story of ships' passage, new worlds, jewels, new crops, and names that could be traced back several centuries when generations were in the same towns and businesses were handed down from father to son.

Grandma began. "And the magnolias were in bloom. Help me, Lord. Amen."

*****

It was not that long ago when all our relatives lived in the same country.

But there were those among the family who had heard of a new land. Where lands were able to be had, and dreams of opportunities were to be seized. A land where young and old, rich or poor, could exist side by side. A place where men could live and flourish.

This was a time before the war of the states. Where North and South were simply a geographic description of two territories that joined borders.

A place where you could see hills and flatlands, deserts and oceans. Where the soil was rich and yield a harvest, sometimes year-round.

Where gold and silver were found, and things of value could be purchased by all or traded. A place where I met my Mr. Hurley, and love could be found. A land that could not only produce a crop but give you a new hope. A new hope for a better life than that of the one you had sailed away from.

Dear ones, I believe if you traveled to Europe and found the place where my family first lived, you would still find a portion of my family tree. Cousins, aunts, and uncles.

When my Great-Grandmother Ottilie Amelie was a girl, and that was not so long ago. Back in Europe.

It was not until her parents were given passage on a ship that her momma worked as a seamstress, for royalty, kings, queens, and their heirs.

Do you see these beautiful jewels I am wearing? These are treasures that a princess gave to my great-grandmother's mother.

They have been a treasure that was carried over on the ship many long years ago.

The ships have carried numerous people over the years to these new lands. It was not so long ago a long-lost cousin took passage on a great ship called the *Titanic*. It sailed from England. He was twenty-three years old and took a job as a waiter on this huge ship. The ship had sailed for days and hit an iceberg. It knocked such a big hole in the hull of the ship that it was sinking in the middle of the ocean. He was going to be our guest, but he went down with the ship. Not many survived.

You see, you really do not know when your time is up here on earth. You could live to be a hundred or not make it to twenty-four. That is why you must always be ready. "Ready for what, Grandma?"

You know, just like the preacher tells us every Sunday. Pray, forgive, and be a shining light for others to see. I always like to say, "Be the best Christian that anyone knows."

Time to prepare for dinner, dear ones.

*****

The boys resumed their checkers game, and Miss Abigaile and Grandma retreated upstairs. Off came the belle skirt and ribbons, and last but not least the princess emeralds and pearls were placed back in their velvet boxes and gingerly placed back into the double secret hiding place where they would wait until another story time called them out.

With the holidays over and school begun again, Miss Abigaile waited each morning for her Mr. Butler. They were in different grades, and there were separate rooms for certain grade groups. It just so happened that Miss Abigaile missed his grade group by only one year, but nonetheless, it was hit or miss for them to see each other.

The only time Miss Abigaile could catch a glimpse was during lunch. Yet it was enough to fill her heart with joy. A glance, a wave, and maybe a quick hello. It all made this young lady happy and gave her a smile that never left her heart, all the way home and back again. The next day she skipped and sang a song of love that no one could hear.

She was in love, a young girl no more. Now a young woman was born.

The week passed quickly, and before all knew it, February 14 was here. The day where Cupid would shoot his arrows, and a new love would be born.

Maybe for someone else. But for Abigaile, she was already in love. And Mr. Butler was her valentine.

A big red box in the shape of a heart was her Valentine's gift from Mr. Buder. It was filled with milk chocolate and another lace-trimmed hankie with Abigaile's initial. That made two hankies she could cherish now, forever.

The winter snows had completely melted, and the buds of spring were peeking out.

In Georgia, one could always count on March first as the date for spring to open up a long fruitful growing season.

With Easter approaching, the red bud trees were dis playing varying shades of purple, and the fruit trees showed flowers of yellow, red, pink, and white. An Easter parade in nature.

School was still in session, and all were looking forward to the Easter holiday.

Especially Miss Abigaile. She was wondering if Mr. Butler would present another keepsake to her.

So much to look forward to.

It seemed like Grandma Abigaile Amelie had a secret. But she didn't utter a word.

Grandma was talking about the trips she had taken, but it didn't give anyone a clue. She talked about Europe, New York, Paris, and Italy. But still no clue. Just about the people and the beauty of the country, but still no real clue. They didn't guess what her clues were saying.

At this time, Grandma Abigaile Amelie was fixing to be eighty years old that summer. Miss Abigaile was turning fourteen, and the boys were turning older also. All summertime birthdays.

All were wondering if Grandma was going to be announcing to the family a plan to celebrate all four birth days this summer with a tour of these cities, she had mentioned. But again, no clue. It was as if Grandma was holding her mouth closed to all. No questions, because they all knew Grandma could keep a secret better than the dead.

School days were coming to an end, and Easter was celebrated by a Sunday church meeting and dinner on the church grounds. All the members were bringing their best dishes; there were so many dishes and desserts that everyone could have seconds and still take-home leftovers.

At River Bend, the Hurley family would be given all the leftovers, and they served their helpers a feast of huge proportions.

CHAPTER 7
God's Message

BE READY.

This was a message that the Hurley family had heard twice in less than a day.

They all decided that Grandma had an ear turned to heaven, and God spoke to her like He did the pastor.

Mr. Buder was waiting for Miss Abigaile until almost everyone had gone home from church. She carried a small yet extremely fine Easter wire basket filled with jelly beans of different colors and a large chocolate Eater bunny. No hankie, but a basket that could hold anything she wanted. Another keepsake to treasure.

It seemed to be young love in bloom. At least Miss Abigaile saw it that way. Parting ways was hard for these two. A quick hug, and off they went.

Home again, and Miss Abigaile requested a special one-on-one talk with Grandma.

Grandma could read her young namesake. It was going to be a question-and-answer session. One where young love and proper responses would be discussed.

As nighttime called to all, Miss Abigaile was pacing back and forth. She had been given wise instruction but wasn't sure when she could use this information. Yet she knew in time all that grandma said was going to be put to good use.

Grandma was still holding her tongue, no information shared. But in her mind, it just wasn't time yet.

What could she be withholding from her family? But Grandma Abigaile Amelie had a plan, and no one was about to change her mind. She had a plan, and everybody would just have to wait.

Six more weeks of school, and Miss Abigaile might not see her sweet Mr. Butler for a whole three months. She was worried about something that had not presented itself yet, and time marched on. School continued.

The end of school was there, and the school party was ready to be enjoyed by all. Just like the year before. Ferris wheel and games, cotton candy and hot dogs. Races and eating contests.

Mr. Butler found his Miss Abigaile and wished her a great summer and told her he would be working at Willow Oaks all summer. "See you next September!" Her heart sank but she knew she had his heart. That would have to hold her heart until school began again.

Grandma was still holding on to her secret. It was coming close to being disclosed, but Grandma had several have-tos before all would know the secret Grandma had been holding on to.

But Grandma had a plan: First plan of attack was to make sure her great-grandchildren all had new clothes, casual and Sunday clothes. So off to the general store for a shopping adventure. The boys hated shopping of all kinds but were accommodating to their grandma's wishes.

Still there was no clue as to the secret she was keeping. Grandma was a good secret keeper.

Her second step, to their surprise, was individual pho tos. Again, still no clue as to Grandmas surprise. Photos were posted into a small blue book that had a special insignia on it.

The kids were still clueless.

By this time, several weeks had passed. In the later part of June, the two Abigaile's were getting ready for their birthday celebration. But Grandma was still not ready to reveal her surprise. Grandma was turning eighty-five, and Miss Abigaile was in her second teen year. Fourteen years old. The boys' birthday was in August, and Mom and Dad were not planning on anything great because they could tell Grandma was cooking up something.

As the two Abigaile's celebrated their special day, a surprise was about to be revealed.

In the month of July, the completion of all grandma's plans was ready to be exposed.

A special meeting was called. The children were ready for another story time, but that was not what Grandma had in mind.

The children noticed something was different. No costume. Grandma was not dressed in her belled skirt or floppy hat. And no princess emeralds. Even Miss Abigaile had a question as to what this meeting could be all about.

At first, Miss Abigaile was wondering if her dear sweet Grandma was okay. She had talked herself into and out of several concerns.

MISS MATILDA'S GIFT
TO GRANDMA ABIGAILE

Then Grandma sat down on her carved chaise longue and gathered her young ones around her. "Dear ones, let's begin. And the magnolias were in bloom. Help me, Lord."

Well, it was the same way with all grandma's story times. Still there was something off.

"Children, call your mom and dad in here."

Concerned about Grandma, they came running. The children were not sure what was going on, but all would be revealed in a flash. By Grandma herself.

"Dear ones," she started. All were ready. "I have a sur prise for my dear grandchildren and you. I have a geography lesson for you all." Confused looks on everyone's face. No one knew what Grandma was talking about.

"Dear ones, I have booked passage for all of us to a country Miss Matilda told me about. The place is called Australia. A geography lesson you can elaborate on for school. Our family trip begins in two weeks. So, get your stuff in order. We leave at noon. Oh, and it is winter over there."

No questions were asked because Grandma had instructed her family in the facts. They knew to not ask Grandma demanded respect; she was after all the matriarch of the Hurley family, and sharp as a tack.

The new clothes, the pictures, now it all made sense.

Grandma also had another reason for choosing Australia. Miss Matilda had given her friend Abigaile Amelie a gorgeous opal ring for Christmas, and she really needed a bracelet, earrings, and necklace to match. The only place to get it right was Australia. So off to Australia was the plan.

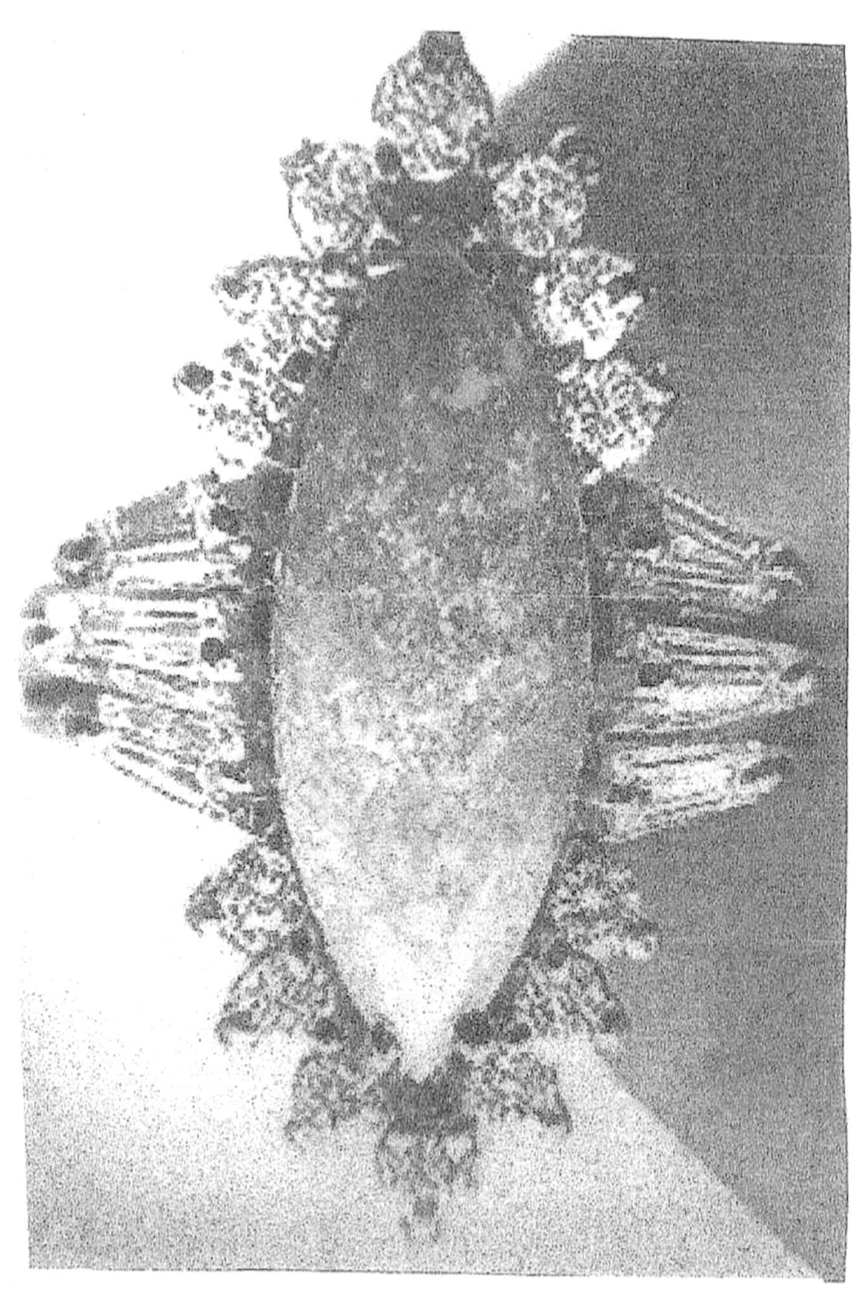

MISS MATILDA'S GIFT
TO GRANDMA ABIGAILE

Miss Abigaile was excited to go, but she was going to miss her Mr. Butler.

It was a long trip ahead for the family, but all were looking forward to the adventure. Grandma could hardly wait to pick out her new jewels, a fall set of precious opals and diamonds to match her new opal ring from Miss Matilda.

Even though the heat of Georgia was at full tilt, the Hurley family had to pack for their trip with winter attire. You see, the summer and winter seasons were exactly opposite in Australia.

Grandma Abigaile Amelie was going through her trunks.

Because Australia was halfway around the world and the seasons were opposite, it presented a challenge for all.

Things were so hectic. The next two weeks flew by. All the trunks were collected, and passage on the ship and the adventure began.

Days and nights of travel, hours of planning the trip, and now they were there.

Plans to see the whales first. Then the koala bears, next the horse races. A rest in between each sight. The Kangaroo Island was a two-day affair. Last but certainly not least on the itinerary, the mines. And then the jeweler. First the opal mines. Grandma had her new ring with her, so she could match the pattern in this rainbow-colored gem. Next the lost river diamond mine, where gold and diamonds could be found. It was the perfect place to find the components to make her new jewels a family heirloom.

And one last excursion in a hot-air balloon.

A geography lesson and memories for a lifetime. Back home to Georgia, and the hot weather was looming.

With trunks back in the attic and all winter clothes hidden away, the preparation for the next school year had to begin.

As soon as Miss Abigaile arrived home, she began to think about her Mr. Butler. She was hoping he had missed her because she surely missed him. But she would be knowing very soon.

Now as for Grandma Abigaile, she was so glad to be back home. As she unpacked and placed all her heavy warm clothes away, she took out her new gems. She smiled. Her new gems, opals, and diamonds.

They were glistening in the sunlight. The rays of sun light were reflecting on the mirrors and walls rainbow colors. No matter which way she held the velvet box, the light of the sun shone the streaks of light in the shape of a rain bow onto every surface.

Placing her opal and diamond necklace on her fair Southern neck took her back to when her Great Grandmother Ottilie Amelie placed the princess emeralds on her neck. Pearls and emeralds, a gorgeous piece of history.

But now the opal and diamonds were not that of yesterday's history but a part of the present that would, one day, become a new piece of history, one where she would place her jewels on to her great-granddaughter's neck. Miss Abigaile would one day pass it on to her great-granddaughter as well.

Now two pieces of history that would be Miss Abigaile s in time, jewels of beauty and worth for the generations to come.

School was just about ready to open, and Miss Abigaile was in high expectations. She was so hoping to see her Mr. Buder on the first day. But she remembered last year. It was harvesting time at Willow Oaks, and he was part of the workers who would help bring in and prepare the soil for the next planting.

In Georgia, depending on the weather, they could plant and harvest three to four times a year. back.

But Miss Abigaile was hoping against hope her Mr. Butler would be there to welcome her Over the summer, Miss Abigaile turned fourteen, and Mr. Buder was now seventeen.

In the history of men and women and the plans of families in the old country, but not in this new land, Georgia, it was the hope that thereafter, Southern gentlemen would meet and marry a young Southern belle. The plans of arranged marriages seemed to be a thing of the old country.

But old or new, Mr. Buder and Miss Abigaile had a young budding romance that could, maybe in time, turn into a long love that would last until death did, they part.

For now, their attraction couldn't bloom too much because they were very young.

First day of school, and their eyes met. "Hello." And school began.

Miss Abigaile was in ninth grade, and Mr. Buder was in twelfth grade.

One might think that Miss Abigaile was too young for Mr. Buder, but the heart can respect and wait for love to bloom for just such a time as this. And that time wasn't ready to be exposed, a love that seemed to be growing roots that would weather the storms of their lives to come. But neither of them had a clue yet.

The Christmas holidays were in full swing at River Bend. Since Thanksgiving, the grand hall had been dec orated with red and greens cords of blue and gold draped across the mantel, and artworks hung in the grand hall.

Great-Grandma Abigaile Amelie was being picked up by her dear friend Miss Matilda. A trip to the post office in town was one of their stops. Grandma was expecting her silver ornaments that would be placed on each of the Hurley family's pillows that night or the next.

She would take each ornament that had been casted and wrap each one separately, each having a paper that matched the bed linens in each room.

This year's silver memento was in the shape of a boomerang engraved with the name and date of their summer trip, *Australia 1934.*

When unwrapped, the Hurley family would place the silver ornament on a tree of the appropriate size to hold the collection of silver mementos Grandma Abigaile had blessed each one with since the year of their birth.

Grandmas tree stood four feet tall. She had all nine ty-three of her years and the sixty-five from her Mr. Hurley, a hundred fifty-eight in total.

Shapes that told a story, snowflakes, baseballs, air globes, cotton balls, indigo flowers, willow trees, great oaks, River Bend, and many more, all having a date and a single word engraved to peek into a memory for each.

Several of her mementos were two of a kind, because she and Mr. Hurley each had the same silver ornament.

Each time the mementos came out of the attic, it would bring a tear to Grandmas eye. Memories and love lost. A personal story of who she was and her life with Mr. Hurley and her life at River Bend. Children and grandchildren, trips and times of importance in the world, a tree with history draped on each and every limb.

Before school resumed, Grandma had one more story time for her dear ones.

With the new year here and the parties and Christmas celebration in the past, it was onward and upward toward a new year.

The holiday decorations were all hand wrapped and placed into boxes and placed back into the attic. Grandma Abigaile Amelie had a bit of hesitation as all the silver ornaments that Mr. Hurley and she had shared were put away for another year.

Miss Matilda and Grandma Abigaile were into their nineties. Both were like, as the expression said, spring chickens. But both knew their time was closer than all the years before.

Even though these two gray-haired beauties were young at heart and very adventurous, they knew that being almost a hundred could become an issue soon.

Perhaps these trips might be coming to an end, but for now, there was life full speed ahead.

Grandma Abigaile was not going to take it lying down. Feisty and still full of life, she had a plan. A plan to reach a hundred plus and see her namesake Miss Abigaile marry and wear the princess emeralds on her wedding day. She also had a plan to see another precious darling child being born into her family.

So off she would go. There would be no stopping someone of such determination, and she certainly had that.

Sunday morning, and church was calling. The night before, Grandma had gathered her family around the great dining table and began to preach. "Tell all your friends that God has a time for all of us to be born and a time to go be with Him. Be ready. Don't be putting off forgiving someone. Love yourself and your neighbors."

Well, you guessed it. Sunday morning, that was the exact words the pastor spoke on.

We were sure Grandma and God had a special phone line. They must talk a lot, because the pastor and Grandma had 80 percent of the time the same message, and we at River Bend heard the message twice. We all thought that it must be pretty important because we always had a chance after those double messages to put it to the test.

The fireplaces were going and the crimson drapes were framing the walk-throughs. The winter wonderland outside was framed in scarlet inside. A picture-perfect scene for any greeting card.

Before the holidays were over, Grandma wanted one more time to share with her dear ones.

Grandma Abigaile Amelie was positive what she would share. It could make you cry, but also make you appreciate the way the Lord had continually protected and blessed the Hurley family and River Bend.

School was only a few more days away.

The night called, and the winter cold had set in Grandma had one thing on her mind. Tomorrow would be her last chance before school began again for her to convey to her dear ones another real-life part of history.

The ritual of hair brushing was going on, and Miss Abigaile asked Grandma if she could try on her new opal and diamond necklace. Grandma was pleased and said yes. Yes, to her namesake.

Next to the double secret hiding place Grandma had for the princess emeralds, she pulled out the cobalt-blue velvet box that held her new acquisition from Australia. The box was opened, and the night light reflected the rain bow colors of the opals that lay within the special box.

Grandma slowly placed her hand underneath the beautiful opal necklace.

Even in the candlelight of Grandmas room, they sparkled like the stars. Grandma had Miss Abigaile sit in front of the dressing table. Grandma placed the opal necklace around Miss Abigaile s dainty neck and closed the locking closer. Grandma stood back, and her eyes looked like she had seen a ghost. The truth was she saw herself in Miss Abigaile. The same as when she asked her great-grand mother to try on the princess emeralds around her neck.

Now there would be a new treasure to pass down. Both admired the beautiful jewelry, and back in the blue box they went. The double secret hiding place was closed, and bedtime called.

Grandma was alone again, and her mind was having a hard time turning off. She was going over the past and her time with Mr. Hurley, her sweet time with Mr. Hurley, her love. As her silver- haired braid lay across her shoulder, she asked the Lord for sweet sleep. She also thanked Him for the time she had with Mr. Hurley and the legacy of River Bend that would live on far after she was gone.

If anyone could have heard her prayer, they might have thought she was saying goodbye to life. However, that was about as far as the east is from the west. In her mind, she was alive with thoughts of all the tomorrows to come. Especially the story time she would share with her dear ones in the next day or two.

The winter winds were blowing, and the snow was falling. The Hurley family was all awake, and there was a sur prise snowfall sunrise. Breakfast was almost ready, freshly baked bread, slab bacon, fresh apple butter, and eggs sizzling in the bacon grease, and lots of gravy to pour over everything. Maybe they could be known as the gravy baby family.

Today was the day Grandma had decided. Story time for her dear ones.

School would start in two days, and she didn't want to lose her opportunity to share another part of history, Hurley history.

Before breakfast had ended, Grandma announced her story time would be following dinner. "Midafternoon," she said, "so get ready."

Grandma Abigaile Amelie was already ready to go forward, but hold the horses, she was thinking. You have a few hours before story time.

This was the boys' last day for hunting. So, the guns were out of the gun cabinet, and coats and hats went on. Off to the woods, and the search was on for a target. Whatever they shot, they gave to their dogs to eat. The rule was "Don't kill just to kill. Kill to eat, or give it to another to eat."

It seemed so appropriate because there were so many who went hungry every day in the twenties, and the Great Depression was such a hard time in our country for all. A very special thought because that was Grandma's topic for story time, but the boys had no idea.

The dinner bell was ringing, and all came in to enjoy the bounty of God's blessing.

Grandma announced again, "Story time in a couple of hours."

This time, Grandma decided to dress up with a different belle skirt, one that would match her new opals. One that was blue in color with pink and green ribbons that ran around the bottom of this enormous skirt. Another floppy hat that was Grandma's Sunday go-to meeting hat, a beautiful blue lace blouse, and velvet slippers that were the same color as her skirt.

As she descended down the curved stairway, her name's sake held her hand. Down into the grand hall she took her place on the hand-carved mahogany chaise longue.

The dear ones were summoned, and the places they had always taken called them to sit and rest a while. Grandma could take a while to convey her message of the past. With all settled and Grandma sitting on her throne, story time was ready to begin. Grandma would always pray for recall and start with "And the magnolias were in bloom."

*****

Dear ones, we have been so blessed in our life here at River Bend.

You know, we are entering 1935, but in the early 1920s there was a true and very horrible time in our country. I will tell you of the devastation this country encountered, then I will tell you of how the Lord protected us all at River Bend.

Now, it was called the Great Depression. It had its start in the early 1920s and had lasted almost ten years.

In this time, there were many who lost their homes because they could not pay. They could not buy or sell their homes, because nobody had enough money. There were many who were homeless. Their homes were repossessed, and they were told to leave their homes.

The stock markets and banks were under attack. Many banks failed, that means they closed, and the stock market closed, and many lost everything.

The economy was down, and no jobs were to be had. Unemployment was the term. Food was in short supply. And during this poor position in our towns, there were thieves. Crime increased.

People had nothing and no hope for their family. They tried to encourage each other, but everyone knew each others pain. It was very hard to tell someone to hold on when they themselves had nothing to hold on to.

But you must remember that even though it was almost ten years until our country was in recovery, we never had our children begging for bread.

First, when others lost their homes, Mr. Hurley had built River Bend many years before, and we did not owe anything against it. Mr. Hurley was a very good money manager, and we always had extra put away for what he called a rainy day.

And during those days of the Great Depression, there were many rainy days. We kept going.

So, we kept River Bend as an asset. We owned it. Therefore, we didn't have to leave. We were not homeless like so many.

Mr. Hurley didn't do the stock market, so we did not lose there. We did lose some of our

money in a bank that collapsed.

We had this plantation, and we continued to plant and harvest our crops with the help of our workers.

We grew our own veggies and had our own cows, pigs, chickens, and eggs.

There were some things we didn't have, but we were able to share with workers and house them and provide food for their family.

It was indeed a different place and time. We never went hungry, and we always had a roof over our heads.

We were able to share with others, and God never let us go hungry. Our rainy-day funds lasted until the crops were harvested, and we were able to sell at a reduced price to replace a portion of that fund.

I am not saying it was easy, because it was not. We prayed a lot and ate a little less. Our clothes seemed to last longer than normal, and it rained enough on our land to keep our plants growing. Our streams never dried up, and our trees always provided shade, and the magnolias were still blooming. The sweet smell filled our home and our hearts with a new hope. Just like when the spring brings forth new life, our hearts saw a rebirth of this country and its people. Yes, it took some time, but it is like the Bible says, God has a time for everything. And I was so happy that His time for this trauma that our country experienced was over.

We all know that when we go through troubles, we are so thankful when it comes to an end.

Boys, it is like your gun. It breaks, and it makes you sad. But how happy are you when you get it fixed or you get a new one? It was that way.

The time that my Great-Grandma Ottilie Amelie came over the waters with her parents was almost lost. Her mom got sick, and her papa was heartsick because he was not sure how he would provide for his wife and young child in a new land, a new everything. He was so excited but so scared at the same time.

Then they landed, and new hope emerged. They came to Louisiana. They opened a cobbler and dress shop, and they were mightily blessed.

One day when things were very quiet, Ottilie Amelie asked her mom about a necklace she saw that was all wrapped up in a tissue paper and velvet cloth. She had never seen it before.

Now do you remember my emerald necklace? Well, this was what my Great- Grandmother Ottilie Amelie saw. A necklace that traveled over the ocean and once lived in a palace where a princess gave it to her seamstress for sewing a dress, her wedding gown, that had roses all over it made of fabulous seed pearls. That dress still hangs in the royal palace in a glass case overlooking the royal rose garden.

Perhaps that might be our next trip. This is what we called the princess emeralds, because that is where they came from. When my Great-Grandmother Ottilie Amelie got married, her mom gave the princess emeralds to her. And from there, it was passed down and down and then to me, and from me it will go to my namesake. Miss Abigaile, it will be yours. Perhaps you can wear it on your wedding day also like we all did.

And, boys, I have not forgotten you. As you grow up and take your love as your wives, you will inherit River Bend.

Your last name is, after all, Hurley. Your great-grand-father Hurley started it, and it shall remain a home and land owned by the Hurley family.

Now I want you to remember these words of wisdom: "Give and it will be given to you good measure, pressed down, shaken together, and running over will be put into your bosom. For with the same measure that you use, it will be measured back to you." Luke 6:38.

This is how we have lived our lives, from the time Mr. Hurley and I began our lives and the lands of River Bend.

I believe that is why we lived through the war between the states and the Great Depression, and we were not burned out nor ever went without food. Yes, we hid our valuables during the war, but we did that so that we were not stolen from. Sometimes bad things are done by bad people. God does not expect you to be walked on or over, so you must protect that which is yours.

You know that if you follow the laws of man and follow the Bibles instruction, you will always come out on top. Not only will you be on the top, whatever you do will prosper. And like I have always said, "And the magnolias will always be in bloom." And the sweet smell of success will follow you all the days of your lives.

So go now and play, but never forget this story, for it will be life to you and all that you do.

*****

The night called, and Grandma was ready for her pillows. It had been long day and a fulfillment of what God told her to say. Dreams of life, love, Mr. Hurley, and her dear ones.

Sunday church and the bet was on. Did Grandma have another talk with God? What was the preacher going to talk about? All the Hurley family had a bet going on. They all got ice cream after church. Who would win?

A few songs, and all were seated. And then the preacher took the pulpit.

The Hurleys glanced at each other. Now was the time for the bet to be won or lost. They held their breath. And the preacher began. "People," he began. "I want to tell you some words of wisdom. There is a rule we all need to live by."

Well, they all knew the word Grandma had given last afternoon they were fixing to hear for the second time. "Give and it shall be given back to you." That was it. The bet was lost by all; weeds and flower beds were going to be prepared by the Hurley family and not the helpers.

They were all correct again. God and Grandma had another talk. To hear it twice had always meant the lessons learned were going to be put to the test.

Grandma was a good sport, and the Hurley bunch all got ice cream anyway, but the flower beds and weeds were still going to get one. By guess who? Hurleys!

First day of school after the Christmas holiday, and Miss Abigaile was excited, hoping to see her Mr. Butler.

No success for the first week, but both met up that next week. Hugs and stories of their holiday celebrations, of gifts they gave and those they received.

Harvest at River Bend and Willow Oaks had been done, and the weeks ahead would give each a time of togetherness that they had never had.

Mr. Butler and Miss Abigaile were experiencing something new. A newness of quality time together and a desire to search out more of each other's history.

Mr. Butler had been so very busy with Willow Oaks and school that his focus on Miss Abigaile had been challenged. But he felt in his heart that his last two years of knowing Miss Abigaile had opened his eyes to a love that might last a lifetime. He knew he was almost eighteen and very young to think of a love everlasting, but he knew that she made him feel special. Like he could swim the English Channel and fly over any mountain. In his youth, he had his heartstrings singing, but not too quick, because his Miss Abigaile was just turning fifteen and had a couple of more years of school.

If Miss Abigaile would have known the depth of his love, she would have compared that love with her great-grand mother and Mr. Hurleys longtime courtship and of the time Mr. Hurley waited for his true love, Abigaile Amelie.

So, Mr. Butler was in waiting mode. Perhaps he could begin his quiet courtship, beginning with Valentines. He would consult his mom as to what a young lady might like for a special Valentines gift. He had a thought but wasn't sure his mom or Miss Abigaile would be agreeable.

A heart-shaped hand mirror with a brush and comb to match, one that the silversmith could make, and engrave on the mirrors back a likeness of a beautiful weeping willow. One that looked like those of Willow Oaks. For he was hoping that Miss Abigaile would become the next lady of his great home at Willow Oak. Her mirror would be just the beginning of the things he would bless her with when she became his wife.

With Valentines approaching soon, he had to get a move on his idea. His mom had told him that all young women needed a beautiful hand set for their dressing table. One that could stand the test of time. A lifetime. For she had had her set since she was a young girl; it had graced her dresser and combed and brushed through her hair and was still looking great. It was given to her by her parents. The silver and ivory had shown some wear, but it was still serviceable. Thirty years plus.

So, it was a yes for Mr. Butler to go ahead. Momma Butler never inquired of her son what was going on, but she knew her son. He was a good boy. He was very mature for his age. He was a hard worker, and he was trustworthy. So, she knew it must be something and someone very special. She trusted her son with all her heart. If he asked for her opinion, she would give it with a breath of wisdom in all her thoughts.

Off to the silversmiths and a short timeline to get his treasure for his valentine made.

Miss Abigaile was feeling like a young lady of certain maturity and hoping that she could show her Mr. Butler of her love but had no idea of how to do this.

Perhaps she would ask her mom, but she knew if she could ask her great-grandma, she could understand because she knew what it was like to be in love with an older man.

Just like she was. Miss Abigaile was sure that the counsel she would receive from her would be exactly the truth.

And she was right. Great-Grandma Abigaile Amelie told her namesake that the way to a man's heart was through his stomach. So that was her plan. She would bake some special heart- shaped cookies for her Mr. Buder. And she would do this without any help from the kitchen help or her mom. Special ingredients.

Now, she would have to look through all the cookie recipes to find the perfect one that her Mr. Buder would gobble up. Miss Abigaile was sure this would make his Valentines Day, and he would certainly know of her love for him.

She had found the perfect cookie. It was going to be a sugar cookie that she could carve into the shape of a heart and decorate with his initial on each one, the letter B. Next, she would have to find the most special container to place her love snacks into. Instead of a square box for her heart shaped delights, she decided to buy a large box of chocolates that came in a heart- shaped box, eat all the candy, and put her sweet sugar cookies inside. But to make it much more special, she would make her own Valentines card. One that could convey her special love for an older man.

Both had some preparation for their special valentine, but for now, both had a plan, and they were determined to complete this task without help. The money it took to buy their gifts they had earned and saved for just such a special occasion.

Miss Abigaile was in ninth grade, and Mr. Buder was in twelfth. He was getting ready to graduate from high school, ready for college. His focus was on business and how to run a plantation, for he was next in line to inherit and help run his precious Willow Oaks, a place where he was hoping to bring his Miss Abigaile for a lifetime, as soon as he ended his college days. She would be eighteen, and he was sure that his proposal of marriage was going to be her graduation and eighteenth birthday present. He had a plan, and so did Miss Abigaile. One for their futures, no matter how long it might take.

But for now, the silver mirror dresser set and sugar cookies were the first of the gifts foremost on the list.

School continued, and Valentines Day was fast approaching. Miss Abigaile and Mr. Buder were both good students, and their grades would show up on their report cards, As and Bs, so scholarships were going to be offered for both.

Miss Abigaile was so very smart that she was going to be entering eleventh grade next September; she had tested and passed all her tenth-grade subjects. Miss Abigaile was sure that her love of books and reading prepared her to graduate early.

She was reading between the lines and was wondering what God was doing for her and with her. She was so hoping that He was getting her through school more quickly so she could be considered old enough to become Mr. B s wife, if and when he might ask. For now, Valentines and sugar cookies were her focus. She would try her hand several times before her gift for Mr. Butler was perfect. But she wanted to do this baking effort and guessed that it would be good practice for the future.

Even Grandma knew her practice runs would give her confidence.

Mr. Butler was in full control and checked daily with the silversmith. Several drawings of the famed willow tree to be carved on the heart-shaped hand mirror. He ordered a red velvet box just as he had for Miss Abigaile the year before. The fourth drawing was approved, and his gift was almost finished.

Just a short time after that, and word was sent to Willow Oaks that Mr. Butlers order was complete and ready for pick-up and payment.

He could hardly wait to show his mom. He was so hoping for her approval. In fact, he was sure that she would be happy for him that he had practiced a speech. One like he might make to his dear Miss Abigaile. He started out, "Mom, I know," and she stopped him.

"My darling," she said, "I trust you." That was all he needed to hear. He knew his plan was a winner.

And Valentines was just two days away.

Miss Abigaile was so nervous. She had committed to baking these sugar cookies and was surely hoping that her Mr. Butler would love them. But until she gave them to him, she didn't gobble one up or take one bite. She set them aside.

One day until Valentines Day, and preparations by both were underway.

The classrooms were all decorated in red and white. A party with cake and punch was planned for each room.

Miss Abigaile was beginning to bake her cookies, and the pretty red heart box was lined with waxed paper, and her handmade Valentines card was ready to be placed on top of her red box. A card that was approved by Great Grandma Abigaile Amelie. A sentiment of young love, but not too mushy, ending with the words, "You are special."

Grandma Abigaile approved! Joy entered Miss Abigaile's heart.

The day dawned, and off to school they went with special gifts tucked away in each of their book bags, with a few notes for each of their friends and classmates.

After lunch, the party was on the schedule. With all their classmates exchanging cards, they could hardly wait until the day was over and these two could share a moment. Miss Abigaile was feeling a bit insecure. Her Mr. Buder was so handsome to her. She began to worry that other girls might find his blue eyes and raven-black hair calling their name.

But this was just a taunt. Mr. Buder was hers from the beginning, and this token he had made for her had special meaning. It was almost like an engagement ring. Because it showed his deep devotion to a young lady he had met and fallen head over hills for two years ago. A hope for the future.

The moment was here. Both Mr. Buder and Miss Abigaile met on the schoolyard and sat on a bench they had deemed "their bench." Excited and reeling with anticipation, they both pulled their treasures out and exchanged gifts. He opened his first. The sweet smell of sugar filled the air. A smile and a taste told the story of his pleasure in her gift.

Grandma was so very right. The way to his heart was, it seemed, sugar cookies. He had six of the twenty-four eaten in just a few minutes.

Then it was Miss Abigaile's turn. Mr. Butler wanted this moment to last forever. He handed her his gift and said, "Wait a moment. I made this for you, and I want you to cherish this like I cherish you and your friendship. This is for you forever."

She lifted the heart-shaped lid and saw a picture of a weeping willow tree. But something was different. The box was heavy. She picked up the heart-shaped picture and turned it over. It was a hand mirror, and below the treasured heart shape was an ivory comb and brush with a willow branch on its handle.

She peered at herself, and tears began to fall. She knew right then, right there, that he was declaring his love for her. She could read his face and he hers. It would seem that from that moment they silently, but openly, shared their abiding love for each other.

Mr. Buder got home, and his mom asked how it went. No words were spoken, but she knew immediately. Her son had given his heart to a lady. She shared her son with another.

Miss Abigaile's heart sang all the way home. With her new heart in hand, she could hardly wait to share her news with Grandma Abigaile. But her news could be read from far away. Grandma Abigaile saw a smile that could stretch across Georgia. A flush color shone on her face, and her ears were pink on the edges. Grandma knew.

The weekend followed Friday, the fourteenth of February, and you could see Miss Abigaile floating on air.

Grandma Abigaile Amelie had a story time planned, and Sunday after church was her target. She knew exactly what her story would be about, love and more love.

But plans change. And now Saturday evening was the story time for her dear ones.

After supper, Grandma Abigaile excused herself and changed into her Southern belle costume. The princess emeralds came out of hiding, and her floppy hat was placed atop her silver hair.

After dishes were cleared, the children were summoned to the great hall. Grandma Abigaile took her place on the carved chaise longue. Her big belle skirt draped over the back, and the fireplace glowed. Her dear ones took their places, and sheer excitement covered their faces. Because every time Grandma shared her history, it gave each of them a life story they could share with others in years to come.

What was the story this time going to be about? They didn't know yet. Grandma never told the same story. She always brought something new.

Grandma started. "God, help me to recall and tell this story with truth and exactness. Thank You, God. And the magnolias were in bloom."

*****

We just had a day that speaks to all about love. Hearts, flowers, and candy. A show of one's affection for others.

There was someone else long ago who gave His creation a gift they never earned. He was born, and then He was accused of crimes He didn't commit. He was tried in a Roman court and found to be guilty. He was sentenced to death. He took stripes on his back, and then He was nailed to a cross. He suffered, and they placed a crown of thorns on His head. He took His last breath and died.

He did all this and never said anything. He did this all so we could live with Him in heaven one day.

Yes, it was Jesus. He loved us so much that He was willing to give us the chance to live again in Him.

This is a chance for each of you, if you haven't said yes to Him, to say yes. We can't do what He did, but we don't have to. The choice is yours.

All the days that I have lived, I ask God every day for His guiding light to show me the way. All the days of war and the Great Depression, God always gave us what we needed, and we gave to others who needed our help. It is man helping man. To this day, we have been cared for and loved by Jesus. So, take this love that we celebrated yesterday and make it your love story. One that will carry you to the end of your life in style. Put Him first, and He will pro mote you to a height you could never reach on your own.

*****

Bedtime called, and River Bend shut down for a long winter's nap. Snow fell, and the ground had a blanket of white to wake up to.

In honor of the Valentines weekend, the sugar ham, toast, and grits were all in the shape of hearts. The butter had been put in heart molds, and one part was placed on each slice of toast. Beautiful red China and silver dishes held the homemade strawberry jelly and the sugar for a pinch of sweet on everything. The orange juice had a drop of beef juice to color its red. It was all red and hearts.

Church was at ten, and all were dressing for the occasion. A short ride to their little church, and all were seated.

The boys were extra attentive this morning. It seemed like something was on their minds. And then the pastor began.

"We just had a special day pass us. It was Valentines Day. I will bet that most of you spent time with your honeys. You might have given a gift to each other or someone you liked. But you celebrated a day set aside for love.

"Well, I want to tell you a story of unbridled love, of a love that has never been seen since.

A love that gives and gives and gives.

"Long ago, we had a dear friend who was born to a little lady. She gave him a special name. She called him Jesus. He played like all children. He went to church with His parents. He grew to be a man. He was from a little town. Just like our small town. He had friends, and He loved fishing. When He worked, He built things. He was a carpenter."

The boys looked at each other. They knew exactly what was going to be said next. They had this story last evening. Grandma Abigaile Amelie was talking with God again on their private phone line.

Another story from Grandma and the pastor. Same story, but this time the boys took it to heart. They both had said yes to Jesus the night before. A Valentines treat they could never get enough of now.

Miss Abigaile had already made that decision two years prior. She had asked Jesus to be her sweetheart forever. It was just after one of Grandmas stories. She felt a tug on her heart like no other. Ever since that time, she felt guided to live every moment with her sweetheart Jesus.

With the fresh blanket of snow on the ground, it looked so clean and bright. The trees were showing off their strength and beauty. The fields were showing off the rolling terrain, and the little animals were chasing each other and leaving a trail of footprints that could trace their every move.

Dinner awaited the Hurley family, and more hearts were telling the story of love. There were vegetables laid out on a large silver tray to form a heart. Beef that had been cut into heart shapes. Red hot tea and pretty little sandwiches filled with peanut butter and red plum jelly, all in the shape of hearts, and a red paper banner that was laid out on the long mahogany table. It repeated the word love over and over again. On each red China plate lay a silver heart with the date 1935. A memento that all would cherish. Grandma knew her heart was full of love for her family and wanted them to see her as a gift of love to them from God, her maker.

Miss Abigaile was still floating on air and felt like this gesture of love that her great- grandma had shared would be a beginning of how she wanted to treat her love, her Mr. Butler.

The year was going by quickly, and graduation was almost here for her Mr. Butler. What to get him for this great accomplishment? It had to be something very special for her love. She knew just who to ask. It had to be Grandma Abigaile Amelie. So the next day would be that time in which her question might be answered. Grandma had fallen in love with an older man. She would most certainly have the perfect gift in mind.

After school was Miss Abigaile's set time for questions and answers.

Miss Abigaile had only one thing to ask her great-grand mother. She knew her Mr. Butler was turning eighteen and going off to college soon, so she had to have a two-for-one outstanding gift for him.

For one so young in love, there was a beautiful maturity about Miss Abigaile.

Great-Grandmother Abigaile Amelie was the voice of wisdom. For all the questions and answers that ever approached, she always had the right answers to everything. So, Miss Abigaile had total confidence in her namesake.

Grandma had only one suggestion. Miss Abigaile was excited. It should be a custom shaving mug! One that had a silver tray with his initial and a mug that matched. Two types of razors with silver handles, and a mirror on a stand.

Miss Abigaile's heart sang. That was it! "Grandma, how do you always know? I must get started right away."

With a plan and Grandmas silversmith, a unique and very special gift was in the works. School continued, and the months seemed to pass by rather quickly.

The silversmith had been in constant contact with the young Miss Abigaile. The design was one of her own drawings. It had a willow tree on one side and an oak tree on the other side, and the initial was a bold and strong profile, again one Miss Abigaile designed.

With odd jobs around the house, she had been gathering funds for her treasured gift.

She almost had enough saved when the silversmith called and announced that her treasure was complete pending her approval. She was short and asked Grandma Abigaile to loan her a little money.

Grandma agreed but told her she would have to pay the loan back. They both agreed, and both Abigaile's made an appointment to pick up Mr. Butlers gift.

Another day of pure joy and happiness for Miss Abigaile. Graduation was just a week away, and Mr. Butlers birthday just two weeks away. A double special celebration for a double special Mr. Butler.

The school year ended, and it marked a new beginning for both. For Miss Abigaile, she was entering eleventh grade. She had skipped tenth grade. Mr. Butler was finishing his high school career and entering a new college career. After the ceremony was over, Miss Abigaile collected her treasured gift and presented it to the graduating senior, Mr. Butler.

Opening the package, Mr. Butler almost fainted. He was a very sensitive young man. He had no idea what Miss Abigaile had gotten for him. But when he saw what was During the time Mr. Butler was finishing his college years, Miss Abigaile had finished high school and began her college education.

It only took Mr. Butler three years to complete his college business degree, and Miss Abigaile only had two more years of college left. She would graduate from college at the beginning of the year 1942. Her Mr. Butler was twenty-four years old when Miss Abigaile graduated from college, and she was just twenty-one.

During the years of their courtship, their bond of respect and love grew deeper. It was when Miss Abigaile graduated that her Mr. Butler presented her with a beautiful engagement ring with the hope that she would say yes and yes again.

CHAPTER 8
Plantations Meet

MR. BUTLER HAD Taken his position at Willow Oaks and made it more successful than it had ever been. His Brothers were both in college at this time and learning more to help Willow Oaks become even more successful. Because Harrison had been so very good at his management of Willow Oaks, it stood to reason that more knowledge learned by his two younger brothers would only prove to be better for Willow Oaks in the future.

On the other end of Miss Abigaile s home River Bend, they had also put into practice the similar practices of crop rotation, and their profits also rose.

These plantations were never in competition because the supply and demand for their products were equal.

So, as Miss Abigaile had accepted Mr. Butler s proposal, the plans for a wedding were in preparation. A summer wedding and college graduation were just one month apart.

At River Bend during the time Miss Abigaile was away at college, her brothers were graduating from college and preparing for their River Bend life. Both boys were interested in agriculture and business management. It seemed to be the way of plantation owners and the new generation of owners. Someone would inherit the land, and it was going to be up to them to make it better than when they received it. So, it stood to reason to learn and put into practice as much knowledge as they could after college.

But probably the most amazing happening at River Bend was the birthday of its original owner. Great Grandmother Abigaile Amelie Hurley. She had made it to a hundred years of age. She still came down the curved stairway, but now it seemed to be just a touch slower. And sometimes a little help was needed. She had made it. A hundred years old and adding days and more weeks and months to her time. Now she was hoping to make it to the wedding of her namesake that she knew was approaching.

The crops were still being planted and harvested at River Bend, and the previous practice of rotating them was definitely paying off. The tobacco plants were drying in the barns, and the indigo was still being processed for its blue dye. Cotton was a staple as well. All was part of the cash crops that most of the plantation in the area produced.

With America needing all these products, it made the plantations a business that always had business.

Because a new war was in full swing in Europe, the masses of Americans were all ready to assist any way they could. That included River Bend and Willow Oaks. They had no one going to war but offered any of their goods for the war effort. The one product that was accepted was lots of cotton. The military used cotton and wool in their uniforms. Backpacks and socks also used cotton.

Grandma Abigaile knew it was her job to help. She always knew that her God would bless the plantation and her prayers for the servicemen and their families to be safe and protected overseas and here at home. Grandma knew that in war there was always the Lord's timing for some, but she always prayed anyway. She knew prayer was always honored by God. And her prayers were honored. No one from their town was lost in the war.

Grandma Abigaile Amelie was turning 102 with her next birthday, and Miss Abigaile was now twenty-one, but shortly after graduation and just before her wedding, she was going to be twenty-two.

Grandma Abigaile had again made her goal. However, Miss Matilda did not. She was turning 107, and one night she just didn't wake up.

This was truly a sad moment for Grandma Abigaile Amelie. A friend of many years and a confidant had gone to heaven, but left a petite friend to carry on life and love in her memory. The trips to town and afternoons shared at River Bend and the local soda fountain would be different now.

But Grandma had a hopeful thought. Her dear ones could take up some of her needs to talk and share her memories. And the others in life would take up her other needs for fellowship.

For now, her main focus was that of the upcoming wedding of her namesake. A wedding dress that would enhance the princess emeralds or perhaps the new neck lace Grandma Abigaile had recently acquired on her trip to Australia. She had promised these two treasures to her namesake, Miss Abigaile. She announced to her dear ones how River Bend was going to be Miss Abigaile's brothers', and since that time, a percentage of all the money made by River Bend was set aside for a dowry for her namesake. After her marriage, she would still retain a small percentage of the net profits of her homeplace, River Bend. But Miss Abigaile never knew. Grandma Abigaile Amelie had this financial blessing planned for many, many years for her. A nice little nest egg for the new couple.

MISS ABIGAILE GRACE
&
HARRISON DARCY

At Willow Oaks, the years where Harrison was in college, his family was going through a trial of their own. His parents were in a car accident, and his brothers and uncles had to run Willow Oaks. After Mr. Butler graduated with degrees from college, he was summoned back to Willow Oaks. His education had prepared him for all types of business that could or would be needed at Willow Oaks. So, while his sweet Miss Abigaile was finishing her college education, he was so busy trying to care for all the needs of his recovering parents and the day-to-day hands- on business of completely running a thousand-acre plantation. With both of his brothers off to college now, the responsibilities fell almost all on the young Mr. Harrison Butler, but he was no stranger to hard work and long hours. Yet he had a brand-new focus. His upcoming wedding to the blond haired, green-eyed beauty he had waited so long for. Miss Abigaile was his love, his new life. His parents had been released from medical care just in time for their first son to marry and leave the plantation for a honeymoon. They were able to assume the regular duties that they had missed for almost two years.

But back at River Bend, before the celebration of the long-awaited wedding, there were many parties and tears for the bride-to-be and a huge dinner party for the groom and bride-to- be.

Gifts flowed into the great River Bend house, and like most gifts that graced the great hall, the sterling silver serving dishes and trays were indeed a sight to see.

As it was the custom for all misters- and missuses-to-be, gifts were given to help the new couple set up housekeeping. Everyone knew the two plantations that were giving their young people to be wed. Some wondered if this was just maybe the start of a merger. But in time all would see that from the beginning of each plantation, there was an unspoken rule. The Hurley name and Butler name was then and still today the only name on ownership papers. And according to the family members that had lived there, it would never change. So, with the past hundred years and several generations, the unspoken word stood.

Grandma Abigaile was doing her part. Words of wisdom and special story time with her namesake, Miss Abigaile, continued.

"And the magnolias were in bloom" started a tutorial of the duties and responsibilities of a wife. Miss Abigaile knew that her grandma was the most important and wise woman she had ever known. Her mom was smart, but Grandma Abigaile was a century old and had seen the world change and had loved one man who was her everything. Miss Abigaile never knew her Great- Grandfather Hurley, but she knew that his love and respect for his Abigaile Amelie held a new family together for many years, and that all the hard work of two could build a home of love and respect for the generations of Hurleys to come.

Miss Abigaile had chosen her wedding dress. A lace gown with a beautiful sweetheart neckline, one that showed off the princess emeralds or Abigaile opals, a similar design like her Grandma Abigaile s. A beautiful lace bodice and a satin bottom tiered with yards and yards of lace from Paris.

Seed pearls were sewn into each layer in the shape of roses. Just like the wedding dress made many years ago, for a princess in the old country.

Miss Abigaile had remembered the story her Grandma Abigaile Amelie had told her. She was so wanting to bring back that memory for her great-grandmother because she could see that it could please her beyond all measure. Her namesake needed to have a reminder of all the love she had shared, and it would keep a bit of history alive.

When you have challenges in your life, some changes need to be made. Miss Abigaile was willing to do anything to tell her grandma just how much she loved her.

Her choice of wedding gown was made to fit the style and era that would fit the princess emeralds.

The color of freshly fallen snow with the seed pearls in shades of ivory to a yellow white, all to replicate the roses that her Grandmother Abigaile had told her about, those that would be able to almost be picked. Picked as if you were in those royal gardens of long ago. Miss Abigaile knew her dress would not hang in a glass case for all to see, but this dress would be a testament to story time and the love her great-grandmother had shared with a little girl from the moments she was born.

The day was June 30, a perfect date for two to become one. The time was sunset, and the magnolias were in bloom. The sweet smell of a beautiful flower that grew naturally in the state of South Georgia, with the grounds of River Bend lit up like a fairground. Family and friends lined up to welcome the bride and her father. The procession had ten bridesmaids and a flower girl who would drop rose petals in front of a bride of such glowing beauty that nothing and no one could hold a candle to her.

Her dress was flowing in the Georgia winds, the pearl roses glistened in the lights, and the princess emerald showed a touch of royalty. But no one knew the history of this amazing emerald set of jewels. Great-Grandmother Abigaile Amelie knew the story. Truly a history of royalty and a gift that was given to her by her great-grandmother by her mother by the princess of Bavaria; emeralds, diamonds, and pearls that all came from the princess that were all mined in a place across the world from Georgia, India. No one knew the dollar value, but truly no one cared, and it never mattered.

Something borrowed, something blue. Emeralds borrowed from Great-Grandmother Abigaile Amelie, and a blue lace hankie from her mom. All that was traditional, and a bouquet of roses, with green ribbons streaming down, all to match the emeralds that would be hers one day. The I do s, and Mr. and Mrs. Harrison Darcy Butler were presented to all as man and wife. A magnificent reception and dinner on the grounds for all three hundred guests.

Gifts were still pouring in, and the party lasted until 10:00 p.m. The lightning bugs were showing off their beams of lights, and the stars made the heavens all aglow.

The newlyweds slipped away earlier and were aboard a train headed to the Big Apple. A stay at the famed plaza hotel and another train ride to the West Coast, California, to see all about the stars of movies. A monthlong honey moon, and they came to transition Miss Abigaile s home to the Willow Oaks Plantation.

As soon as the new couple arrived back home, and all the wedding gifts and Miss Abigaile's belongings were in place, the news came.

Harrison was going to be the owner of Willow Oaks along with his two brothers. His mom and dad were going to move to a new state and spend their remaining days traveling and enjoying each other's company.

The two had almost lost their lives earlier and wanted to make the rest of their life one that could make memories with no regrets. Instead of just existing in a life they had for many years, they wanted to be like Christopher Columbus, discovering a world outside of Georgia.

The move was on for Mom and Dad in just two months.

The newlyweds were enjoying each other, and plans to rearrange the bedrooms at Willow Oaks were in process. But until Mom and Dad left, things stayed the same.

Miss Abigaile never knew such love. She could only think of her great-grandmother and her honey, Mr. Hurley. They shared their love and their life, and it made the next generation.

It had only been three months since Abigaile and Harrison had been married, but she suspected that there could be a new Butler on the way.

She shared her news with her Mr. Butler, and you could see a smile unlike any other across his face. He loved her so much, and now his love had even more purpose. A new little Butler to share with and more love to give.

Even though he had a new responsibility with Willow Oaks, his love overshadowed the thoughts of all the hard work that was ahead of him.

They waited a month before sharing the fabulous news with all the family.

Harrison's mom and dad were very excited and would certainly make plans to be back at Willow Oak for the birth of their first grandchild.

Abigaile asked her Mr. Butler to let her announce the news to her great-grandmother and her parents. He agreed. Now Abigaile was on point. But what was the proper way to tell her news. She was most excited to tell her great-grand mother because she knew that this would give her another point to look forward to and strive to be here at River Bend a few more years before she told the Lord she was ready to be in heaven and see her Mr. Hurley and her great friend Miss Matilda.

The time was set, and Abigaile made her way back to River Bend. Her parents met her, and Grandma Abigaile Amelie awaited her entrance into the grand hall where Grandma would sit on the carved chaise longue and tell her the stories of the Hurleys' past. Abigaile recalled the times when the stories and Sunday sermons seemed to collide. God and Grandma Abigaile had a private phone line and talked frequently. Conversation between her and her brothers had made them bet on story-time history and Sunday sermons.

The glad tidings were announced, and joy filled the room. Abigaile was in tears when she saw her great-grandmother begin to cry. They both knew that this new life would prolong an old one.

It was another prayer answered for Grandma. A new little person. Grandma knew she would see her great-great grandchild being brought into this world. Grandma began with "What shall we call this new gift? Will it be a boy or a soft pink petite little girl? Both would be a huge blessing. And when will this little person be due?"

"In June sometime, late June."

Grandma Abigaile was doubly excited. It was her birth month also. The two Abigaile's could share another birth day together, and now a new little person could make it three.

Secretly Grandma was hoping for a pretty pink little bundle of beauty but knew God had a special gift in mind to bless many others.

Grandma had already designed a new silver ornament and now had one more to add to her order. This would be a very special Christmas. A new love, a new hope, a new little person to join the Hurley family soon, something great to look forward to.

All Grandma Abigaile s dear ones had left River Bend. School and a new husband had taken her dear ones to a different place. Now Grandma had to store up in her mind stories that could be told when all would be home for Christmas. But in the meantime, it seemed too quiet.

In the day's past, there was the noise of life and youth all around.

This was a time for her being alone. Even her dear friend was gone; she had shared so much with Miss Matilda.

Grandma Abigaile was a little lost. Yet she knew there must be something that an old Southern lady, who still had some spunk, could do and feel the zest for life again. But nothing was on the horizon that she could see. So, she was in the waiting mode.

Thanksgiving was approaching with the hope for all to join together at River Bend.

The table had some of the leaves taken out to accommodate a smaller group. But just like clockwork, the meal times still called the family that was still there to join in breaking bread together. A more select menu was adapted to fit the needs of an older group: bacon, ham, and eggs only graced the table twice a week. The homemade breads were only served three times a week, and more fruits and vegetables adorned the silver trays. The garden still produced an abundance, so they ate more from the land than before.

Grandma Abigaile never wanted anything to go to waste. After all, she was the matriarch of the family, and after a hundred years plus she had learned how to abase and abound. She did, however, like more rather than less. She had learned much, and she knew that even when there was less, she could always share with those who had none and still have enough.

Thanksgiving was here, and the leaves had to be placed back onto the table. The whole Hurley family would be home. Mr. and Mrs. Harrison Buder would also attend.

A banquet was planned: turkey, dressing, mashed potatoes, gravy, cranberry sauce, green beans, beets, and a green salad, and that was just the main course. For dessert, pecan pie, cheesecake, carrot cake, milk chocolate brownies, and Grandma Abigaile's favorite bread pudding with fresh whipped cream. And, the favorite of all, homemade bread with freshly churned butter, all served on silver platters. And in honor of Miss Matilda, the beautiful green and-gold-banded China graced the tabletop.

The table was dressed in fine linen, and a floral arrangement stretched almost the length of the great mahogany table.

The boys had made it home from college, and Mr. and Mrs. Buder would soon be arriving.

Grandma Abigaile was hoping to have a little bit of time to share a story or two with her dear ones before every one would have to leave.

After Thanksgiving Day dinner was inhaled, and the table was cleared and food put away, an afternoon nap was on the menu.

Then Grandma might have some time to share with her dear ones. But if not, she told the Lord she could wait.

Well, she was going to have to wait for story time. Everyone had other plans and they were not at River Bend.

Mrs. Abigaile, the new Mrs. Buder, was two months pregnant, and the morning sickness was an all-day affair. Her petite little body never knew such a feeling. It was one of joy and one of sickness all at the same time, but that is pregnancy! And all the joys of a new husband, a new home, a new baby were almost overwhelming.

However, like all the Hurley women before her, she knew she could get through this temporary issue and come out on top a winner.

Besides, the thought of a new little person growing inside of her was such a good feeling that she was willing to go through whatever it took to bring forth proof of her and her husband s love, truly a child that was conceived in love.

As for Grandma Abigaile Amelie, she was overjoyed with the news. She was going to be a great-great-grand mother. It was indeed something new in her life and perhaps just the zest she had been praying for.

Again, she began to think about the gender of this new Hurley. What could be our colors? Pretty and pink or baby blue? And names! What might they be? So many questions, and no way to know the answers for another six and a half to seven months. In the meantime, Grandma would com pile a list of names for both boys and girls. Names of the new century and those of the old century and then those of family. Those were the names of distinction that had the most meaning for this petite, gray-haired, green-eyed Southern lady of over a hundred years of history and family.

Grandma was on the hunt. Butler family names. She was so sure that there could be the perfect combination of Butler and Hurley names that would bless all. Names of distinction and family-honored heritage.

The search was on. How long back into history should she go? And the Lord told her, "As far as it takes to honor both families." So, Grandma was sure she was on the right page, just really hoping that the new Mr. and Mrs. Buder would feel the same way. But then, if God gave Grandma the go-ahead, why should she be concerned? Grandmas zest had returned.

Christmas was just a few days away, and the annual Hurley Christmas party was just around the corner. The grand hall, entry, and dining room were all aglow. The outside of River Bend had a new look.

Since the summer wedding of Miss Abigaile and Mr. Butler, there were streams of lights that graced the trees and bushes of River Bend. They had not been turned on since the wedding, but there was no reason to think that they would not work. So, on they would go.

The switch was flipped, and the glow of a noonday sun lit up the surrounding grounds of River Bend. Lights that almost challenged the sunlight of summer. Inside, the house was declaring the new joy to come. Blue and pink, in lots of different shades, new hand-blown glass ornaments, and lights that mimicked the shades of baby boys and baby girls.

It was a completely unique and different look that would take all by surprise.

Grandma oversaw all the buying and placements of all the new Christmas decor. She was thinking to herself, would anyone get the subtle message? The message of a new life to come? If not, maybe she would be setting a new trend for a different color at Christmas except the standard reds and greens. No matter, this was her way of announcing to others, family and friends, the joyous news.

Grandma had also changed her silver ornament to one of a hobby horse with the date engraved on its saddle, 1942. It was a date to remember for all. Great-great-great grandparents and uncles-to-be would all remember, especially for her namesake and her new husband.

The party was quite amazing. It seemed like every per son that was invited showed up. When the lights were lit up, the path to River Bend could be seen for almost a mile down the way. Tons of food and party favors and a new offering, photographs for the honored guests to take home, and one of Grandmas hand-blown glass ornaments that would grace any Christmas tree of any size.

There were a few who asked about the unique decor, but for the most, none were really interested as to its meaning.

As usual, Grandma retreated a little ahead of the other Hurleys and heard her feather pillow calling. Her cotton nighty lay awaiting her to step inside and crawl into the feather mattress that always cradled all around her and helped her to drift off to dreamland.

Grandma Abigaile Amelie's life had a new zesty step in it. But tonight hoped for sweet dreams of her love, her Mr. Hurley. The winter winds blew hard, and a light mist of ice-covered River Bend and the small town of Buder, Georgia.

All were amazed how the harsh winter storm was halted until the Hurley Christmas was over, but then Grandma had prayed for just the right weather and enough food and ornaments to meet every guest's arrival and departure.

Several weeks prior to Christmas, Grandma had picked up her commissioned silver ornaments, and as always, she placed the memento on everyone's pillow. The trees in each bedroom were adorned with eighteen to a hundred silver ornaments, Grandma having the most And now each had one more to add to their tree. It was a beautiful history of the Hurleys'.

A precious silver treasure that told a story. No matter how old you might be, it could carry you to the occasions of memorable times shared with brothers, aunts, uncles, parents, and one very special great-grandmother. Mr. Hurley had started this tradition many years ago, and Grandma honored his love for family memories in the same way. Every year of this family's life could be seen in their specially decorated tree.

Great-Grandma Abigaile Amelie was feeling good and looking pretty great for a woman of her years. God had been good to her. She missed her friend, Miss Matilda, but knew she was still needed at River Bend.

Christmas was a day away, and all her dear ones were going to be home. She had planned another story time for her great-grandchildren. She dressed in her costume of a Southern belle, and this time she would wear a floppy hat with blue and pink velvet ribbons. Her eyes of green and her belle skirt all brought out the colors of Abigaile's opals.

This was the last time Great-Grandma Abigaile Amelie would be wearing her opals. You see, she had a plan. A plan to bless her namesake with a part of her inheritance. She had already blessed her with the princess emeralds at her wedding, and now Grandma's opals were about to be family jewels that would have a new home for many, many more years. If there was ever a time of pink and blue, it was now, an opal set that could herald the upcoming bundle of joy that was expected in just a few months. But Miss Abigaile had no idea.

Mr. Butler's mom and dad had already left Willow Oaks and were going to have their first Christmas away from the only place they had called home for more the thirty years.

But it was a new adventure that they had both agreed upon, and now was the perfect time to do just that: start.

Even though this was the Butlers' first Christmas together, they wanted to share it with a little hundred-year-old lady.

Grandma Abigaile Amelie was getting ready for her crew. The noise level might not ever be the same, but the conversation of life and love could make up for the herd of turtles that once ran the halls of River Bend.

Part of the conversation was that of the boys' plans for River Bend. And Grandma Abigaile was thinking of baby names. But all were waiting on the call to join Grandma Abigaile in the great hall for story time.

When would she call her dear ones? No one knew, but all felt it was coming soon, so everyone stayed close. This was the first time Harrison Darcy Butler would join Grandma for her God-given story time, some of which were stories of Hurley history, and others were sermons that were always taught twice, one from Grandma Abigaile, and the second on Sunday from the pastor. It must have been pretty important because God, Grandma, and the pastor shared a party line, and all had the same story. Grandma's dear ones were blessed to hear the message twice, inquiries to the Lord later what, where, and when this important message needed to be taken to heart or put into action.

But no matter what you heard, and it was different for each one, it was a call to action in some way, shape, or form.

Grandma Abigaile Amelie descended the curved mahogany staircase. With a little help, she entered the grand hall and called for her dear ones to gather.

Dressed in her Southern belle costume and the floppy hat, all could see she was ready for her famous story time. Miss Abigaile noticed that her namesake was wearing the famed opals that all started with a Christmas gift from her dear friend Miss Matilda.

The blue and pink that were the base colors in her opals matched the Christmas decor that told of the upcoming blessing. Grandma had this plan, and today, right now, was the beginning of her Christmas blessing.

Mr. and Mrs. Butler made it into the grand hall and took the place where Miss Abigaile always sat.

The boys and Mr. Butler and Miss Abigaile were waiting, but there was silence. One where you could hear a pin drop. And then Grandma began. "And the magnolias were in bloom."

Even though these were all adults, it was like children waiting for a dish of ice cream. Quiet and awaiting their prize for good behavior. Just waiting for the jeweled nug gets of wisdom.

*****

Dear ones, we have shared many story times together. History and genealogy of our family and special words of instruction to enlighten your lives from the Lord. Tonight is special. We have to be thankful for everything, knowing God will take care of us no matter what. We are family with history, history of struggles and victories of blessings and the ability to share our bounty no matter how much or how little we had.

We have seen the great sea and landed on new ground.

We saw poverty and oppression. We took our faith in Jesus and offered ourselves as living sacrifices to be sent to a new nation.

We met new people and made lifelong friends. We shared new love and built a new home and family in a new land. We have dedicated our very lives to each other. We have sent our bounty to men and women in war and treated others as we wanted to be treated. We have traveled the world and built a plantation of over two thousand acres. A few acres, one at a time. We planted fertile land and yielded crops that made us money. And with that money, we built a church. The one we now attend. We have shared our love of life and this country and that of the Lord and built memories that will be shared for years to come.

And now we are here during this joyous season of Christmas when we celebrate the birth of Jesus. We too have a celebration of new life. Our own Miss Abigaile will give birth in June to a new family member. We will be honored to share in this miracle of life.

We do not know the course of this child's future. But we can rest assured that with lots of love, he or she will reach new heights that we probably will never know.

Just as my hundred-plus years have seen many, many changes, this new little person will also see many, many changes in his or her life.

We must strive to show this blessing we are receiving the rights in life and instruct them that disobedience comes with punishment.

We are to instill in this child the love of the Lord and remind them of His love for them.

We should tell them how much fun it is to take care of the needs of others. To remember to give out of love, not necessity, and remember the greatest command of all is love.

Take to heart this lesson: We were oppressed and found acceptance. We had nothing and now we are blessed with bounty. We worked hard in this land for others, and here in this new land we work hard for ourselves. We were offered a chance to be born into a land where uncertainty was a definite but were given a hope for freedom. Freedom from oppression and depression to a promise of self-worth and victories that could follow you all the days of your life. A chance to excel at your craft and gather means for your family without giving it to a hard taskmaster. A chance to grow a family with hopes and dreams that can be reached. We had less and now had more. We had nothing, and we were given the chance at life liberty and the pursuit of happiness. We were citizens of Europe and now have a citizenship in this great USA.

No one ever guessed or could imagine the wealth of knowledge we were given when we, our forefathers, said yes. A yes that landed us into a new land. New loves and new hopes.

It is that way today We looked toward heaven, and God gave us a child. The remembrance of His birth, which we celebrate at Christmas.

Jesus said yes to His Father so many years ago, just as we said yes so, many years ago. But we will perish in time, but His gift that He gave will last forever.

We celebrate our love for each other with treasures of this world, but Jesus was the treasure from another world, heaven.

Remember we are here to lay a foundation of love that will end in time, but Jesus and His love will last forever."

*****

Grandma ended with, "And the magnolias were in bloom. And the sweet smell of love and commitment will allow you to be blessed no matter what you lay your hand to."

Mr. Butler had never heard such a speech—no, story— but it hit him hard. His eyes began to fill with tears, and a new seed of hope began to be planted within. What was it? Only time would tell.

But for now, his plate was full. A plantation to run. A new wife and a new baby. A new love that he never knew he could enjoy and dare to dream with.

And then Grandma Abigaile stood up and took the opals from her body and placed the opal ring upon Miss Abigaile's finger. She took the bracelet that matched so beautifully and wrapped it around her namesake's delicate wrist, then took the necklace that graced her aging neckline and gently laid the Abigaile opal necklace about Miss Abigaile s neckline.

This was indeed a surprise, but Grandma had this treasured moment planned for quite some time.

Mr. Butler was shocked for the second time in a short period of time. He had never seen jewelry of such beauty. The worth of such a rare treasure was unknown, but with ninety carats of opals and twelve carats of diamonds, it surely was something Mr. Butler couldn't imagine. And that was just the necklace.

Grandma knew its worth for it had only been a few years since she designed and commissioned her opals from Australia.

The boys knew Grandma Abigaile should bless Miss Abigaile with these treasures, for they would in time inherit River Bend. She would be left out except for ten percent of its cash crops. And it was only the female in their family who would enjoy and wear such an opulent piece of jewelry.

You could hear a pin drop. The only thing that broke the silence was the laughter and tears of this Christmas moment. A Christmas miracle and a summer dream. All in one.

But this was not about money, it was about love. With courage and confidence. The plan of this gray-haired beauty had met its completion. There was only one more word Grandma Abigaile had to say.

This was a treasure that could have been made for a queen, but she knew in her heart it would be worn by a servant. A servant of God, one who knew He was her only desire.

Since Miss Abigaile and Grandma Abigaile were joined in love and name, they had talked and walked with the knowledge of God as their most important possession, and nothing or no one could or would change their commitment, not even the princess emeralds or Grandmas opals.

The new year approached with a bang, and Miss Abigaile was beginning to think about the remodel of their new master bedroom and the proper placement for baby's new room.

At River Bend, Grandma Abigaile was busy with plans for a baby room. She was considering making Miss Abigaile s old room a beautiful soft nursery. She was thinking pink It seemed that everything she was drawn to was in soft and pretty shades of pink. Grandma was having a block when it came to baby blue colors.

Grandma was wondering if God was telling her something, or was she still drawn to a replacement for her namesake? But again, time would tell the story.

Sunday morning, and it was the last day before the boys were due back at college and new jobs.

With leaves still in the grand mahogany dining table, breakfast was calling. The boys' favorites were being served, honey ham, pancakes with fresh maple syrup, homemade apple sauce, and a tropical treat left over from New Year's, pineapple and bananas. All served on the gold and cobalt blue China. Piles of everything placed in a flower design on large silver serving trays.

The boys were like vacuums. You had to get your serving first or maybe miss out altogether, but it was like Grandma said, take charge and you will never miss out. So, there was enough for everyone; no one went hungry; the boys just wanted more because they were last in line.

Dressed for church, and the Butlers met the Hurleys at that little church that the Hurley family helped build. All were seated, music began, and the pastor entered. All stood up, and hands raised a moment for spiritual awakening. But all were ready. Would the message be the same?

As Grandma's head was bowed out of respect, the boys shared a quick glance toward each other.

If you could have heard what they were thinking, it might sound something like this. *Hey, remember all those times Grandma gave us the Sunday morning message ahead of the pastor? Do you think this is another one of those times? Hl bet we hear it again!*

And the pastor began. "Sit down and say hi to your neighbor. Well, we have just entered a new year, 1943. But make no mistake about it. Last year ended with a very important celebration. One that has been marked for almost 150 years. It was a birthday celebration. But there was a reversal of gifts given.

"We didn't give any gifts, but the one who was born gave us a gift. I knew we didn't receive this gift realized until later, but it all began at the birth of this special child.

"We all gave each other gifts at Christmas, and some we will treasure for a lifetime. It is that same way with the gift that this child gave us. He said yes to His Father and thus gave us a gift of a lifetime."

Well, the boys knew what was coming. It was the sermon they'd had last night from Grandma.

That phone line that God, Grandma, and the pastor shared was very busy. They shared thoughts and wisdom that needed to be passed on. A second notification was especially important for the Hurley family and the new family member, Mr. Butler.

Miss Abigaile's parents, Bertie Mae and Edward Darnell, were hearing this message for the first time.

You see, every time Grandma was calling for her dear ones, Miss Abigaile's parents always seemed to be doing something else. Besides, Grandma Abigaile was, it seemed, the live-in babysitter. It gave the kids' parents a chance to do anything they wanted, and the children were well taken care of.

Since Mr. Hurley, her love, and her two sons had passed, she gave herself completely to the family members who were remaining.

That was a love job, but a joy that made her life have purpose, and River Bend was expecting to survive. For no matter the trials that were set before Abigaile Amelie, her faith in family and God gave her the strength to face another day and take her hope and love to places that others could not imagine.

There were many who faced like experiences and perished. But this feisty petite little Southern lady showed a strong backbone and faith in her God that gave her victory. River Bend would survive, as would the Hurley family. Grandma Abigaile retired to her room and took out her journal and penned a sonnet to her love.

A Love Sonnet

I have longed for your touch for many a year But only emptiness came and filled me with tears I have looked to the heavens and cried to the Lord
He brought me a namesake all pretty and pink
With hair all golden and eyes that are green I looked in the mirror and saw all that
An image of me and all that I was
My love runs deep and fills up my heart But I still missed all the songs
You once sang to me
Those of love and life and children to be Only happiness you promised
But soon did I see
The love of my life was lost to me Struggles and pain tried to cripple my heart But I took up the word and took it to heart
I learned the way to carry my cross
To search for new life in those that were left
And I found a reason
Even though I had lost all that I bore

But this little old lady Took the bull by the horns I
shouted out loud
You will take no more prisoners
I will not cave in
I will fight the good fight Devil, you will not win. For
God is my refuge My lamp and my light
And now I have won I will still fight
I will honor Gods name And praise will I sing
He will keep me and love me Till my time will He call
Good night, my Dear Love Please wait for me
My time is not done
For this I am sure Yet time draws nearer And plans do I
make
I pray I will bless All that I know
And meet you once more As the young girl I was
Not like the woman of old that I am Gray hair and
wrinkles
My step has less spring
But we will stroll through heaven And dance in His light
Sweet dreams to my love Till morning I wake
I will love you forever And true I will be
To the one true love
That was given to me By my God of all time Hugs and
kisses
I lay my head down My pillow holds tight Sleep does
come fast My dreams will I dream My life does continue
Until home I am called So, wait for me, my love
For my journey is not done I will love you forever Your
red hair I will see
And hug you forever and ever to be

Grandma Abigaile lay her head down, and her little body sank into the old feather mattress that once held her and Mr. Hurley. Her love everlasting

Grandma Abigaile had made a lot of promises, but this one she knew best. She would

love him forever without any end. God blessed her time and time again.

It could not have been a more fitting end to that night, and the birth of a new family member.

CHAPTER 9

A New Dream

GRANDMA ABIGAILE was on point. She wanted to get her new remodel started. A new room for a new little person.

Mrs. Butler was dreaming as well. The first thing on her list was the master bedroom. The bedroom that Harrisons parents stayed in for over thirty years. It was time. New drapes and new furniture that suited a younger generation. What color could stand the test of times? Color that would cause a feeling of peace to all who entered. Miss Abigaile would gather samples of paint color and fabrics to help her decide on the room's decor.

Because she might have to keep that room the same for maybe years to come.

This would be Miss Abigaile s first attempt at interior design. Her college education was that of a teacher. She always loved children and books and wanted to help mold little minds to be productive adults in this great USA.

But her career to teach and form little one's minds had to be put on hold. Her main concern now was for her unborn child and her new husband.

While Miss Abigaile, the new Mrs. Butler, was busy at Willow Oaks, Great-Grandma Abigaile Amelie was just as busy at River Bend. She was doing the same thing as her namesake. Fabrics, paint samples, and the possibility of new furniture as well for new great-great- granddaughter or grandson.

But everything that Grandma looked at was still pink with lace and satin and more pink in varying shades.

But this was exactly the same problem that Miss Abigaile had. Everything pink. Nothing blue. Pink, pink, and pink.

Grandma was assisted in the attic with a crib and a colorful hobbyhorse that her namesake had when she was a baby. All came down to Grandmas remodel project, and it was beginning to take on the appearance of a nursery. It was a pretty and pink explosion that said little girl. Not a hint of little boy anywhere. But Grandma had it in her head girl, girl, girl. Soft sweet delicate little girl, a gorgeous little girl that might one day inherit the princess emeralds and Grandmas opals.

Now all that grandma was thinking about was what family names might grace this new little person. One that could carry a little person into adulthood and beyond.

It would be a special joining of two families that would bless all. So now Grandmama was on point again. She would research Mr. Butlers family and their names, and she was sure she, with the new parents' permission, would reach a beautiful girly name.

Of course it was not something set in stone, but Grandma had special skills, you know, that private party line that she, the pastor, and God shared.

Miss Abigaile just wanted a healthy baby, and Harrison was so excited that his love was having his baby. Neither one cared. Or you might think. But Abigaile was only thinking pink, and Harrison was hoping for a son. Baby boy blue was his mindset.

Now what color could be safe? Green, white, yellow? Maybe so, but it just didn't feel right.

Abigaile was still looking at pink, pink, pink, just like her great-grandmother Abigaile.

Of course, Bertie Mae and Edward Darnel Hurley were just so excited they were going to be grandparents.

They felt that Miss Abigaile's room would make a perfect nursery. So, they were on board with Grandma Abigaile's remodel. Both Bertie and Edward had pink on their minds. So far that was four for baby girl and only one for a baby boy. Harrison was outnumbered. But again, only time would tell.

Abigaile was back on the master remodel and asked her new husband how he liked blue.

From all she had read, it was supposed to be a very calming and restful color.

Both agreed. The very old color green was out, and the new master color was a pale shade that matched the summer sky and the morning glories that filled the plantations trenches.

Harrison was going to get blue one way or the other, but the truth was it was one of his most favorite colors. So, he gave in to his love and her desire, but it was his desire also.

This remodel was Harrison's gift: to Miss Abigaile for Valentines, and Miss Abigaile's gift to Harrison was of a much more personal nature: the baby that was being formed had begun to move. She took his hand and placed it on her tummy and right at that moment, that very moment, he felt the tiny flutter, like a butterfly, the first of many more to come.

The gift she gave him made him cry. And he did not hold back the tears.

He thought back so many years ago when he first met this blond beauty with eyes of green. From that time to now his love had bloomed, and now that tiny flutter showed her love for him.

It was indeed a match that was made in heaven from the beginning of time.

As Grandma would say, "For just such a moment as this." And the magnolias were in bloom, and so was Miss Abigaile. She was beginning to show the world her love.

But back at River Bend, Grandma was in full speed ahead. She had the nursery to complete. White walls and new white drapes finished the bones of the nursery. Now it came down to some really hard choices. How could you finish this special room without the reality of gender?

Great-Grandma Abigaile Amelie had never been so torn. But in her heart, she was still thinking baby girl. Pink and pink. Bertie and Edward were of the same mind. So, they all decided to finish the new nursery for Miss Abigaile s baby in different shades of blush and lavender. The perfect combination for who they were hoping, for, a beautiful soft delicate little baby girl.

A huge surprise. Moments of yesteryear hidden in the secret shadows of a home that was built out of love. How much more beautiful could it be?

Miss Abigaile knew exactly what she would do with the money. She would frame this memory of the past and present it to the Buder family and hang it in the formal entry at Willow Oaks. This way, all could enjoy this treasure that had stayed hidden for almost a hundred years.

This was also a testimony to the Butlers' hope and faith in God because, after all, it was He who kept them and all they had safe for a century.

Halfway through her pregnancy, Miss Abigaile was getting anxious. The master remodel was not finished yet, and she had not even started on new baby Butler's room.

But like always when Miss Abigaile was in a dilemma, she would go to her Great- Grandmother Abigaile. She had planned a day trip to River Bend the next day. Hoping that her namesake would have some words of wisdom to help calm her down.

She had not seen her Grandma Abigaile since New Year's. An excitement of massive proportions could not be hidden. Miss Abigaile arose early the next morning. She was ready to go by 8:00 a.m. She was planning an all-day visit. But she had no idea what Great-Grandma had in store for her namesake, for she was planning on showing Miss Abigaile the new nursery. All pretty and pink, with her old hobbyhorse that she rode on as a child. Grandma Abigaile had it freshly painted in blush and lavender to match the other decor for her new great-great- granddaughter.

This hobbyhorse was one that came from a display at the 1901 New York World's Fair and has been in the Hurley family home ever since. Grandma Abigaile's grandchildren and all her great-grandchildren and next her great-great grandchild would enjoy the ride no matter if God would bless this family with a girl or boy. But secretly she was still hoping and expecting a sweet soft delicate pretty and pink little bitty girl.

Miss Abigaile was almost home. River Bend was where she was born and grew up, and the place where she married her Mr. Butler. She was trying hard to feel at home at Willow Oaks, but she still felt uneasy. Mr. Butler was trying to make her feel at home, but he knew it might take a little time. The master remodel was the first step, and the second a special place for their new little person.

CHAPTER 10

New Beginnings

GRADUATION, MARRIAGE, NEW home, new baby, new master bedroom, new baby's rooms. So much news, but Miss Abigaile was still not settled.

Perhaps the best solution to this problem was the up-and-coming visit to River Bend and a loving talk with the wisest woman that young Miss Abigaile ever knew, her mom, Bertie Mae, being a close second.

A later breakfast was calling for the two Abigaile's. Something of a lighter fare, a French pastry called a croissant and a plate of fresh fruit and a pot of hot tea in some of the China cups that came from Miss Matilda, two sets of green plates and emerald China to enjoy the reunion.

And next, the stroll upstairs to the room Grandma Abigaile Amelie was in the process of changing for her great-great-grandchild.

The door opened, and so did Miss Abigaile's eyes. Her mouth was open, but no words came out. She was completely dumbfounded. Both Abigaile's turned toward each other. Another one of those smiles as big as Texas happened.

It was as if the problem Miss Abigaile was having was solved in one glance. Yet no words had been spoken, yet. Just at that moment, that small little butterfly flutter awakened. It was almost like a window had been opened to this wee one and she could see her Great-Great-Grandmothers room designed just for her.

Miss Abigaile saw her old hobbyhorse and the new paint colors and began to cry. One might think it was hormones, but it was the memories of her youth and the times she spent in this room at River Bend.

An explosion of blush and lavender engulfed the room. It was the epitome of femininity, no baby blue anywhere. As much as there was no way to know, it seemed as if Grandma and God must have had another phone con versation, a party line exclusive.

There was no question in Miss Abigaile's mind. Grandma was trying to tell her something, but it wasn't a surprise to anyone. Miss Abigaile was also on the pretty and pink, girly sweet, and soft-little-girl mode of thinking, but she knew her Mr. Butler was secretly hoping for a boy.

Inside the girly nursery, there were two rocking chairs. Grandma took one and Miss Abigaile the other.

It felt so familiar. The two Abigaile's together again. And then Great-Grandma Abigaile Amelie stopped rocking and said, "Darling, you are the light of my life. I love you to the stars and back.

"When you were born, and your mom and dad, who is my only grandson, named you Abigaile, my heart sang, and the magnolias began to bloom again.

"I began to look at life differently. You see, I had two children. Both boys. They grew up and worked hard with their daddy, lots of hard work. One of my boys never married. And your daddy's father met a darling young lady, and they married. They had your daddy, and your daddy met Miss Bertie Mae, and they married. They had you and your two brothers. And my heart sang. "My Mr. Hurley and our two sons died way early in their lives. Your daddy's mom also passed away soon thereafter. Your daddy had no mom and no dad left, just me and Miss Bertie Mae.

"Our family was small then, and with lots of prayer and the blessing of you and your brothers, I felt like the Hurley family had a fighting chance to live on. Our plantation could also live on.

"I never thought that the hell we went through to obtain this land and keep it, even in war, could have matched the loss of my loved ones. But I was wrong. My heart was so broken. And then you were born, my darling.

"I saw a light at the end of the tunnel. I think it all started when you were named after me. An old little lady that had seen a lot of life and the joys and hardships that followed.

"I honestly thought that my life was about to come to an end. I was eighty plus, and I had outlived my husband and our two boys.

"My faith had taken me far, but the hurts of this life had hit me on top of my head and tried to pound me into the ground. God gave me you. A mirror image of me when I was a girl. I never knew that you were a gift that gave me new hope, a hope for more life. I was not aware of this at first, but it truly only took me a few seconds. I was holding a precious little person. When you held on to my finger with your tiny little hand, I felt a surge, like electricity, enter my body. One like I never knew before. At first it scared me, and then it was like the power unleashed in rushing waters. No sounds, no overwhelming emotions, but a peace that surpassed my understanding. And a desire to live bigger than I had ever known before.

"I thought that at my age I experienced just about everything, but I was only approaching the beginning of the blessings that were in store for me. With you, I truly began to look at my life and all the years I would have left to share with you and your brothers.

"From the time that you three were able to sit still, I have shared stories, stories of this plantation and those of family. We have traveled together and marked with silver ornaments the memories of our lives together. We looked at those mementos of years before you were born, and now we marvel at the blessings of family, our Christmas celebrations, and friends we have shared the season of Christ with.

"But some of the most memorable times you and I shared were those when we brushed our hair together and you helped me take your princess emeralds on and off. Your eyes and those emeralds complemented each other. The day you married and wore the princess emeralds just like I did thrill my heart and took my breath away. And now this new addition to our family. I could not be more blessed to be here, and now for another generation to be born. I cannot tell you that I know for sure that this little one will be a pink little bundle. I cannot seem to be able to think baby boy, but I will redo if necessary."

Another butterfly flutter, and both Abigaile's knew the signs of life within. It had been many, many years since Abigaile Amelie had known that feeling of life but savored the newness of life with Miss Abigaile.

"And now, my dear one, we share a joy that only women can know. Life being formed within. A miracle. Never a mistake. But a blessing that God has many plans for. This beautiful gift will be brought into this world, and many will be the times of joy you and Mr. Butler will share, and perhaps some pain as well. But the joys will outweigh the pain. And the magnolias will be in bloom from the moment of this little one's birth for you and your love.

"And as a Great-Great-Grandmother, I will share stories with her just as I did with you. Or maybe with him. Dear one, do you have any questions?"

"Yes, I do. Can you teach me how to listen closer to the Lord, Grandma? What makes you think this baby is a girl?"

"My darling, it is just a feeling inside me. I cannot explain it. All I know is that all I can see is pink."

"Grandma, do I fix my nursery for a girl?"

"Darling, dear one, fix it as neutral as you can. Then you can add pink or blue when the baby comes. You know that there have been boys in the Butler household for many years. So, baby boy things are plentiful."

"I might get a few fluffy pink things that would say girl just in case."

"Great idea. I just knew you would know what to do."

The rocking stopped, and down to lunch and a peek at Grandmas second surprise was just around the corner.

A whole group of family and friends had joined together for an impromptu baby shower.

While Great-Grandma had Miss Abigaile in the new baby nursery, Momma Bertie Mae had called all the ladies to gather for a surprise gathering for the new momma-to-be and to present gifts for the upcoming little bundle of joy.

It could not have been more perfect. Miss Abigaile got to visit her namesake, and Momma Bertie threw a party.

The day could not have been any more special.

Cake and punch and gifts. A party for everyone.

It had been several months since the wedding and now a baby. God is good, and all the time God is good. Presents opened, and three-quarters of the gifts were pink.

Soft pretty pastel pink, all with flowers and lace. Satin lined blankets and stuffed animals and Madame Alexander dolls. Everything a little girl would need for two years to come.

Hugs, kisses, the car was loaded with presents for the new baby and lots of cake for Mr.

Butler.

Mr. Butler was alerted to the party and was excited about his wife's arrival back home, and the cake.

During the time Miss Abigaile was gone, Mr. Butler had made huge strides with the carpenter who was doing the master bedroom and bath. A completion date was given, and samples of tiles and paint swatches were left for her approval.

Neither one had an idea of the process for remold. College seemed like a walk in the park compared to the decisions that faced this young couple. It might have to last thirty plus years. And after all, the house was over a hundred years old and posed problems due to its age.

The cake was retrieved first and immediately set in the kitchen. Mr. Butler figured the gifts could wait to be unloaded, but the cake, the cake had to be eaten right away. Why? Because it might go bad

Surely Miss Abigaile could understand because Mr. Butler had this sweet tooth. Anything baked, full of sugar, eggs, and flour to coat his tummy. That was his downfall. He just loved sweets. Miss Abigaile remembered when she baked her famed sugar cookies, half were gone in just a few moments. That was way back when. But the years had not tamed his sweet tooth. She began to think the years only made it more pronounced. He liked the taste of salty and sweet together. So, dessert was always served with the meal, and not after.

The party cake was a strawberry-filled angel cake with layers of pretty pink icing and sliced strawberries with white magnolias on the top. It was Great-Grandmother Abigaile s reminder to her namesake of the story times they shared, and when God gave her a new hope, from the moment her great-granddaughter was born, and she was given the name Abigaile, after her Great-Grandmother, Abigaile Amelie. She saw the trees outside filled with fragrant white flowers. From that moment, the magnolias were in bloom again. The sign of new life and new hope. At that moment until now, the magnolias have been in bloom no matter the season.

Their bond had only gotten stronger through the years.

The party packages were retrieved from the car and placed on top of the marble entry table. One by one, the boxes were unveiled to Daddy Butler-to-be. The tiny little garments and toys were truly a shock. So tiny. "So very,

very tiny," said Mr. Butler. "There are so many little pink garments. So much little girl stuff. What are we going to do with all these pink things?"

Miss Abigaile smiled and assured Mr. Butler that God would work it out. It must have given him a sense of peace because he never asked again. And again, time would tell the story.

It was Easter in two weeks, the time for all projects to be finished. The master bedroom and bath and the two nurseries at River Bend and Willow Oaks. Miss Abigaile had only eight to ten weeks to go until Miss or Master Butler would arrive.

As for Grandma Abigaile Amelie, she was hoping to have another birthday partner.

But until that time, she needed to get busy with her name search. A list of possible family names that might be their new additions legacy.

As Grandma Abigaile began her search, she could only imagine what it would be like to be a fifth generation. She had seen life begin and end, but to live this many years gave her a different insight to the blessing of this special little person. Girl or boy, they would be part of her own blood line, one of her and Mr. Hurleys union.

This name would have to reflect the families that were joined together in marriage. One of love and commitment.

One of lasting union and respect for each mate that was given by God Himself.

Mom and dad names. Aunts and uncles. Grandparents. Grandma Abigaile Amelie began to feel overwhelmed. So many names with character. So many with strength and honor and a history of distinctive individuals. How could she choose? But it must flow. A name that would join the first and last name as a sonnet. It must be a name that had poetry in motion. Romance for a girl and strength for a boy. These were the final words that characterized Grandma Abigaile's search.

A list of his family names and all hers, but again, only girl's names were coming to her. Grandma was in a quandary. Again, was that party line open and the voice at the other end talking, or was Abigaile Amelie just hoping for a soft pink baby girl that she could hold and dress up like a Southern belle, something like she did with her own namesake?

But again, only time would tell, and until the reveal, she could only hope.

Grandma Abigaile Amelie was back to her search. How could Grandma present her findings? Was Mr. Butler going to be on board, or would he revolt? No, Grandma Abigaile trusted herself. So onward and upward to her goal.

Names of those who had gone before and a few new names that were celebrated with movie stars.

The list was not too long. But it certainly made a statement. There were only two that stood out for a boy, Rhett James. Rhett after the character in Gone with the Wind, and James after one of Mr. Butler's family members and Jesus's disciples. It was a name that flowed well over the tongue. Rhett James Butler.

And a name of grace and royalty, Sophie Grace. Sophie after her daddy's great-aunt, a lady of many talents and a beauty no one could match. And Grace after her momma, a woman of noble character and a heart of gold, always a giver, never a taker.

You would have guessed that Mr. Butler would have cared, but he didn't have an opinion.

His main focus was Willow Oaks and anything his darling Miss Abigaile would need.

One could tell the time was coming close for the new Butler to be introduced to this world.

Great-Grandma Abigaile Amelie had finished the nursery at River Bend. Miss Abigaile had the nursery at Willow Oaks complete also. All seemed to be in readiness.

Miss Abigaile's brothers were home from college and were anxiously awaiting the blessed event. It was the end of May, and Baby Butler was due in two to four weeks. Miss Abigaile was increasing in size day by day. Her walk looked more like a duck waddle. Sleep was not easy, so naps were Miss Abigaile's only relief.

Harrison's parents were due to arrive back at Willow Oaks. Their plan was to be there for the birth of their first grandchild. Their old room had been completely changed, and what they all saw was what looked like a New York hotel room. A true improvement over what they had left. They could not have been prouder of their son and Miss Abigaile, and super excited for the blessing coming their way.

But babies have their own schedule. No one could really say because from the beginning of time no birthdays were set in stone for new life. We hope and plan, but after all, God says there is a time to be born, and there is nothing that will change that.

Miss Abigaile's brothers, Carter and Edward, could hardly wait to be uncles. They were planning to teach their nephew how to ride horses and hunt squirrels. They had gone together and bought his first gun, a Red Ryder BB gun, a new release from Daisy Outdoor Products Co. They also had his name all picked out. Jefferson Edward Darcy Butler. They would call him Jed Butler. A name from each of the men who would help him be a man. Harrisons brothers would have to wait for baby number two to get their namesakes.

All the men in the Hurley and Butler family had this plan, his name, what he would wear, where he would go to school, and, importantly, how to fish, and, even more important, how to hunt. Everything from foxes to squirrels and big game. You see, that was the sign of a real man. And of course, how to run and maintain a plantation. From a very young age, this was the avenue that all these Southern gentlemen were taught to follow.

And the time marched on. Miss Abigaile had prepared the nursery for their little bundle. The time was so close. Every family member was on alert. Every time the doorbell rang, a car approached, or the phone rang, the family was ready to go to the hospital. But no news yet.

Miss Abigaile's brothers were preparing to meet their nephew, and Great-Grandma

Abigaile was waiting for her new birthday buddy to meet her Great-Great-Grandmother. Harrisons parents and Miss Abigaile's parents were on pins and needles. Everything and anything sent them into baby time, but it just wasn't time yet.

Every morning, every evening, the phones were busy. No info yet, but Miss Abigaile had been feeling a little different.

June 15,1943, and Miss Abigaile called her Mr. Butler. "Darling," she said, "are you ready to be a daddy? Please take me to the hospital." Harrison had been in town for new seeds. The co- op owner had been on alert for the last thirty days, knowing that babies have a mind of their own. After all, he had eight of his own. So, he was very familiar with the process. After he alerted Harrison, it was like a comedy show.

Mr. Butler dropped his packages, turned around, and lost all sense of direction. He dropped his car keys twice and bumped into almost every display. He looked like a wind-up toy. And then a friendly hand helped him to the door and helped Mr. Butler outside. The store owner, Mr. Sawyer, said a quick prayer. Mr. Butler seemed to gain composure, and off he went. He only had five miles to get to Willow Oaks. But it seemed like forty miles. He broke speed limits and passed everyone like they were standing still.

Miss Abigaile was at the front door waiting for her chariot to arrive. She could see Mr. Butler approaching by the cloud of dust that filled the air. On the way back to Willow Oaks, Harrison realized that he had just left.

And he was right back where he was, not to pick up seeds but because a new family member was coming.

He was so nervous. This was his darling Miss Abigaile.

All he could think about was that the mystery of girl or boy was close to being unveiled. Harrison had seen many animals give birth, but his Miss Abigaile, well, she was his love. And this was his baby.

Harrison was an excited daddy-to-be. Miss Abigaile was in a panic. Her water had broken, and contraction had gotten stronger. Already three minutes apart. A rush back down the road. A streak of lightning-fast driving, and the hospital was in sight.

Miss Abigaile had already registered, so she just walked right in. A wheelchair, and down the hall to a private room where this new little person was about to be introduced.

Harrison was escorted to the waiting room, and he took a seat next to one more daddy-to-be.

At first, Harrison was without words, then he said, "How long have you been here?"

"Only eight hours," the other man said. This shocked Harrison; he was frozen in place. For all he knew about his plantation animals, he could not comprehend that type of time. He then asked if everything was okay. "Yeah. Our little one is just not ready yet. But all is okay. Thanks for asking," the gentleman said.

Then the tables were turned. The other daddy-to-be asked Harrison about his wife. He said, "We just got here."

A nurse came out and told Harrison that it was just about time.

You could have knocked Harrison over with a feather. "Already?" he said. "Yes," the nurse said. "You are just about going to be a daddy, Mr. Butler."

Just then, the Butler and Hurley entourage all came into the waiting room. Two sets of grandparents.

Four big strapping young men were all excited about being uncles. Then a grand entrance by Miss Abigaile's namesake. All turned, and Grandma Abigaile smiled. "Has she been born yet?" It was a shocking revelation.

"What?" they all said.

"Well," Grandma Abigaile said, "has she been born yet? Tomorrow is my birthday, and this is the perfect gift for me."

As if this new little bundle could hear. She was entering this world. Grandma Abigaile had a prophetic word spoken, but none seemed to hear. Everyone was still holding on to the surprise. Grandma Abigaile was not ready, yet she knew that feeling of truth within her. So, she was waiting for her new granddaughter to be introduced to the family.

Everyone heard a baby cry. It was in the next room. It was for the daddy-to-be whom Harrison had met when he came in. It was not the Butler baby.

Then another cry. This had to be Miss Abigaile's and Harrisons baby. There was no one else in the maternity ward. Oh my. The nurse came out. Before she announced the sex of the baby, Great-Grandma Abigaile said, "It is a baby girl, right?"

"Yes," the nurse said. "How did you know?"

Grandma Abigaile said, "It was easy. Jesus and I had a conversation."

Well, that was a confirmation to all the Hurley clan. She did have a party line straight to God. From that moment they all knew that God spoke directly to Great-Grandma Abigaile.

"Yes, it is a baby girl."

Grandma Abigaile raised her hands and said, "Praise the Lord." And everyone chimed in. "Is my wife okay?"

"Oh yes, she is just fine. Would you like to see your little girl?"

The nurse asked all to stand back and asked Mr. Butler, the new daddy, to step forward. Out came the new family member. She was so tiny, sweet, soft, and pink. Don't touch! And the new little Miss Butler was off to the nursery, where everyone could see this beautiful little wonder. A blessing from God.

Well, you guessed it, Grandma Abigaile and God had talked, and Miss Buder was born.

Now the question was what was going to be her name.

So, the Red Ryder BB gun would have to wait. Or maybe the new uncles could teach their

niece all about hunting and fishing.

Then it happened. Names, lots of names, were offered up. And each of the family members were sure that they had a winner.

Names like Alice, Ida, Genell, Camille, Ursel, Mary, Rochelle, and Gabriella. They all sounded pretty good with the last name Butler. And, of course, Jed was going to be put on hold. And then the name Scarlett was spoken. Well, it was a nod to the movie Gone with the Wind. No Rhett, but they could all live with Scarlett.

But none knew the answer yet. Because the new momma and daddy had not announced their decision.

A name is a very important thing. Because it is something that you will carry with you your whole life.

And then the waiting room was quiet, and all were waiting to hear what Great-Grandma Abigaile would suggest for Miss Butler's first and middle name, but Grandma Abigaile was silent. She was not ready to discuss her great-great-granddaughter's name yet because Miss Butler's parents had not spoken. Out of respect for her namesake and her husband, if asked, Grandma Abigaile would say, "I will be very happy to give my darlings a name, but for now I have no name." All were puzzled. Everyone knew she had talked to God on their party line. What did He say? No one knew. However, nobody would be kept in the dark too long since Miss Abigaile was in the hospital for the next seven days. The birth certificate would have to reveal the name all had been waiting for, so everyone had to wait.

WILLOW OAKS
BEFORE RESTORATION

WILLOW OAKS
BEFORE RESTORATION

Restoration

DURING THIS TIME Of anticipation, Harrison was also planning for a huge surprise for his beloved. Miss Abigaile had presented him with an heir, and he wanted to present her with something new a well.

Miss Abigaile was preparing to arrive home at Willow Oaks when they arrived at the decision of what to name their gift from God. They were both unsure. They had agreed upon a boy's name but had not considered the proper name for this pretty and pink little bundle.

Harrison had grown to love Great-Grandma Abigaile and had seen and heard of her talks with God.

It was as if the thought hit them both at the same time.

"Let's ask Grandma Abigaile. Maybe God already told her." So, knowing that Grandma Abigaile was coming to visit again, they made a plan.

Grandma Abigaile was getting older but not too old to drive her new Cadillac. She had chosen it herself just a few years before. So, for her, it was still new. An ivory color with big whitewall tires. A ride as soft as being on a cloud, she always said.

It was the last day before Miss Abigaile and her new baby were in the hospital, and Grandma Abigaile was on her way to visit.

From just the two of them, Harrison and Miss Abigaile, now there were three in their family. None of them could ever have guessed God's timing for a family, but here they were. Grandma Abigaile entered the room, and it was as if sunshine entered, even though the hour was late and the sun was going down.

Grandma Abigaile Amelie stopped at the nursery first and was simply glowing with pride.

She had witnessed a miracle and had an answer to her prayer.

Harrison and Miss Abigaile welcomed Grandma, and from the moment she entered the room, she could feel there was a question coming.

"What's up? Both of you have a questioning look on your face! Is everything okay? Is my great-great-grand daughter, okay?"

"Oh my, yes. Yes, she is great! We have a question for you. We don't want to put you on the spot, but we have a dilemma!"

Grandma was very excited. A younger generation was asking a dinosaur. She had passed the century-old mark. But in all those years, this was a woman who had seen peace and war, marriage and loss, children and loss, and a rebirth of hopes and dreams. She counted it all a blessing because she had faith. A faith in the God who had created her and had her days numbered. And He was not done with her yet, so at her birthday party she had turned 103 years old and was still going strong. Maybe not as fast but still going. She felt blessed to have seen her namesake's child. She considered this to be the icing on the cake of her life.

"Now let's talk, children! What is your question?"

"Well, Grandma." Harrison was turning beet red. "We have a problem."

"My goodness, what is it?"

Harrison shouted out loud, "We have no name, no name for our little girl."

"Are you asking me what I would call her?"

"Yes, we are. We know you talk to God, and He talks to you."

"Yes, He does. I have talked with God," Grandma said, "and from the time you had announced this blessed event, I asked God for a name. A name of beauty and godly char acter. This is what He, God, gave me. Just this one, only one, no more, no options. Sophie Grace. Sophie after your great-aunt who was a lady of many talents and a beauty no one could match. All from your side of the family,

Harrison. And Grace after her mother. A woman of noble character and a heart of gold who was always a giver and never a taker. This is the name, I believe, God gave me for your daughter."

Both smiled. It was perfect. Both families represented a legacy, a name of honor and destination, from the pages of generations present and past. "This was going to be our daughter's name. Sophie Grace Butler, our little princess."

A picture of pure perfection.

And Harrison and Miss Abigaile Grace were home ward bound with the newest family member. Harrison had picked up his two beautiful women and escorted them into the new Cadillac he had gotten for just this occasion. A new baby and a new car. This car was similar to Grandma Abigaile's but years newer, a new chariot for his new family. Harrison could not have been prouder; his chest was so puffed out it almost popped his buttons off, and off to Willow Oaks they went. Little Sophie Grace had a new room, and so did Miss Abigaile Grace.

But when they arrived back at Willow Oaks, there was a something different.

The house that was built a hundred years ago had the beginnings of a fresh new look. During the times of plantation ups and downs, the house at Willow Oaks had fallen into disrepair. The interior of this beautiful old home had also seen better days. Since the master suite remodel and the new nursery, it seemed to highlight the fallen look of this grand old house. It seemed to light a slow burn underneath Harrison, because it was now up to Harrison to fix and repair everything that had to do with Willow Oaks. The whole time he had lived there, he never noticed the fallen steps, peeling paint, and the dry grounds of the house, but now it was like a light had been turned on. This would not be a proper place for his new family. That was why the push to begin the cleanup and restoration of the grounds and this gorgeous home, a place where his family could sit on the porches and stroll among the new gardens. He had a picture in his mind and was attacking it like a starving person might attack a plate of food.

Miss Abigaile Grace was ecstatic. She could see it all in white like the home she grew up in, River Bend. It was a super surprise. The new look for Willow Oaks.

This was now the picture of home for her new family that she had secretly envisioned. And now it was all coming true, with her love, Harrison, and their precious little girl., with a name that God Himself approved. This was home.

Grandma Abigaile Amelie planned her weeks around trips to Willow Oaks. Each time she pulled up to this grand old house, she saw a rose beginning to bloom, but the most important focus of her visits was all about her namesake and that amazing, beautiful, pretty little pink bundle of femininity, her granddaughter Sophie Grace.

The months passed, and all boys were back from college. Harrisons brothers were both graduating from college and were going to move back to Willow Oaks, where all three brothers would assume full ownership of Willow Oaks. They were all willed Willow Oaks in a living will by their mom and dad, because Mom and Dad had realized that Willow Oaks was not that huge focus it once was. Since the accident, they seemed drawn to a place where new adventures and people needed them, and they needed it as well.

While the exterior of Willow Oaks was emerging like a beautiful butterfly, the interior was still in yesteryears. Even though the master suite and nursery had an overhaul, the rest of the house was still on hold.

But until the time when the Butler boys graduated, there was a lot to do. The summer had ended, and Thanksgiving and Christmas were on their way.

Sophie Grace was going to have her first Christmas, and Grandma Abigaile Amelie was designing her special silver ornaments to celebrate this occasion. Grandma Abigaile's darling would be six months December 15, and she would surely be able to enjoy her first Christmas with all the lights and decorations.

Grandma Abigaile would have to add one more ornament to her silver order. Just one more for a very special little darling, her Sophie Grace.

And then it came to her. The ornament would be a dress with carved flowers on it and the date 1943. It would be one more to add to every individual Christmas tree. For Sophie, this was her second memento. Because even though she was not born yet, the Christmas before, it was a memory of the big announcement.

This was Grandma Abigaile's way of remembering special moments in their family, and she would always say, "And the magnolias were in bloom " With Grandma Abigaile, it signified new life, spring, and a fragrance that reminded her that life is beautiful if you take time to enjoy each and every moment, for all too quick what and who you love can be gone and you have missed the beauty of the moment. So, for Grandma Abigaile Amelie, it kept her focus up and not down. Her glass was always half full and never half empty.

Miss Abigaile and Grandma Abigaile had weekly vis its, and there seemed to be a peace that fell each time they shared hugs. Grandma prayed every time, and so did Miss Abigaile. Little Sophie Grace was growing, and her baby blond hair was turning darker and darker. Her little blue eyes were staying blue as the sky; her little hands were grabbing hold of everything. She had rattles and little teething toys, but when this little one saw her great-great-grand mother, she reached out with both little hands and made little noises. Smiles and little hugs were exchanged. No one could deny that this special little girl had a bond with this gray-haired lady of a hundred years plus. Grandma Abigaile began to tell Sophie Grace a story.

"My little darling," she said, "when we were expecting you, we were all very excited. You know you were an answer to our prayers. Before you were born, God and I talked about your name. You were named after Great-Aunt Sophie. She was the most beautiful lady and had many, many talents. And your second name, Grace, was given to you after your mom. I have always known her to be a very giving person and a lady of godly character. You see, my darling, you were sent here for just such a time as this, so the magnolias could still bloom for me and all the others who will get the privilege of knowing you. As you grow up, there will be much for you to learn and much to do as you mature. But if you keep your eyes on Jesus, you will always be blessed, and God will take you to marvelous places, and you will meet your love there. Your mom and dad will be there to help you in your life, and I will pray always for you until I am no more. Blessings, my dear sweet baby girl."

Now you would have thought that Grandma Abigaile was talking to an older child, with the ability to completely understand or at least somewhat comprehend part of Grandmas love instructions, but no, it was a conversation with a teeny tiny six-month-old. Yet one could see that this little one never took her beautiful blue eyes off her great-great-grandmother. And she smiled so big you would have thought that she was given one of her favorite foods or toys. But no, it was just simply two that shared family and God. Sophie was a gift from God to her dear sweet Great-Great-Grandma, and Abigaile was a gift to Little Miss Sophie Grace.

This was how their visits began and ended. Each week you could see Sophie Grace growing and glowing with new excitement. Everything was brand-new, and she was curious about everything. Grandma Abigaile seemed to come alive like never before. She had a spring in her step, like having a new pair of PF flyers on her size 5 feet. Her strength seemed to be energized like a bunny. She bounced up the curved stairway at River Bend and sat with her darling in the perfect pink nursery that was designed just for this pretty and pink little girl.

Each week there were two visits. One at River Bend and one at Willow Oaks. It was a treasured time for all. Grandma Bertie was always there hugging and loving on her only grandchild. She was making the best out of every moment she had with Sophie Grace. Bertie Mae had heard Grandma Abigaile s stories many times and took to heart the ones that instructed her dear ones in seizing the moments and never, but never, waiting for another time to love on your family. It was like Grandma said, "They could be gone, and you lose your chance to love."

This was indeed an instructive message that Bertie never forgot. Bertie Maes family were busy with political issues, and she never knew she was missing that tight family bond until she married Edward Darnell Hurley and moved to River Bend, where she was welcomed graciously and loved on like she had never known.

So, for Bertie Mae, for the first time in her life, she felt a part of a family where they were more concerned about her instead of policies and politics.

Now it truly felt like the priority in Bertie Maes life was in order. God first, family second, and everyone and everything else last.

So, the whole time she was raising Miss Abigaile and her two boys, she made Grandma Abigaile s stories come to life. With many years of wisdom under her belt, Grandma Abigaile could instruct others in family, love, God, and the things that matter most in life.

She would always say you only have one life and one chance to live it; don't forget who you are and what you were sent to do and who you are to bless along the way. One way, one life, one chance to make a difference, and she would always begin and end her instructions with her signature words. "And the magnolias were then and always will be blooming, if you allow them to."

Take charge, she would say, and walk as though you were meant to make a difference, and everyone will respect you, and God will promote you.

CHAPTER 12

Southern Love and Secret Dreams

GRANDA ABIGAILE HAD A trip to town to pick up the silver treasures she had designed for her dear ones. Christmas was just two weeks away, and all the decor for River Bend had been taken out and was on full display. The annual Hurley Christmas party for family and friends was coming up.

Grandma had her Christmas gifts for friends all completed and beautifully wrapped, all placed on the entry table at River Bend. The house was decorated again in different shades of pink. Fuchsia to pale pink. The glass ornaments that Grandma Abigaile had made last year were all artfully placed on top of the mantels and around the branches of the huge Douglas fir Christmas tree.

Grandma Abigaile was saving the baby-blue decor for baby number two. But if two didn't come, she could always use them with the cobalt-blue decor, but for now, the pink was the theme for this special Christmas. This was all in honor of the newest family member, Miss Sophie Grace. But before the annual Christmas party, Grandma Abigaile had taken her love for family and wrapped her new family history ornament and placed one under each pillow. She had taken the Butlers' mementos and placed them under the pillow in Miss Sophie Grace's crib.

Grandma Abigaile had a zip in her step that night for this was her way of saying I love you, my family. All would be able to see her creation. She was also planning for her next year's memento. But she was not sure how many silver ornaments she might need to order. Her grandsons could be married and even expecting a new little Hurley, and her namesake could be with child again. It was truly a wonderful thought. But for now, the pillow ornaments and the Hurley Christmas party would keep her busy until after the first of the year.

Grandma Abigaile had so many silver mementos, the limbs were drooping, but it could hold more if needed. There was a consideration for a new type of display for the family history tree. But Grandma said that nothing could be so perfect and looking like a tree of family history than a Christmas tree. "After all, it is all about our family, the family we came from, and the first family we all came from, Christ. And the Christmas tree represents Christ for me."

So, the family vote was yes for the Christmas tree, forever.

The Hurley Christmas party was just a day way. The beautiful Miss Matilda's green and gold China graced the table and sideboard. Pink roses and red poinsettia were everywhere, in short vases and tall crystal-goblet-style vases. The tall Christmas tree was framed by the two walks through windows, and the new pink brocade drapes made a very elegant picture. With all the presents dressed in shades of pink just like the hand-blown glass ornaments, it was a jaw- dropping moment.

Each year, Grandma Abigaile and Bertie Mae had joined opinions and always came up with a winner. It was a treat for all who were invited to share Christmas with the Hurley family.

Christmas Day greeted them with a fresh blanket of snow. It was a ten-inch snowfall. It literally crippled the small town. Church services were canceled, and no one moved from their houses. It was a first for the Hurley family. No church on Christmas morning! It put a different tempo in the house at River Bend.

Instead of a rush to get to church, there was a slow laid-back approach to the day. Breakfast was more of a brunch, and supper was at 4:00 p.m. Then a snack at 8:00 p.m., and stories of Christmases past, but as full as the house was, it still felt empty. This was the second Christmas that Miss Abigaile was not there.

But of course, that was not going to change. Willow Oaks was Miss Abigaile's new home.

A home where Mr. Buder and their precious Sophie Grace were making it their family home.

With Valentines on its way, Mr. Butlers plans were made to be finished with the total restoration, inside and out, at his Willow Oaks. A project that only took a little more than eight months. Some of the longest months. It was like a pregnancy but so much noisier and smellier, Miss Abigaile always remarked, but they would have a prize in time.

From the broken-down ravages of time, the beautiful Southern Willow Oaks was alive again. The porches were filled with furniture and potted ferns everywhere. No mat ter which door you came out of, there was a porch swing and flowers, all dressed in white, just like a beautiful bride.

The gardens and trees had been broken and destroyed with harsh winter freezes year after year. This time of resto ration had removed the scars of war and winter ravages of winters past. For what was beautiful a hundred years ago was dead and now reborn to last another hundred years plus.

In all the years past, the focus was not on the rebirth of this astounding home but on keeping the plantation and the crops for each year that had passed. There were births, deaths, war, and the Great Depression, and the struggles the Butler family had been handed, like most of the United States population.

The times of rebirth for the Butler family and Willow Oaks had come slowly but had reached a fullness of blessing in all areas of their lives.

So, it was no surprise that the restoration of finances had been seen, and money was not in short supply. Therefore, college, clothes, and cars were paid for without a layaway plan or payment schedule; the Lord had restored that which had been stolen.

For Mr. Butler, that is Harrison, he had begun to place more importance on family and Miss Abigaile's God. From the time Harrison met Miss Abigaile Grace, he noticed something different. He could not put his finger on it, but he truly was drawn to her beauty inside and out.

What was this? She seemed to shine from within like the sun, moon, stars, and all the summer lightning bugs that covered the trees where the magnolias were in bloom.

Harrison was compelled to come to the light that was within Miss Abigaile Grace Hurley. It would only be revealed as their young love bloomed from a tight rosebud to a flower in full opulent beauty.

When each met at school, there was only one who claimed her mate; she revealed her choice early on to her Grandma Abigaile Amelie. When Miss Abigaile announced she too had fallen in love with an older man just like her Grandma Abigaile, well, you guessed it. The seed of love was planted, and you see now the blooming flower was full of life and love.

With a destiny that was planned by God Himself, a beautiful little girl was born.

For some people, the end of everything is just the end of school, work, or relationships. But for Harrison and Miss Abigaile, it was a beginning. One of new dreams, new hopes, new lives. And some dreams that were not ready to be revealed.

Everyone dreams, and plans are made, but life takes us in unique and different paths. Yet hopes and dreams can make or break us. For hope deferred will make the heart sick.

For Harrison it was that way. He had a dream. A dream he had since he was a boy. He loved automobiles. The design and unique qualities of a machine that could cover terrain and travel at speeds no horse could ever achieve, an interior of wood and leather for comfort, windows that allowed vision all around, a smooth ride like being on a cloud, and an opportunity to travel anywhere in complete comfort.

This was truly a secret dream. One day own and sell many of the automobiles of Europe and here in the United

States. Where? He had thought this was a pipe dream, so where never entered his thoughts.

For now, he was owner and manager of a thousand plus-acre plantation. And it was a family business, because that was the way of family lands. You were born into a fam ily and were expected to fulfill your duties and continue to grow the land into a bigger and better place than when you received it.

Harrison knew what was expected of him, and his brothers, but still had this deep-down obsession. Maybe one day, maybe someday, but not now!

The remodeling of the beautiful Willow Oaks home was now complete, and the gardens were brought back to life once again.

With this accomplishment, he felt he was fulfilling one of the many duties of ownership and a family legacy that one day might be willed to his beloved Sophie Grace.

But for now, his dream could not be any more than just that, a dream, a hopeful vision of what one day could become reality.

So off to the duties of plantation life and those of being a new daddy.

How could anyone be so blessed, for he truly believed that his life and his duties were set in stone. How could there be anything that could change a family obligation like he had been given?

But every once in a while, when he got into his Cadillac, his mind would recall those moments when he was a child, and his dream of cars and more cars began.

He could enjoy those secret dreams over and over. But like all secrets and dreams he would share with his love someday, perhaps she too held a secret hope and dream unspoken.

It seems to be a very common thing that we humans share. We think that we are the only one. The only one who dreams of better times, different clothes, babies, and the new home that seems so unreachable.

We work hard at our jobs and try to plan for those dreams to come true, but sometimes that door with your dreams does not open. Yet it still lingers in our heart, but when we let loose those ideas sometime, something better comes along, and we cannot remember what we held on to for so long.

Grandma Abigaile Amelie would always say give it to God; He will give you more than you imagine.

And so, it was true. Miss Abigaile was the answer to her dream. The dream she had to share her love and wisdom and her princess emeralds with her namesake.

Grandma Abigaile Amelie had a dream of a love and marriage, children, land, and home. And that door opened. Her dreams came true; now her life was in the fall her days, and she simply thanked God for each new day when she met the sun and breathed again.

Grandma Abigaile had seen life, love, and dreams that came true.

And now was the time to help another's dream come true.

So, Grandma Abigaile was on the party line with God. She had some ideas and was going to research to see where her help was most needed.

It was still wartime, and so many were still dreaming of better times.

Some dreaming of cars. Some of houses; then there were the prayers and hope for loved ones to come home.

Grandma knew she had to start small and pray each time to be a help for the dreams to come true and not embrace anyone or step where she was not supposed to go. She was hoping to enlist the help of Bertie Mae and her namesake, Abigaile Grace.

Sugar was in short supply during this war, and River Bend had been growing sugar cane for several decades.

Grandma Abigaile had a sweet tooth, and since sugar was in very short supply during the war, she thought that this might be a place to start, because a dessert after a won derful meal just feels good.

Could this be the place to start? Grandma Abigaile would be going to her prayer closet where her phone line to Jesus was located.

For the enlisted helpers, this was a plus.

Both Bertie Mae and Abigaile Grace had another thought that they wanted to bring to the table and the phone line to Jesus.

A food bank, where those in need could come to enjoy the bounty from River Bends fields and the gardens from Willow Oaks.

Grandma Abigaile had prayed and asked her dear Jesus for peace and an understanding that she knew where to go.

When Bertie and Miss Abigaile approached Grandma, a flood of tears fell from Abigaile Amelie's eyes. She knew the answer was forthcoming. The two enlisted help. They suggested the food bank, and manna fell from heaven. This was the answer to her prayers.

"How soon can we get this started?"

"We can open a store in town or the barns here at River Bend! Make a list, my dears, and so will I. It shouldn't take too long to implement our plan. With spring approaching, we will plant a bigger garden and take over left over sugar cane and prepare it for the food bank and the sweet tooths of our area."

They were all on board. This was the blessing that so many had dreamed of. Thus, the dream Grandma Bertie Mae and Miss Abigaile had going was to be that door that many were dreaming of: food for their table and some sugar for the sweet tooth we all have.

This was a dream that could come true. And also, a possibility for more to be involved, not just today but for many months and years to come.

It was indeed a good idea, but Grandma said it was a good idea.

Before long, the gardens were producing a harvest, the barn at River Bend was the location for the food bank. Word had gotten around, and there were others contributing produce, chickens, eggs, an occasional pig or calf. The food bank had to make arrangements for drop-offs and for food distribution. River Bend and Willow Oaks were busier than ever before.

Grandma was in hog heaven. She was making a difference. She would always say it is better to give, and she was surely doing her part.

Miss Abigaile, Grandma Abigaile, and Sophie Grace were all about to turn a year older. For this was the month of June, Grandma had more years under her belt, and Sophia Grace was just beginning.

The Georgia heat was taking a toll on Grandma. She would have to rely on others to distribute food in the food bank at River Bend. But Grandma Abigaile did not stop her. While the others volunteered in the barn, she was taking calls and receiving personal letters requesting assistance. Grandma could see this was a God idea because everything came together so easily, and many offered more and more food as the weeks went on. There was much food and so many hungry people. It reminded Grandma Abigaile of the Great Depression when the lines for jobs and food were a hundred to two hundred people long, but there was always enough; no one ever left hungry or was turned away.

It seemed like this good idea had caught on. It was a huge success. There were some who came every week. Then there were those who only received once. But there was always enough of everything for everyone to get what their family needed. There were some who would drop a penny or nickel on the table to help further the blessings.

And that it did. Seeds for the garden, flour, and some cloths were offered for sewing garments.

It was something that no one had ever seen before. People helping people without keeping score.

Grandma had people asking for lodging, but there were none available. Once in a while, River Bend and Willow Oaks had one of their helpers leave. Then Miss Abigaile and Grandma Abigaile would go through the housing requests. Just like before, there were requirements, work, and food, and lodging. A package deal, for one or a family.

June was here.

Where and where shall the perfect party take place? Because there were two birthday girls at Willow Oaks, the decision was made. With the beautiful restoration that had taken place, it gave the lady of Willow Oaks opportunity to show off her skills at interior and exterior design.

Grandma Abigaile was completely astonished at the completed rebirth of a home that she had seen go to seed. This was a testament to what she knew should and did happen with her namesake at the helm of this ship.

The exterior and interior were dressed with loads and loads of pink—pink balloons, pink flowers, and pink fabric draped everywhere. Pink punch and pink cake. Pink plates and napkins and pink party favors.

Little Sophie Grace was dressed in a fluffy little pink dress that matched her momma's dress. They were a picture-perfect photo.

And then Grandma Abigaile Amelie arrived, and the birthday girl joined her party mates. She too had a pretty pink dress on, and a pink feathered hat sat atop her gray hair like a bird had landed there and was protecting a nest of eggs. She too was a portrait in motion.

With Bertie Mae in the picture, there were four generations represented.

Pictures were being snapped from every angle. As the photographer kept saying "These are moments frozen in time. As some are lost in time, these photos will take you back to the times when you shared special moments together."

So, the photographer went wild. Lots of memories were snapped for over two hours, hundreds of pictures that would fill a beautiful pink photo album celebrating this auspicious occasion.

There were lots of people celebrating birthdays everywhere but very, very few that had reached the age of 103. Some of these photos and an interview would be posted in the local newspaper, and photos would be wired all over the United States.

To reach a hundred years plus was a testament to genes and healthy living, but the stories behind a hundred years of living were a unique and pleasurable story to be shared by hundreds of the newspaper s readers all over the world.

The time was midafternoon and the year 1944. The war was still a driving force for families with members overseas.

The food bank was in full swing; more people were donating, and more needs were being met. Things had been going so well, and there was so much more response than expected... Another distribution center would need to be located; maybe some of the volunteers could take turns, and more than one day could be arranged for the needy.

Before the party for the three beautiful Southern ladies was over, and the majority of guests had left, Grandma Abigaile Amelie gathered her little Sophie Grace and asked her little princess if she wanted to hear a story.

Of course, Sophie Grace couldn't talk, but the smile and hugs seemed to say yes.

Grandma Abigaile began, "My little darling, I want to tell you a story about myself and your momma. And the magnolias were in bloom. Before your momma was born, I was having a hard time. I was thinking that my life was coming to an end. My love, Mr. Hurley, had passed away. That is, he went to heaven. And both of my sons had also passed away. I had this big plantation to run, and I felt like there was too much to do and not enough time to do it.

"Then your momma was born, and she was given my name. Abigaile Grace was her name. My name is Abigaile Amelie, but her first name was the same as mine. She looked at me, and my heart began to sing as never before. Since that time, we have shared many times like this one. Holidays and birthdays and trips together all over the world. I am getting a little bit older now, and I may not be able to travel, but God has given me some new ideas. Perhaps as you grow up you can assist me and your momma and her momma to help others in need." Then Sophie Grace fell asleep.

Abigaile Grace noticed something special happening. She saw a unique and very special bond was being formed right before her very eyes. The soft voice and the tender hugs that she had enjoyed when she was a child seemed to be her little one's as well.

The thought went through Abigaile Grace's mind every now and then. Her dear Grandma Abigaile Amelie was getting older. Really older, and she wondered what life might be like without her grandma.

And then Sophie Grace awakened, and the thoughts of loss was lost. Life was right in front of her, along with excitement for all the special moments they would all be sharing.

The summer was in full swing, and Harrison's brothers were home from college. They had both graduated and started their plantation education.

There was much to learn. During the time that brother Harrison had taken over as owner, there had been several changes made.

Harrison's brothers, however, were beginning to talk about some changes of their own.

Willow Oaks was now owned by three Butler brothers. They had to be in agreement with everything as equal owners. It was going to be a struggle at first because they had not worked together for over five years, but it was like all life. It would surely work its way out in time.

Both of Harrison's brothers were now eligible for military service. The war had been going on now for the U.S. for almost three years, and no one knew how much longer it might go on.

Both Butler boys were summoned to the draft board in Georgia.

Fear had filled the Butler household; there was a delay in their reporting date.

Everyone had been praying, but now it was an "every moment, every second of every day" thing.

So many of the towns young men had been called up, and now two more were in danger of the war that Hitler started. As Americans, there was not a one who fled the country. All were filled with a pride of country and considered it an honor to defend their country. But the boys were not going to be army bound. They signed up as new Marine recruits. Again, the time was postponed for two months, and before Thanksgiving, the Butler brothers were on their way to training camp. Both were assigned to the same base camp.

Harrison and Abigaile Grace were the family that saw the boys off to boot camp.

It seemed so very strange again at Willow Oaks, after Harrisons parents had left Willow Oaks to pursue their new life. It was another transition from having family support to becoming a single member owner again.

But for Harrison and Abigaile Grace, they knew God had a plan. What plan? That was certainly not evident yet, so it was another "one day at a time" situation.

Grandma Abigaile and Bertie knew this was going to be a chance to help. They were on board; they wanted to help in any way they could.

Perhaps some of River Bends helpers could lend a hand when harvest was due.

But there was a kink in the plan. The family was ready to take charge when word came that the boys might not have to go overseas.

They might be stationed Stateside.

The Hurley family and the Butlers were overjoyed.

This Christmas might truly be one of miracles. Loyalty, patriotism, valor, leadership—these were traits taught to all recruits, no matter what branch of service.

For in peacetime or in war, the U.S. believed these young men were representing a freedom. One of country, family, love, and a right to be free from oppression no matter your color or creed.

There was an unspoken promise among these groups of men and women. No man or woman would be left behind. No matter the cost, our soldiers would be brought home.

And home in the U.S. was where the Butler brothers were sent. After boot camp they had shown such amazing abilities with their fellow Marines that recruiting offices begged for these two Stateside! The men that these two eloquent Southern gentlemen were replacing had aspirations of seeing the war firsthand.

But Harrison and Miss Abigaile knew exactly how it had happened. They prayed, God heard their prayers, and God answered their prayers.

As for Grandma Abigaile and her party line, the request had been made long ago. And there were no questions in Grandma Abigaile's mind. She was thrown a curveball at first when the Butler brothers received their orders to report, but Grandma was diligent. No ifs, ands, or buts. Just God telling her all would be all right.

So, Christmas was a true miracle of the birth of Jesus and the saving of two more young men from war. Why? one might ask. Well, all grandma knew was that God had another plan for the uncles of her darling Sophie Grace.

Grandma Abigaile had been doing some research of her own, looking up more information about the military and the parts of the country in peace and war, and the security they would all feel in wartime and in peacetime.

It was a two-and-a-half-year commitment that the Butler boys had made. The pride that this town and these families had was simply phenomenal. Banners were hung in the windows of all who had servicemen and -women. The American Legion national emblem was a blue star.

And in this small Georgia town, there were many. For some, it would be a family member who was overseas, but for the Hurleys and the Butlers, it was for two who were serving Stateside. It was not going to be in their hometown of Thomaston, but that didn't seem to matter; the Butler boys were in the United States.

Before they took up their new post, they were scheduled for a visit home. But of course, they had several more weeks of boot camp to go.

In the in-between time, Christmas had come and gone. Sophie Grace's first Christmas, and her uncles couldn't see her smiles and excitement.

Grandma Abigaile Amelie had her silversmith very busy. This year, and it was the first, she had designed two ornaments for her family's trees.

A silver design that said family. But it was not the family we knew and loved, it was the family that represented in this war. It was a round medallion. One that was simple but gorgeous. A circle that was never ending, one that was a display of how we felt as a unit. One country united. It had the engraved letters WWII on it.

Grandma Abigaile always said we need to support our troops, those at home and those overseas. This was her way of showing her family how important our country was.

So those at the Hurley household and the Butler home all received this memento of Grandma Abigaile's love.

For her second design, she decided on a simple Christmas tree. One that had round balls placed on every limb. One ball for every person in their family, past and present, and the year 1943. These were a beautiful representation of life, love, and memories of family.

God had given Grandma Abigaile Amelie so much, yet she had so much she had lost also. The season had given Grandma Abigaile another rea son to proceed in her life. Silver ornaments, the annual Christmas party, and one new little darling, Sophie Grace. But the season was still a little less than the years before.

Her namesake was living somewhere else, and her new darling was not as close as she would have liked.

The year had been very busy with the food pantry, yet it was still lacking.

But Grandma was not sure why. She was going to have to get on her party line hoping that God could shed some light on her feeling of emptiness.

And in a flash, the light came on. She was missing all the holiday hustle and her namesake. Now all she had to do was plan more projects and get back to her weekly visits with her darling Sophie and her momma.

The snow once more blanketed the grounds at River Bend, and all planting and harvests were at a standstill. But in these parts, people had a saying, "Just wait around a little bit, and it will change." It did. The sun had peeked out of the clouds, and the snow slowly disappeared. It was like sugar melting in water. It was a sweet sight. Things began to get back to a winter norm, and the snow melted away.

River Bend was still donating cotton to the mills at Thomaston, Georgia, for the needs of the servicemen and women who were serving our country, particularly during this time of war, but as for Grandma Abigaile Amelie, she had decided that River Bend would continue to donate even after the war.

Grandma Abigaile had discussed her wishes with Bertie Mae and Edward Darnell. They were completely in agreement. So, a document was drawn up and filed with the legal wants of one little gray-haired lady named Abigaile Amelie Hurley.

When the boys, Carter and Edward, came back from school, they would be made aware of this commitment to the military.

As for Grandma and Bertie Mae and Edward Darnell, they were praying that the war would be over, and their young men would stay here at River Bend.

As for Grandma and Bertie Mae and Edward Darnell, they were praying that the war would be over, and their young men would stay here at River Bend.

News of war was still reported, and the summer was drawing near.

Grandma was busy with her food-distribution centers, and more contributions were coming in than her two centers could handle. Bertie Mae and Abigaile Grace were on the hunt for another outlet for the needs of many to be met.

Weekly visits were set in stone. Grandma Abigaile would hop in her Cadillac and drive over to Willow Oaks. Her namesake and darling Sophie Grace were always excited to see her, and a beautiful lunch was served.

Before nap time for Sophie Grace, Grandma Abigaile Amelie would hold her little darling and ask her if she wanted to hear another story. Of course, Sophie was too young to answer back, but the smiles and hugs again said yes, and Grandma Abigaile Amelie began.

*****

My darling, this last Christmas was very special. The tree in your room had two new ornaments. Your Grandma Abigaile has made special silver ornaments for each family member, and you are our newest member. Your momma will tell you all about our family as you grow up. She will tell you how she got her name. She will bring you to River Bend and walk with you in our gardens. She will tell you stories of her princess emeralds and how they were handed down to all the girls in our family. They traveled from across the ocean to our new land, Georgia.

This was a land where I met my Mr. Hurley, your grandfather. He had flaming red hair and beautiful eyes. I looked at him when I was just a young girl and fell in love with him.

Your momma fell in love with your daddy in somewhat the same fashion.

And the magnolias were in full bloom. It was spring, maybe not in season as we know them, but it was spring in our hearts, now that love was in our hearts. That is how our families began, and one day in your life, you will have spring flowers blooming in your heart. No matter where you are or how old you are. It is like me, my darling. I am

102 years old and lots of springtimes have blossomed in my heart.

Sweet dreams, my darling. Hugs and kisses from Grandma Abigaile. I will see you soon.

*****

Before Grandma Abigaile left Willow Oaks, an update was shared: the food pantry. Another potential, but not certain, location was up for consideration. It would help those in need in another town that was close by, but the drive was thirty miles away. Both were praying that someone from that town might recruit some townspeople to pick up the food and separate it into single portions for those in need. Another one of the party-line discussions Grandma Abigaile and God would talk about.

Before their next lunch date, there would have to be answers, so God and Grandma had to talk fast.

When Grandma arrived back at River Bend, one of the first things she saw in the window was the blue star. It reminded her, once again, to pray. The war was still going on. Everyone was so tired of the horrible reports. All were hoping for the war to be done and the boys over there would be coming home.

It was birthday month for that three birthday buddies, and everyone was turning a year older.

Grandma Abigaile was turning 103, Sophie was turning a year old, and Abigaile Grace was twenty-four. Milestones for all these Southern ladies.

Because of the special time in June, a party for all three was planned.

Bertie Mae was in charge of the big birthday bash. Now the first and only decision was the gifts. How to shop for one who has lived a hundred-plus years? As for the other two, it was very easy.

Decorations and invitations were ready. Three birthday cakes and birthday favor galore. Bertie Mae had a hundred invitations sent out. There were over eighty that said yes to the RSVP. It was a midmorning party with lunch, just so it would not interrupt little Sophie Graces nap time. Carter and Edward were home from college, so they helped their momma with all the party needs.

So many people arrived to help these three beauties celebrate. Most of the focus was on Grandma Abigaile. She was dressed in her best Sunday go-to-meeting attire.

The pink party plates offered each guest pink petit fours, red strawberries, small bite-size finger sandwiches, a veggie tray, olives black and green, and a pink lemonade punch with strawberry ice cubes floating in four giant punch bowls.

There were people everywhere. Young and old, men and ladies, boys and girls. After all, when you have lived for a great number of years you acquire a loyal bunch of friends.

All the guests were enjoying this amazing party. For the small ones, there were also pony rides. Four small little horses where the young guests could play cowboys and Indians. Carter and Edward were in charge of pony rides, and for the guests that were Abigaile s age, there was chess and checker games for the men and cigars out on the veranda. For the ladies, something very different. Bertie Mae had secured the help of one of the prominent decora tors in Georgia. Something for the discerning homemaker, because Abigaile knew that a pretty place to hang your hat made the whole family happy.

And for Abigaile Amelie's friends of age, there was a gathering in the grand hall. A place for each to recall a part of their history of love and loss.

In all, the party was fabulous. Sophie Grace was taken up to the nursery designed just for her. A long nap for Grandmas Abigaile's little darling. During that time, the friends of age were still gathering and sharing memories. Gentlemen were enjoying cards and checkers, and the ladies were learning new ways to make their homes more welcoming.

It was a party that carried into early evening. Bertie Mae was so impressed that she offered her guests dinner. Grandma Abigaile always said He would provide.

It seemed to be a miracle. Like the loaves and fishes in the Bible. There was more than enough for everyone. Bertie and Edward barbecued chicken, and a huge salad was served. Bertie Mae had never seen this type of a miracle. It was truly amazing; there seemed to be more left over than when they started.

Whenever Grandma Abigaile was involved with food stuff, there was a multiplication of the blessing. It was a story that everyone noticed.

So, with the leftovers from the birthday party, more at the local food pantry were blessed.

You could always see God at work.

Mama Bertie Mae and Daddy Edward Darnell were sole caretakers at River Bend, until their sons were home from school for good. The boys only had one more semester to go and one half of a semester of internship, then home late April 1945. The summers were very busy at both River Bend and Willow Oaks. Crops were ready for the summer harvests, tobacco leaves were hanging in the barns, the cotton was ready for the mills, and the indigo plants were blooming.

It was like bees buzzing around a hive; workers everywhere, and honey being developed everywhere.

Both Harrison and Edward Darnell were busier than a one-arm paperhanger.

With plantations and home duties, both families at Willow Oaks and River Bend stayed very busy.

Grandma Abigaile, Bertie Mae, and Abigaile had their hands full. More people offered extra produce and a lamb or pig to help supply protein for the needy. The local butcher would prepare the meat in small one-to-two-pound pack ages; the meat was always offered in ground- meat style.

Each time, meat came in a pasta product, and rice helped those who received a possible meal suggestion.

The food pantry was a once-a-week offering. There were three locations now, and the neighboring town had volunteers who drove thirty miles back and forth to bring the needy the much-needed assistance.

The summer brought forth such an abundance of all kinds that they, Bertie Mae and Grandma Abigaile, were going to consider some type of refrigeration. At least at River Bend, and the store that was being used for distribution.

But this was a huge cost, so this endeavor would need a plan to pay for this need.

During the time that the food pantry had been helping, there was an article in the paper that noted that the needs of many were being met. And the driving force behind the blessing was a little hundred-year-plus lady. The story told of how she had been through the Civil War and World War I and now World War II. She had seen it all. She had been hungry, but she never went without nourishment of some sort, and if you asked this little old lady, she would tell you that God was always watching over her and her family, and she was all ready to share what she had with those who had nothing.

The wire photo service picked up the food pantry story and the human-interest story of a century-old woman and all her memories of war.

The wire photo service picked up the food pantry story and the human-interest story of a century- old woman and all her memories of war.

But the story of her life was one page and done. No one could have guessed the impact that the food pantry story would have on the rest of the U.S. Small towns and larger cities took up the cause. All over the nation, people were flocking to the new food pantries that offered to many the food that they needed to feed their families.

With war still in force, the people who were left at home, theirs was a different kind of war. A war where there was not enough of some necessities. Meat, dairy, coffee, dried fruits, jams, jellies, lard, shortening and oils, sugar, butter, canned goods, and shoes. You would need a special coupon to buy shoes, gasoline, and tires; all these things were in short supply.

So, the story about the food pantry hit a ton of Americans right at home. For the owners of farms and dairies, they were deciding to assist their neighbors. Even though they had offered some in the past, somehow or the other, they felt a heartfelt sympathy that they had not had before. It was a desire that was spurred on by the article, but Grandma Abigaile knew who had begun the whole blessing.

She had asked for help from God but did not know how He would do it.

Odd as it might seem, there was a small box in each place where the food pantry was set up and it offered a place for a penny or two to be donated to help the effort. Anyone could donate. As for the need Grandma and Bertie Mae had, there was a gift that was sent over by the newspaper. It was a refrigerator. It was a thank-you gift that was given to the newspaper by Sears.

It was called a Coldspot, Just for Grandma.

And once again the party line between Grandma Abigaile and God had produced an answer to prayer.

God gave the food pantry a big brand-new Coldspot Sears refrigerator.

Now how could anyone explain this blessing? No one tried. A big thank-you and a formal note sent to the newspaper and Sears by Grandma and Bertie Mae.

But Grandma had decided that every food pantry should have a refrigerator also. So back to her party line with God she went.

She never heard of anyone else getting a refrigerator from Sears, but she was completely confident God would answer her prayers somehow. If not Sears, someone else would provide.

CHAPTER 13

Bumps in the Road

FOR GRANDMA ABIGAILE AMELIE, her cup had run over with blessings.

She had opened a food pantry, received a refrigerator, and had a birthday party with her dear one and her little darling. She had lived for many, many years and saw three wars begin and each ending. And many hopes and prayers to see war number three ending soon. She has had a love and children. Births and deaths, grandchildren and great-great-grandchildren. And the amazing plantation that had grown to provide for all her family. And she began a food source to feed those in need.

For Grandma Abigaile Amelie, it was not the money and things that it bought for herself but the blessings it would provide for those in need.

The article in the newspaper really didn't cover her hearts cry, but it did shine a light on a current call to the public to get involved. And that it did. But this was not the only thing on Grandmas heart.

Food was one way to help hurting people, but the kids were hurting. Many of the children had worn out their toys. There was a whole group of children whose dads or moms were off fighting the war, and Christmas was coming up.

Grandma had the food pantry up and running, and it did not have a problem. In fact, it was like this. The food that came in seemed always to multiply to fit all the cries of the needy. The refrigerator kept the excess fresh until the next distribution. And sometimes, the extra food helped out the lonely traveler.

Grandma and her crew were ever so committed to the food pantry.

While the needs of the hungry were met, the hearts of the helpers were filled with joy and a knowing they were Gods hand extended. This checked all Grandma Abigaile's boxes.

Thanksgiving was just two days away. Carter and Edward were home for the holiday, and just in time.

Grandma had a holiday surprise for the food pantry.

There was an extra amount of sugar, two hundred chickens for the River Bend food pantry, another 240 loaves of bread for bread pudding and dressing, fresh oranges, and some extra potatoes.

The news spread fast, and more than a hundred people arrived at River Bend.

But it spread panic in all the helpers. Grandma said, "Let's pray."

As the food was being distributed, some said, "I don't need," and that was how God made it Thanksgiving for everyone. Almost everyone had put one to five pennies in the little box that sat where they picked up their care packages.

Grandma Abigaile and her party line with God struck again with answers to her prayers.

As Grandma Abigaile finished her Thanksgiving at River Bend, she began to think about her silversmith. She had not gotten her design completed for her ornaments. The food pantry had her attentions divided, but she knew time was of the essence, so she would have to get started.

Bertie Mae and the boys offered to take over the food pantry so Grandma Abigaile could concentrate on the annual Christmas party and the silver ornaments for her family. Not just the silver ornaments but the favors for her Christmas party guests.

Christmas decor was planned many months before.

The theme was that of the United States, red, white, and blue. A party and its colors to encourage all guests. The only thing Grandma Abigaile had to buy was the white hand-blown glass balls that would join the already secured red and blue glass balls and teardrop ornaments that had been used in years past.

For the guests Grandma chose a beautiful blue star that matched the star that hung in so many windows throughout the homes of Thomaston, Georgia, and the whole country

Along with the decision about the favors for the Christmas party guests, Grandma Abigaile had made a quality decision about the silver ornaments for her family. It was part of her patriotic duty. She had decided to make a silver reminder of the free country we all live in, a flag that resembled all the breezes that waved through this amazing land. Stars, forty-eight in all, one for each of the states in this great land; and stripes, thirteen in all, that represented each of the original colonies. A beautiful sight, home of the free, and land of the brave.

She had the United States of Americas symbol replicated as a memory of freedom and family. She said that we are a family, those of us who get the privilege to live here.

It was a really tight squeeze. Grandma Abigaile Amelie's favors were done just a week before the annual Christmas party.

That would leave her only a few days to pick up and wrap all as she had always done, but she was truly up for the task. Of course, she had Carter and Edward to help. They had never wrapped anything before, but Grandma had hope they could catch on quickly.

When they were all done, the count was almost fifteen.

While the favors were set in place, the entry showed signs of a beautiful party about to happen.

Grandma had also picked up her silver ornaments from the silversmith. She was so excited.

The wrapping for her memory ornaments were going to be hers and only hers to wrap.

While they were in her room, ready for wrapping, she sat a moment and quietly smiled. This was a special Christmas. She had lived and loved and been renewed. Truly her life had been a history book in the making; the newspaper had documented well. She had seen so much change in her life. But the one thing that never changed was her love for the one who created her. Amazed at the number of days she had lived; she began to question what was left for her to do. She had raised a family, farmed, and grew a plantation to supply for her family and their needs.

She had received much and given a lot. But somehow it didn't seem complete. "God," she cried out, "what do You have left for me? Please show me. Speak to me!"

The party line was open, but Grandma couldn't hear anything. She just kept praying, "Please, Lord!" For now, Grandma would have to put her prayer on hold. She still had some details for the party to work out.

She missed her namesake. They would always work together with Bertie Mae. It was like getting a normal job, done with only half the help you once had. However, there really wasn't a choice. That was why she recruited her boys, Carter and Edward, to assist.

Grandma knew she could count on them, but it might take a little longer, and she might have to assist where she never did before.

Grandma was thinking maybe this was one of those extra jobs God had in mind for her to do.

She was going to use this opportunity to help Carter and Edward learn what it takes to do inside chores. Like most men, the outdoors was their domain. But it was always a plus to find a boy or girl who could do some of both. And this was something that the modern man and woman could always use if they never married.

But for now, the party and its details were all rolled out, and two young men who knew nothing about indoors work could say they helped. Yet in truth, they were simply being prepared for all the life that was facing them.

With only a few months left before graduation, they felt very unsure of their future.

They knew they would be inheriting River Bend, but no one knew if the military would be calling their number like the Butler brothers.

It was a sobering reality. But only time would tell.

This was something that Grandma Abigaile prayed about all the time. She would cry out for her family and for the others who were involved in this horrible time in the world.

Grandma always believed in the goodness of mankind but couldn't get past the man named Hitler, who had the devil alive in him. She always said you can disagree with another and their beliefs, but to kill is wrong. And it was a cruel thing and an inhumane thing that was happening.

Grandma was upstairs hoping and praying when her guests began to arrive. The doorbell rang over and over again. She descended the stairs and met her guests with open arms.

This party helped to encourage family and friends alike to show hospitality, and hope was felt by all. The blue stars were given to all, and the red, white, and blue theme gave everyone a sense of power. The kind of power achieved when people join together in unity of spirit.

This is what America is. A people who joined together to help others in need. For those who had lost loved ones already in the war, they said it was worth the sacrifice. And for others, it gave a hope that this war would be over soon. Even though the pain and the loss of sons, husbands, wives, and daughters was a very raw subject, one still felt the since of pride. That was the one common bond they all had. Unity and America.

Grandma was in touch with so many. Those who lost their brave soldiers and friends, she too had experienced the same trauma in two other wars. Grandma had survived two wars and now almost three. The time and memories of those times left her with a heartache that came alive with tears of hurt, every once in a while, for the hundreds of families.

Even though it was Christmas, the air of patriotism was all about. The night ended with several songs, and one that said "America the beautiful." It was a special night to remember, and the decor was all every American could hope to see.

It made Grandma Abigaile know in her heart that the family ornament she had chosen was perfect, and the next night she would place her treasured family memory under each family members pillow.

This would be another sparkling gift that would grace each person's personal Christmas tree. For some, like Grandma, the tree was loaded down with family memories. For others it showed a history of their shorter lives.

Truly a treasure of history for each family member, even the newest family member, Sophie Grace.

The only thing that crossed Grandma Abigaile s mind, once again, was whether her job here on earth was done, but she began to consider the party for next year and what her choice might be for her treasured family silver ornament.

If one looked at the signs, one could make an educated guess. Grandma had more to do here on earth. She just got sidetracked now and then.

Christmas celebration and church Sunday morning. Grandma Abigaile got her Cadillac out of the garage; she was driving everyone to Sunday Service.

Edward and Carter had talked earlier and wondered if, like before, they would hear from the pastor a story about the war and the part of Christmas in it. But what Grandma was hoping for was a special word or that special feeling about a new project.

The boys were right. They got the same message in church about the war and their part in it as Grandma preached at the party. They simply exchanged glances with each other and knew there must be more for them to do. They would have to explore possibilities.

But as for Grandma, she got a thought for something new. It was like a seed in the ground to her. She would have to take some time to water and fertilize the idea. Then she would have to see how to develop this new idea.

With Sunday dinner ready after church, the smell as they entered the great house was like warm fuzzy gloves on a cold winter's day, so inviting and comforting.

Everyone discussed Sunday service, and all knew their part in this war and how to get more involved.

The family was all together again; even Miss Abigaile and her new family were there.

This was a time to celebrate together the time of the birth of Jesus but also to open the presents each one had been blessed with.

Grandmas red and blue China and stemware dressed the table as if it were the Fourth of July. When Grandma said the blessing, she added an extra thank-you for the freedom, Jesus gave us when He came to earth as a baby.

Everyone ate until they almost popped. The table was cleared, and Grandma Abigaile took her seat on the story telling chaise longue. But no story today, just visiting.

Grandma wanted to visit with her namesake, Abigaile Grace, and her little darling. Carter and Edward were out fishing in the river that flowed down their property line.

Harrison and Edward Darnell retired to the men's parlor, and business was their topic of conversation.

Abigaile Amelie took the time with the ladies and her little darling and talked about a possible trip down South. Texas way down South. She had heard about a place that was built in 1929 and had an indoor pool and spa. The place was called Mineral Wells, Texas. It was 870 miles away. But Grandma knew her Cadillac could make the drive smooth as silk. It might take two to three days to get there, but it could be a girls' vacation. Perhaps Valentines might be a good time to go.

Bertie Mae had questions. What, where, when, and how. What is the name of this place? Do they have snow there?

Is it a hotel? Do they have bathrooms for each room? What about food? Who would take care of the food pantry?

Grandma Abigaile had all the answers. "It is called the Baker Hotel. Built in 1929. Fourteen stories tall. Loads of rooms with private bathrooms. It does not snow there except when you don't expect it. Hardly ever. There is a five-star restaurant. And we might get our guys to oversee the food pantry for the two weeks we might be gone. And perhaps the biggest call to this hotel is the healing mineral springs that their pool and spa have running into them. Oh, yes, and by the way, movie stars! They all come to the Baker for rest and relaxation and the healing waters."

Bertie Mae stood up and gave a resounding "I'm in, let's do it." Then Abigaile Grace joined in. "Yes, let's do it." It was an all-in. Now, just the right time. The trip was on.

Meanwhile, back in the men's parlor, business was still being discussed. The how-tos and how-not-tos were all being decided. Little did they know, they were about to be hit with news and a directive they could not refuse.

A girls' trip had been decided, and the when was up in the air. But it was a sure thing.

Grandma said it was now or never.

Perhaps they had to wait a day or two, but before the new year, the girls had a dinner meeting planned with all the guys, and their announcement would be known.

Christmas Day ended, and the Butlers left for Willow Oaks. Abigaile was so excited she could not hold in her news. But she had promised to wait until the dinner meeting. Bertie Mae went to bed singing, and Edward Darnell knew the girls had hatched a plan. He just didn't know what or maybe who might be involved. Yet after so many years of marriage, he knew sooner or later the secret would be revealed. That left Grandma Abigaile. No one guessed she had hatched this trip idea, but if she was asked, she would take full credit for the whole idea. In fact, this would be the first girls' trip ever for her.

She had always traveled with all the family members. Never just with the girls. She was wondering if it might be different or not. But no matter, she was up for the challenge. She had traveled across the world, and that took weeks. By all standards, this should be a piece of cake. She was feeling good, and her Caddy was ready for the trip. The oil had been changed, and the tires were still good. Grandma had studied a road map and had a route all mapped out for the journey. This must have taken some time for all the details to be organized, and her plans placed on paper where and when the dinner meeting would take place.

So, by all standards, she did not just suggest the idea. Grandma had hatched this plan days, if not weeks, before the family Christmas dinner.

Grandma Abigaile Amelie knew she had one more trip left in her. She could not have picked better travel mates than Bertie Mae, her dear Abigaile Grace, and her little darling.

So, bedtime for Grandma Abigaile was sweet. She knew this was one more thing that God was wanting her to do. Plus, she had another idea that came to her Sunday at church. The new idea was just a seed, but Grandma was sure that the party line between her and God was talking volumes to her.

Around the town of Thomaston, Georgia, you could see all the children playing with Christmas toys. Grandma was noticing that there were some new, but most were repainted. New clothes for dolls were made out of flower stalks. Some food was in short supply, and toys for children were in short supply as well.

Even though the food pantry had helped to feed some families, the children seemed to be left out in some way. The brave men and women had given of themselves to protect their country, but the country didn't do enough for their families, and the children needed to be kids. Grandma knew this had to be her next project.

She had such love for little people. It was truth in action. A need to help her little ones feel like kids and not be hurt by the state of this country and the loss of one of their parents.

But first things first, the girls' trip. Grandma and Bertie Mae needed to get four copies of their plan for their girls' trip to Texas. The next thing that would have to be decided was the date. The girls had talked about Valentine's, but Georgia's weather had been erratic since Thanksgiving.

Perhaps sometime in mid-March might be a little bit bet ter. All the girls agreed, and the dinner would alert all the boys to the plans. Now they were in concrete, and the boys were going to take over all the food pantry and the harvests at both plantations. Grandma and Bertie knew it would be good, and she had complete confidence in her gentlemen and Mr. Harrison. This would also be spring break, so Carter and Edward would be home to be a help.

The dinner went off without any problems. The reservations were next, and the girls would be off. It just so happened that the date Grandma Abigaile chose was the same time that Hollywood's Clark Gable, Judy Garland, and, Grandma's favorite, Dorothy Lamour were scheduled to be there. This made it super exciting.

The stars were there for the healing waters, and Grandma Abigaile Amelie was bringing her stars with her. Her stars were Bertie Mae, Abigaile Grace, and Sophie Grace. In Grandma's eyes no one could outshine her stars, not even her favorite movie star, Dorothy Lamour.

So, the spring break girls' trip was booked, and the smaller suitcases were taken out of both attics. They knew Grandma's Caddy was large, but they would have to con serve on suitcases. Because only so much could fit in the trunk, they were hoping for a laundry service when they got to the hotel. This was an adventure like none they had ever known. No trains, no plane, no boat, just the open road in a not-so-new Cadillac, almost nine hundred miles away, and no men. These ladies were ready to hit the road, but there were a few details that had to be ironed out still.

Gas stations, food stops, and a place to stop and sleep for two nights at last. Grandma Abigaile, as she liked to call herself, had been looking forward to time with her female family members.

But until that time, would a Georgia snow or two be forcing all travel to cease? After all, January was the coldest and most unpredictable time of year. Unseasonable rains, ice, and snow were never present at the most unexpected time, but showed up at the time when almost everyone had something important to do.

The great thing about time was that the snow and ice would melt after a few days and things could return to normal.

The Butlers and Hurleys were counting down the days, and January was gone.

Abigaile Grace was so excited about the girls' trip she forgot to plan something special for Harrison. But he had not forgotten his dearly beloved. Since the first Valentines when they met, he had a very special something planned for her.

After Christmas, he had talked with Grandmas Abigaile's silversmith. He had a beautiful silver flip-top jewelry box large enough to hold her princess emeralds and her great-grandmother's Australian opals. And there was one slot in the silver box that would hold a new ring he had made for her. A beautiful platinum band that held a heart-shaped diamond that measured a half inch across. According to the jeweler, it was twelve to thirteen milli meters and eight and one half in carat weight. It was an engagement ring to match her single wedding band. As for Abigaile Grace, she made his favorite chocolate-chip cookies. Like one of her first Valentine's gift's, she had gotten for him.

Edward Darnell was inspired by his son-in-law. He too went to Harrison's jeweler. It had been a couple of years since their twenty-fifth wedding anniversary. His gift to Bertie Mae was a trip. Just the two of them. But things got in the way; she knew about the trip and was willing to wait.

But Edward Darnell was not. So, he decided to act.

The jeweler showed him several wedding sets. Bertie Mae was partial to yellow gold. There were five that fit his starting budget, but they just didn't seem right. As he was glancing in the jeweler's case, he saw one yellow-gold set. It was a cut emerald stone with two smaller round stones, one on each side. Edward Darnell's face lit up. "That is, it. That is Bertie Mae all over." Then he looked at the price tag. He almost fainted. It was triple his budget. Triple it was, but Bertie Mae had given him so much, how could money dictate what he wanted to give his love? Bertie Mae was worth every penny and more.

So, both Bertie Mae and Abigaile Grace were to be blessed, and they had no idea. Abigaile Grace was getting an eight-and-a-half-carat heart-shaped diamond, and Bertie Mae was getting a fifteen-carat emerald cut diamond set in yellow gold.

And the day for love had arrived.

Candlelight dinners at River Bend and Willow Oaks were planned. Bertie Mae planned Edward Darnell's favorite meal: post roast, roasted potatoes, and pickled beets. Abigaile Grace had Harrison favorite's also, roasted pork loin with cherry-glazed carrots and homemade bread. The dessert was apple pie for Edward Darnell and chocolate pudding with whipped cream, and Harrison's chocolate chip cookies.

A dream came true for these two men.

Because it was true. The way to a man's heart is through his stomach, and they were both enjoying their fill.

Bedtime, and the lights were just about ready to be turned off. Harrison was remembering he hid his Valentines gift under Abigaile Graces pillow. There was no way she would not notice. And so, it was exactly that way. She lay her head down and hit a hard object. The lights went on.

She quickly uncovered the prize; all wrapped in red paper and red rib bons. Unwrapped, the silver box revealed its beauty. She was delighted. She set it aside and prepared for bed once again.

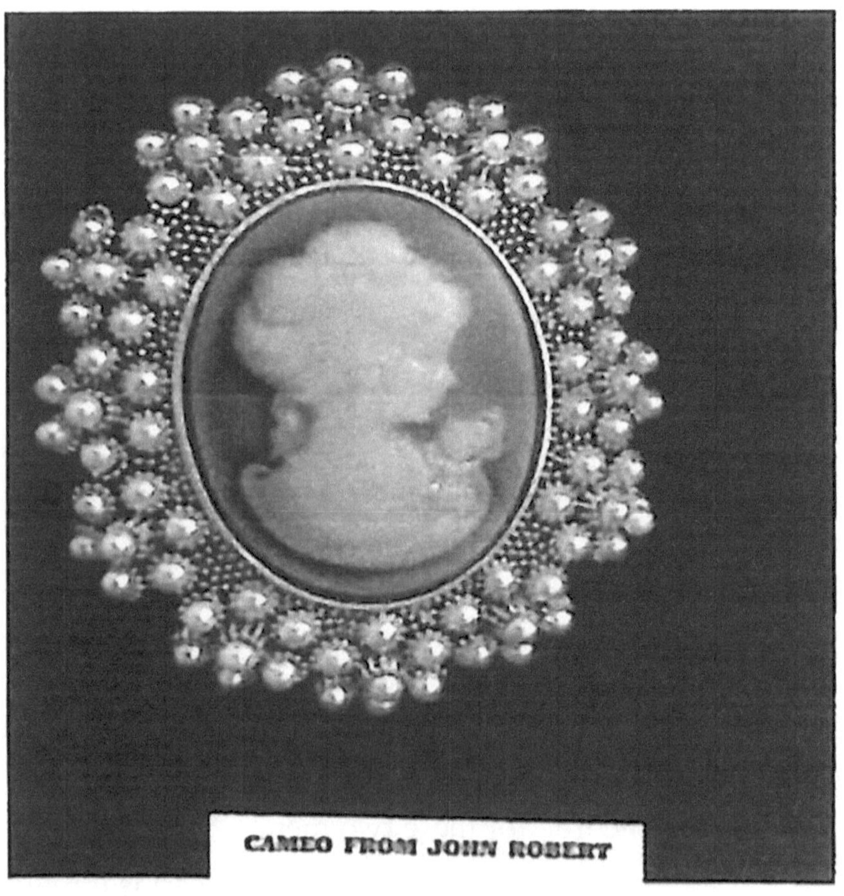

Harrison almost laughed. Abigaile asked what was so funny. "Well," he said. "Open it." She agreed, and her jaw dropped. Even though the light was dim, the diamond glistened in multiple rainbows of color. She cried. She quickly got up and got her wedding band and asked Harrison to place the new ring upon her finger. It fit like a glove, like Willow Oaks did now. She slept with her new ring on. Every several hours, she woke up and stared at her Valentine gift. A heart from her love. This was a memory of great love she would always carry.

At River Bend, the dinner was a candlelight delight. It was just like when they were first married. Dessert was served, and Edward Darnell reached inside his jacket pocket. He drew out the box that held the Valentines gift for Bertie Mae. Edward Darnell was dreaming.

As gently as Edward Darnell had been when he asked Bertie Mae to marry him, he held her hand in his and told her once again of his love for her. He removed her wedding ring and lay the old set on the table. He gently opened the ring box and removed the new wedding set. He asked her to close her eyes and placed the new yellow gold beauty on her finger. "Open," he said. She was completely speechless.

She ran to turn on the overhead lights. When the bright color of the stars shone through the prisms of light and danced across the walls, she knew it must have been a lot of money, but she didn't care. Edward Darnell was right. It was Bertie Mae. Once before, Edward D. had told Bertie Mae that she spelled *small* "big." And *big* was spelled "bigger," and *bigger* was spelled "huge." It fit her.

The dishes stayed in place, and they both danced to a Bing Crosby record and swayed to the beat of the music. He was still dreaming.

Bertie Mae couldn't stop looking at her new ring. She couldn't wait to show Grandma Abigaile and Abigaile Grace, but it was late. It would have to wait until morning.

Besides, Grandma Abigaile had a Valentine's date herself. She had met a younger gentleman of age ninety at one of her food pantry meetings. Edward Darnell was reliving every moment.

When she looked at him, she felt her heart do a hand clap. He had red hair with a mix of almost solid gray. You could see the red hair in his sideburns and beard. He was almost six feet tall with big broad shoulders and a little bit of a tummy. Compared to Mr. Hurley, well, there was none. His great big heart and his love for his family, and his red hair. Well, you could imagine it all over as it once was.

Grandma Abigaile Amelie was a little less than five foot tall, and they looked a little like Mutt and Jeff. One very short and one very tall. But they had found a place in each other's heart that made music. Marriage was certainly not a thought, but each found a joy in being with each other.

Their Valentine's date was a dinner at his favorite Italian restaurant and a movie called The Road to Utopia. It seemed a comedy was just what both needed because of the heaviness of the war, but both had been praying for the war to end soon, very soon, so all the boys could come home. Grandma's friend was a blessing that she never expected.

She called him Jack even though his name was John Robert. He told her it was a nickname given to him by his momma.

He had picked her up in his Oldsmobile 98. At the end of their date, John Robert presented her with a beautiful cameo surrounded by seed pearls. All the Hurley ladies got Valentine gifts, and Mrs. Buder got a gift as well.

This was February 14 and just one month away from the famed girls' trip.

The next morning, the party line that connected Willow Oaks and River Bend was in use. Exchanges of their Valentine's gifts and the full description of their treasure was the topic of the whole conversation. Bertie Mae was still staring at her new wedding set. She considered this set a gift, and her twenty-fifth wedding anniversary trip was still going to have to take place.

Grandma Abigaile Amelie was acting like a schoolgirl. She was smiling, giggling, and dancing around like she was ninety again. She didn't move quite as gracefully as when she was younger, but she could still glide across the hard wood floors and hold her arms out as if she had a partner.

Now Abigaile Grace was a touch more distracted. Little Sophie Grace was just over one and a half years old. She was demanding every waking moment of her momma's attention. When Abigaile Grace was on the phone, little Sophie was trying to talk as well. So, the description of her treasure needed more than just a onetime description. Every time momma began to talk, so did little Sophie Grace. After several attempts, Abigaile said, "Let me call you back."

It was easy enough to distract her little one with a set of different toys that did not make any noise; well, it was a noble effort. Sophie Grace had decided to make her own noise. She began a melody of her own making. It was almost like singing. But the highs and lows had such a dramatic difference, it hurt Abigaile's ears. But Sophie, well, she had such a happy going on within herself you could not help but be amused.

Abigaile Grace took the moment of silence to make her return call. Two shorts and a long ring, and River Bend answered. Grandma Abigaile answered, "Oh yes, Miss Abigaile."

"Yes, Grandma, I also got a treasure. My Mr. Butler gave me a beautiful heart-shaped diamond ring for Valentines. It is so pretty." Abigaile Grace was also wanting to know if John Robert had given her grandma a prize.

"Well, yes, he did, a gorgeous brooch. A cameo with seed pearls surrounding it with filigree. It is in gold and can also be a pendant. He had seen it in a catalog, and he said it had my name on it. So, he bought it just for me."

"Grandma, did he kiss you?"

"Child! That is private, but yes, he did, and I kissed him back."

Grandma Abigaile was not at all embarrassed. In fact, it felt good to be wanted.

As the time passed, the girls' trip came closer and closer. Bertie Mae was going to take on the position as driver, and Abigaile Grace and Sophie Grace were going to be the naviga tors. Grandma was in charge of food and lodging. It was a perfect match. Grandma had miscalculated the days it was going to take to get to Mineral Wells, Texas. She had to take the speed limit max of thirty-five miles per hour, the Victory Speed Limit instated to reduce gasoline and rubber consumption.

How many miles, then how many hours? Instead of two days, it was going to take eight hours a day, 280 miles each day. Maybe an extra day of travel in the car, so it was three and a half days to four in the car instead of two.

It was almost doubling their travel time, but there was no train that would get close to this small town any quicker. So, the trio decided on the Cadillac, Magnolia Express. For that was what Grandma Abigaile called her car.

Grandma Abigaile was footing the cost, so no one could fuss about it. It just might be a touch hard on Sophie Grace, and Momma.

John Robert offered to drive the trio. Maybe he could take a little bit of the time off their travel time by switching off with Bertie Mae. But while the offer was gallant, the trio said no. They were going to take this time to be together, just the girls.

During the time of preparation for the girls' trip, Harrison and Edward Darnell had tried to formulate a plan. One that could cover the plantation harvests and the food pantry. John Robert was offering his assistance at the food pantry. He would do something different. He was going to talk with all the volunteers and try to make a day that each could commit to with one backup.

Grandma had never tried this, but men have a super kind of organization ability, and Mr. John Robert Huebner had those skills. He had a graph with place, people, and times. According to John Robert, it worked in the textile mills he worked in. The mills never stopped running, and production was up by 20 percent each year.

Well, that solidified the plan. Now, step two. The harvest. Harrisons brothers, Aaron and Jeffery, would be home for spring break.

John Robert had them on food pantry duty and pick-up and delivery service for all donations. And during the off times, they would be helping with some of the harvest. It seemed like everything was in readiness for the girls' departure.

After breakfast the next morning, the bags were packed and placed into the Cadillac Magnolia Express. A soft pallet was made to fit the back seat. This is where Sophie Grace would play and nap for the next several days. Grandma and Abigaile would trade places and keep Sophie Grace occupied.

The first night, they stopped and could hardly wait to exit the Magnolia Express. Food and sleep. They all needed both.

Second day, and all felt renewed. With Georgia in the rearview mirror and Mineral Wells calling, they were on point. Back in the car, the memory of yesterday's trip was felt. Their backsides were already numb, but it didn't seem to matter. They were headed to Texas, and nothing was going to deter them.

In the meantime, back at River Bend and Willow Oaks, the first food pantry open house was underway. Aaron and Jeffery were still in the service Stateside.

Carter and Edward had their first taste of what it was like to be totally responsible for everything and everybody.

The food pantry had an 8:00 a.m. beginning and a 4:00 p.m. close time.

Harrison and Edward Darnell were busy with the beginning of harvest. The tobacco leaves were being cut and moved to the barns at River Bend. The cotton was being stripped at Willow Oaks.

Both Mr. Hurley and Mr. Butler had their hands full. Yet when the business day had ended, they forgot they had to fix their own dinner. This was a first for all the boys.

What would they eat? The ladies had always fixed their meals.

As for the girls, they were enjoying eating out for every meal. It was truly a vacation for them all. No cooking or cleaning.

Two more days in the Magnolia Express. Just two more days to go, and then Texas would be in view.

Everyone was getting excited to almost be there.

Grandma was expecting to see her favorite movie star, Miss Dorothy Lamour. As for Abigaile Grace, she was hoping to see Clark Gable.

Breakfast at the hotel, and only fifty more miles to go.

The soil was different there. A different color. The trees were large but not as huge as the ones in precious Georgia.

Only one more hour in the Magnolia Express. Sophie Grace was content, and all was well.

All her favorite toys and snacks.

Bertie Mae, well, that was a different story. The miles and the time couldn't pass quickly enough. She had driven 870 miles and was so ready to be out of the Magnolia Express.

11/15/22, 5:12 PM
Google Image Result
1942 Cadillac
Magnolia Express
Hyman LTD

1942 CADILLAC
MAGNOLIA EXPRESS

CHAPTER 14
The Baker Hotel

THE DATE WAS MARCH 15, 1945. The sun was shining, and there was the sign. Mineral Wells, Texas. They had arrived. They followed the signs to the famous Baker Hotel. It was a tall brick building, huge in size, with windows everywhere. They drove up, and a valet helped them unloaded the car. He also pulled the Magnolia Express into a special parking place. And then it happened. Dorothy Lamour walked by. What a surprise. The front desk had a bellboy who lived to help these Georgia beauties to their rooms. Grandma had one, Bertie Mae another, and Abigaile Grace another with a crib in it for Sophie Grace.

With all their bags unpacked, the trio headed down stairs. Sophie Grace was singing. Her voice was carrying throughout the elevator and the hotel lobby. Heads turned. Most might have thought it to be a disturbance. Yet it seemed to bring smiles to everyone's face.

With all their bags unpacked, the trio headed down stairs. Sophie Grace was singing. Her voice was carrying throughout the elevator and the hotel lobby. Heads turned. Most might have thought it to be a disturbance. Yet it seemed to bring smiles to everyone's face.

This hotel was known for its healing waters. None of the guests were Sophie Grace's age, but it really didn't mat ter. She was a picture of health, and it gave the people who were seeking healing hope. A hope for restoration within themself.

It was a beautiful sight. A very young beauty and an older gray-haired beauty who showed hope. Yes, an encouragement that displayed young or old, the hotels waters could help you to be restored. No matter your ailment, this could be your place to find healing.

It was a picture that the hotel wanted to advertise. The hotel requested that pictures of the two, young and old, be taken to place in their brochure. It might also be put in the newspapers.

Grandma had one interview with newspaper people already. Perhaps another would not be too bad. But she couldn't speak for Sophie Grace; her momma would have to say yes or no.

As the Georgia beauties strolled the grounds and dined at the five-star restaurant, Grandmas Hollywood favorite passed by them over and over. At dinner, there was a command performance by the golden-voiced Judy Garland. During her song, Sophie Grace began to join in. Miss Garland came over to the table, where Sophie was, and held the microphone to her mouth, and the music was a harmony of love. The Star Gazette began snapping pictures left and right. Sophie Grace was cooperating completely. Smiles and giggles. Hand raised, and the Georgia beauty was going to become famous. "Duo sings at the Baker Hotel."

With 460 rooms, there was always people checking in and out; servicemen were there as well. The array of people was beyond comprehension. From all walks of life.

The Baker Hotel was the top resort in the State of Texas. It rivaled one of the big hotels in New York.

The manager of the Baker was offering free lodging and food for the Georgia beauties for their whole two-week stay in exchange for a photo shoot of the youngest and oldest guests to ever stay at the Baker. One very impressive newsman wasn't offering anything except a big newspaper spread.

Both wanted answers. The Georgia beauties would consider the offer once again.

For all purposes, it was a gift from heaven. However, they didn't want to act too quickly before they could pray about it.

After a day at spa and its healing waters, they were all in agreement.

Photos and a newspaper interview coming up. Since Grandma Abigaile was paying for everything, Bertie Mae and Abigaile Grace gave her the total decision. With a two week stay and the cost of food, Grandma said it was well worth the little amount of time it could take.

It didn't take long for the hotel manager to arrange for the photographer and a copywriter to engage these Georgia beauties.

Grandma Abigaile was asked to wear something casual, not a Sunday dress. And Sophie Grace a play suit. This would give the hotel brochure a sense of vacation to those studying brochures for the healing waters of the Baker Hotel.

Everything was set up in the lobby, then the pool area, and next the mineral springs were used for the background for the healing waters advertised at the Hotel Baker.

Grandma and Sophie Grace wore pink and green out fits. These colors looked cool and fresh in the light of the camera's pictures.

After the photo shoot, Sophie Grace was taken upstairs for a nap. Grandma Abigaile also retired to her room. An evening appointment for the copywriter for the hotel brochure and their two-week holiday would be paid for.

In the meantime, Bertie Mae called home. Edward Darnell answered and told her how much he missed her. It had been a week since the Georgia ladies had left. The menus for breakfast, lunch, and supper became mundane. It was eggs, peanut butter sandwiches, and some type of pasta with meat sauce.

Edward Darnell tried to make Bertie Mae feel like they were getting along well, but the opposite was the truth.

It was only one more week before Carter and Edward had to back at school. Then Harrison and Edward Darnell would be on their own. John Robert offered to take up the slack when the boys left. However, no one could take the place of his Bertie Mae, but he would take any and all help that was offered to him.

Bertie Mae was so excited to share the news about their all-paid vacation.

It seemed like everything and everywhere Grandma Abigaile Amelie went or did was blessed. Bertie Mae said their granddaughter was famous. She told of her duet with Judy Garland and the brochure that would hold pictures and stories about the waters at the hotel. She instructed Edward Darnell to go and bag up as many newspapers as he could find and place them on the dining table to be catalogued in the family history books for each of the Hurley and Butler members. It would take five for the Butler household and four for the Hurley house, so Bertie Mae instructed Edward Darnell to go one more for good measure. That was the Star Gazette only; the brochure was a different story.

The hotel manager was giving Grandma a hundred brochures to take with her to hand out to friends and townspeople. Of course he was trying to drum up business. But Grandma Abigaile Amelie simply saw it as a really nice place, and if the waters had any restorative relief, she wanted to share the blessing.

Edward Darnell didn't want to hang up. He was so missing his love. But it was time. Hugs and kisses flew over the airwaves, and then the return to plantation business and Grandmas food pantry. The one thing that Edward Darnell knew was that when the food pantry was in force for that day, he and his family of men would eat good on the leftovers.

The dinner bell was calling the Georgia beauties. This time they rode the elevator to the top story and were going to enjoy prime rib and corn on the cob. Along with the view of the wide- open spaces of Texas, Guy Lombardo was the entertainment for the evening. A soft easy-to-listen- to music filled the skyscraper room. It was like being in the clouds and hearing the music of heaven and the angels singing.

Grandma was so pleased with her decision to promote this marvel. This was a blessing, free rooms, all three, and free food for their two-week stay.

It was Grandmas party line again to God. They were talking again. And God was directing this trip to bless His phone partner.

The calls that traveled long distance on the phone lines were Ma Bells money crop. For every time someone called home from another country or a neighboring town, she would cash in. But Grandma was given free long-distance calls as well. So now Bertie Mae and Abigaile Grace felt they could call home every day and not break the bank.

During Grandmas absence at the food pantry, the helpers asked about where she was.

Finding out that she was well, they began to pray for her safe return.

With three more weeks before the Georgia beauties would be home, Edward Darnell could not eat another peanut butter sandwich or another plate of pasta.

When the regular food pantry patrons found out how long these gentlemen were going to be alone, food began to arrive nightly at River Bend, ready to be served, and enough for a leftover lunch. The next day, Edward Darnell and Harrison felt as though God had heard their prayer. As for Carter and Edward, they would be back at school in just a few days where their dinners consisted of cafeteria delights. And they could not wait to get back to it. They too were getting really tired of the nightly pasta meals. Well, that is until the food pantry people started bringing those fabulous homemade meals.

They had all agreed to tell no one, until a little more time had passed. They wanted those ladies to feel sorry for them having to do all that hard work, but they hadn't planned on John Robert spilling the beans. He had made it a regular nightly vigil to call his lady, Grandma Abigaile Amelie. Grandma Abigaile disclosed her free long-distance offer. So, after the first few calls John Robert had made, she began to call him on the hotels nickel.

Grandma Abigaile could not have been more pleased when John Robert told her how the River Bend and Willow Oaks men were being taken care of by the food pantry people. Although she never expected it, truly it was an answer to her prayer. She knew that the men in her family were not used to cooking for themselves.

It was time for the interview with the local newspaper. Grandma Abigaile was all prepared. Yet when they came in and began to set up, Grandma stopped in her tracks. She said, "I will be right back."

It was a party line from God calling her. The answers to some proposed questions left her mind completely. The only thing on her mind was the war. In her heart, she felt a joy well up within her. She had prayed with such diligence for the men and women and their families. She had a peace unlike she had felt before. Grandma wanted to tell the newspaper about her hope, her dream about the war coming to an end. But the local newsmen only wanted to hear about her life as a Civil War survivor. Also, her story of one who made it through World Wars I and II. Well, almost through World War II. She was a hundred years plus, and her time here on earth had seen many changes in the physical stature of people. But that was not the only thing she had lived through.

From the horse-and-buggy days to the amazing decades and the automobile, the inventions of safety pins, grain elevators, sewing machines, telephones, refrigerators, Ferris wheels, zippers, cotton candy, special toys, the mousetraps, the airplane, and so many more. These were the types of things these young men wanted to know about. How did she travel and cook and keep food so it would not spoil? Grandma Abigaile was a little put off by their interest in her past life but quickly noticed it was because of the age. They were only in their twenties. She was so hoping to talk about the war and the needs of Americas soldiers.

But it was a two-part interview, and Grandma was asking her party line partner (God) to direct the news interview to the war at hand. Not the horror of it but the hope all Americans had for the torment of war to be over, and their heroes to be coming home.

The night before the second interview, only seven days since they had arrived at the Baker, there was a buzz among the military.

Grandma was sitting next to several military people at breakfast and picked up on some of their conversation. They had been talking about Japan and its surrender back in September. She asked if this had anything to do with Hitler. They were not allowed to discuss the topic because of the nature of it, but one let it slip. He had heard of Germany s Hider going into hiding.

Well, that was Grandmas answer. She just knew the war was coming to an end. She could not wait to talk of the end of war with the newsmen, but she knew that she could not yet discuss this topic because she might be causing a problem for some people's emotions, so she would answer the questions with pure joy and peace, trying to encourage their readers to look forward to life like she had done for a hundred years. It was March 28, 1945, and the girls' trip was progressing beautifully.

Sophie Grace and her momma were enjoying the food and the pool filled by the healing mineral spring right outside the hotel.

Bertie Mae was trying to iron out some kinks from being in the driver's seat for four days, and Grandma Abigaile Amelie was talking to everyone.

One might have thought that she was Hollywood royalty. It seemed that everyone wanted to talk to this century-old Southern belle.

Along with being the new face of the Baker Hotel, she was the latest article in the local and wire photos in all the newspapers. She was indeed a celebrity in her own right.

From the time that the girls left Georgia, it had been thirteen days, four days for travel and nine so far at the hotel.

So much had gone on since they arrived. They had seen Grandmas favorite Hollywood starlet, Dorothy Lamour. They had pictures taken for the Baker Hotel's brochure and been the guests, all expenses paid, for just being them.

And all along the men of River Bend and Willow Oaks were working hard to fill the shoes of three Georgia beauties and one very small little person. And this little one could melt the heart of any and all who saw her, chestnut brown curls and blue eyes that would rival the tropical oceans.

Only five days left to enjoy the hotel extravaganza. The weather in Texas was delightful. The humidity was nonexistent, the breezes were forever relieving some of the warm temperatures, but most of all, it was the people; not just the hotel staff but the locals were the picture of hospitality. Grandma thought they all had an accent, but it was told all over the hotel that the girls from Georgia had an amazing accent.

So, it was a two-sided coin, each showing the same picture, deep accents.

April 6 or 7 would be a date circled on the calendars at River Bend and Willow Oaks. Due date for these Georgia beauties to be back home.

Grandma Abigaile and her crew were going to have to make hay while the sun was shining at Hotel Baker.

More days by the pool, spa treatments, massages, manicures and pedicures, and some of their special skin and hair treatments. That was before breakfast, after breakfast, before lunch and after lunch, and before dinner and after dinner, the five-star restaurants and room service and laundry service, for no one wanted to go home with dirty clothes, and no one wanted to leave without seeing the shows that the hotel and their Hollywood stars were in.

Grandma had been talking with John Robert every day, as was Bertie Mae with Edward Darnell, who told his honey that April 5-6 could not come soon enough.

It was not about the work or the meal preparation; he missed his wife. John Robert had told Grandma Abigaile he felt lonely without her smiling face to greet him.

The work at the food pantry had gone smoothly, like the ticking of a clock.

Harrison had something special for his bride when she arrived home. He was juggling the plantations' harvest and planting, plus the job at the food pantry, but this was a treat for his love and little girl.

John Robert did not spill the beans on this one; his lips were closed. Harrison almost gave it away when he told Abigaile Grace to look for another swimsuit.

The time at the Baker was going by so fast. Bertie Mae told her daughter she was ready to go home. Abigaile Grace agreed with her momma. They decided to talk to Grandma Abigaile about maybe leaving a few days early.

As God and Grandma Abigaile had the party line quite busy with prayer requests, they were hoping that God would talk to Grandma, and she would suggest an earlier departure.

Grandma Abigaile had one more newspaper interview. The paper had asked for one more visit. They had such an amazing response to the human-interest story. They simply wanted to explore more avenues with this Southern lady. They were just trying to sell newspapers. As for Grandma Abigaile, she was going to use this opportunity to stand atop her soapbox and preach however God opened up the door.

No matter if it was about family, their plantation and how it was acquired, or the food pantry and maybe, just maybe, the war, for her, you could not have picked a more passionate person than Grandma to speak about these or any other subject.

You know, to live to such an impressive age, one can and does acquire many types of knowledge. Lessons of life, love, and victories, how to survive when others are perishing, and how Abigaile always credited all wisdom and victories she acquired to be the blessings of her God. Even her Mr. Hurley was a gift to her when she was very, very young, a plan for a family that was going to be in the making. From the mid-1800s to now, she gave credit exactly where credit was due.

Grandma Abigaile was ready and set. Now she just needed to go. But they weren't there yet.

A short recess before they could get started. But Grandma was all fired up. It was like a bonfire had been lit under her, slow to get started, but then a full blaze of orange and blue flames. It would light the day or night with controlled fury. Not the kind that reached out and hurt you, but the fury of passion, a passion for right and family. "All in" was her motto for everything. She was a force to reckon with.

Her determination and fire had seen her through a hundred-plus years of life, and she could herald her rules for success.

CHAPTER 15
A Gift for All

NOTHING OF VALUE comes without effort." This was how the interview began.

"Miss Abigaile, you have been through many days, you have lived through many changes in your life! Is there anything that has guided you to look forward instead of backward?"

Well, this was Grandmas chance to attack with gusto, all her beliefs and the times of victories. But she could feel a gentle voice telling her to hold back. There are many who will agree with you hut there are those who are not ready to take a path like you, the quiet, still voice said. Grandma felt as though the wind was just taken out of her sail. But she really did understand. She remembered her dear friend Miss Matilda. She was a friend who shared all the same things as Grandma did but was not as into God as she was until the last days of her life, so she took a very gentle approach to the newsman's questions.

"Well, I guess you might think that the time I have shared with others for all these years taught me to look forward, as you said. Yet it is the times of life when troubles have tried to overcome me that have taught me that my arms can't hug anyone from behind me, my eyes are located in front of my head, and my feet walk forward. I have taken the stance that the things that are yesterday are meant to be in the past. Not that we can't and shouldn't learn from yesteryear, but to cry over things, continue to beat yourself over the head with the problems of fights or those of our country or the mistakes we have made or not hugging others in crisis. Look toward victories in your traumas and walk forward, not revisiting all your mistakes. Remember God said He would, when you ask Him to, forgive you of sin and the memory of your sin as far as the east is from the west.

"I am not preaching to you, but no matter if you believe in God or not, this looking forward is the beginning of healing and the beginning of new seeds of hope planted to bloom. Yes, to bloom just as the magnolias in my Georgia bloom, and display the beauty of nature with the sweet smell of life being renewed, for just like young ones need to be encouraged to walk and talk, we need to see each day as a gift. Granted, we are not promised all the bells and whistles of fun and happiness, but we can look at each day as a new way to give and be a good receiver." While Grandma Abigaile was talking, the gentlemen of the press were sitting with their mouths wide open; you could have thrown popcorn or jelly beans inside and win a prize like at the fair.

Grandma stopped and gathered her next thoughts. The press had left the ballroom doors open, and a crowd was gathering.

Who knew what was going on? But many of the hotel guests were drawn to a look-see and the music of Grandma's voice.

There were many who had already encountered Grandma Abigaile's wisdom.

But the things she was talking about were like a newspaper, printed in red. It stood out like, one used to say, a sore thumb. It got the attention of so many who were seeking the healing power of the waters of Mineral Wells at the Baker Hotel.

The newsmen had a myriad of questions yet to ask, but decided to take a break before the next round.

During their break, Grandma was bombarded by those who had wandered into the ballroom.

The questions were asked in rapid-fire sequence, one right after the other, but Grandma was the ever-diligent godly woman who saw the hurt and pain in each person's face and in their quivering voices. "How do I face the pain and smile?"

All were amazed with the answers. If you were there, listening to the question-and-answer session, you could have seen and felt the compassion that this small demure Southern belle of Georgia was delivering. "Smile," she said, and pray."

Her answers were so enlightening. To Grandma the answer was easy: Jesus. But it was like the quiet voice she had heard earlier said, "Some are just not ready yet."

The pure and simple instruction of going forward was one that they all could understand. The newsmen were ready again, but Grandma was not ready yet. She was still seeking to answer the multitude of questions that were presented to her by some hurting people. She would be ready in just a little bit.

The hotel management heard the commotion and sat in on the last of the words of wisdom from their new face of the Baker Hotel. You could almost hear their wheels turning. They were listening to Grandma and planning at the same time. With paper and pen in hand, notes were being taken, and one simple word as a little reminder to what the future could hold for Grandma Abigaile and that of the Baker Hotel.

The newsmen had just two more questions that they wanted to present to Grandma Abigaile

She asked for a few moments to compose herself.

Bertie Mae gave Grandma a great big hug and then whispered in her ear, "I love you, Abigaile. Can we go home? We miss everyone."

Grandma sat down and felt a tear fall from her face. What Bertie said went straight to her heart. The party line had been a two-way conversation before now. Grandma knew that with the time that she had spent with her namesake, the party line had a new voice on it. Bertie Mae was her heir apparent after she was gone; she was hearing like Grandma did, from her heart. Bertie Mae was the next in line, not Abigaile Grace.

It was like God was preparing another to take Abigaile Amelies place, but no matter the timing, Grandma knew she would give it her all until that time came.

Bertie Mae looked at Abigaile Amelie and saw the answer in her eyes. Now, tears of joy were falling from Bertie's eyes. They exchanged hugs, and the interview was almost ready to resume.

Everyone in the ballroom could hardly wait to hear the answers that this petite lady from Georgia was going to share.

The newsmen began. "We have covered topics that are ranging from wars and your amazing century of years. Now we want to sum up our story of you and your wisdom for our readers.

"If you could, in your own words please, tell us about how you got through life and still have a zest for it. After all, you have seen a lot of this world, and you have gone through it. There has to be something that carries you on to the next day."

And Abigaile said, "Well, I have always believed that truth is always the best answer anyone can give. Never tell a lie, because you can never remember the false testimony over the days, months, or years. Give and then give some more. Be that hand extended. There is someone who needs you and your hugs and kind words. Feed those who have less or maybe who has nothing. Be available to stop your plans momentarily to help another fulfil or complete theirs. No matter how large or small, provide a word of wisdom and let others talk. You have two ears and one mouth. Listen more. Let your blessings be there to assist others in despair. If possible, have a warm blanket for those who are cold, and a cold iced tea, Georgia style, for those that are passing through or helping in your fields. Clothe the needy.

"I am not saying that you continue to give the hungry food. But you must teach a needy nation to fish. For if you will continue to give to an unteachable people, they will never learn to feed themselves.

"During this time of war, we should always assist a people whose loved ones are not at home. Yet when this war comes to an end, we must teach all of us to be a part of life again. We must plant seeds of hope and water them until they are able to withstand the storms of life again. "Our nation has been through many changes. I have seen us recover from two major wars, and I hope now this war that has reached our borders will quickly be over, and that would make three big wars for me, WWI, WWII, and the one that hit my home. We called it the Civil War, or the war between the states, but there was nothing civil about it.

"How could you talk about that time in history without thinking hate, for that is what it was all about. Hate. A time when a gentle nation turned against itself, when brothers fought against each other, when towns and homes were burned, and family members lay on the battlefield or in the forest, rotting.

"This was a time of such unrest on our own soil."

"Yes, I can remember this time well. But in all the turmoil around us, we prayed, and God saved our children and our home. We had friends who lost both and never recovered, but as for me and our house, we served our God, and He carried us to another day and then another.

"In this land, there have been people born to be the inventors of new and mostly helpful items. I have been the proud owner of many of these marvelous inventions, and I am very sure that there will be many more of these in the future. But make no mistake, there will never be a more wonderful invention than Southern ice tea."

At the last moment, the newsmen couldn't help but laugh out loud. Some of the group that was listening in on Grandmas interview burst out into fall-on-the-ground type of laughter.

Complete disruption at the Baker Hotel; the ballroom was filled with laughter. You couldn't help but be intrigued about the happenings going on in the great ballroom.

There were people going in and coming out of the ballroom. They were like children in a candy shop. They couldn't wait to get in and retrieve their candy surprise.

Grandma Abigaile Amelie was part of history in the making, and everybody wanted to be a part of the experience. It wasn't just about seeing a lady of a hundred-plus years; it was about the wisdom of life she was handing out.

Some of the younger generation of this age stood with anticipation, hoping that each could and would grab hold of the brass ring and be successful. But this was not what Grandma Abigaile was about. She was asked about her rules for life and how she followed a principal laid out by God Himself. She never quoted the Bible verses but would offer answers to people who were needing hugs and wisdom from one who had seen a lot of life.

Of course, she would always end with these words. "Help is there if you know where to look." There were those who would ask about where they should look. Grandma had a two-word answer: "The Bible."

For those looking for healing at the springs at Mineral Wells, it was something they could get on board with if it could help with the physical healing they were seeking. Grandma told them that so much of the physical healing starts with peace. Her piece-of-heaven peace came many years ago. She told them of when her Mr. Hurley had passed away. "I needed to be strong for everyone else, yet I felt so weak within myself. I felt all alone. I had children who were grown and a plantation to run. Workers who depended on me for their well-being.

"I went to church and prayed my whole life. My par ents gave me everything a child needed at that time, but my heart was broken. The love of my life had left me, and I didn't know what to do, then one day I opened my Bible up and started reading. It was a storybook at first. Chapter after chapter I read. It was like a pot of water on the fire. The water is cold at first, and then a little time with the fire under the pot, the water begins to warm up, and then it boils.

"The story was just a story that the preacher talked about on Sundays before my Mr. Hurley died. Then I realized that I depended on others. My focus was on my family and our land. I was consumed with the worry and headaches of this world.

"During the Civil War and WWI, we always prayed. I was trying to follow my heart, but I didn't give my everything to God.

"I have always been a giving person, but I gave to everyone else. I thought I had God in my pocket, but I took my church clothes and my Bible and showed up on Sunday. That was all.

"Then after Mr. Hurley's passing, I looked into my Bible. Like I said, it was a story. Then I began to warm up, like the pot of water.

"I cannot say that it made a lot of sense to me, but the pages that were encased in the red leather book seem to call me. I found myself reaching for my red leather book more and more.

"Some of the hurt my heart felt seemed like it was melting away. Happiness was reaching out to me.

"I was looking at things differently. Yes, I still was responsible for the same people, places, and things. But now my emotions were stronger and not so fragile.

"My hope is for you all to look at the big picture. I know it is very hard to look to the future when all you are in is the present, but I can assure you that my hope had to be for the future. I had the past, and then the tomorrows were all there were.

"My time today, here, was to spend quality time with my family in a new state I had never seen, a place where people joined together for hope, a place where my life could help give a new insight to those who are younger and going through some of the struggles of life like I did.

"Perhaps not in the same exact way that I had, but struggles just the same.

"I have never been so blessed to have lived, loved, and been a part of this changing word.

Yet in all my struggles and all my years, I have learned one, maybe two things

"Love others and let that love cover the hurts others inflict, and to give and then give some more.

"You can never go wrong if you forgive and give until you are no more.

"For the burden you carry on your shoulders only weigh you down, and it makes that weight too heavy to proceed forward with ease.

"Yes, many are the trials we have all faced, yours different perhaps than mine, but each one of us is designed to be individuals. So, what is right for your neighbor may not be your path, but that path will never kill, steal, or destroy another. Be on guard to look up and not down, and to proceed with caution, for you never know what, when, or where you might be headed.

"I believe we all have a path that will lead us to be a blessing. Look before you leap, and be a hand that extends a beautiful magnolia in bloom with a sweet aroma that causes a smile.

"I will join my family back in Georgia soon, and know this, I will never forget this special time.

The newsmen and onlookers all agreed. "Please, one last word of wisdom."

"Well, okay. Treat others like you would like to be treated."

As the Baker Hotel s manager saw the massive response to their new face, they called down to the kitchen and sent up sandwiches and drinks for everyone.

All who were there enjoyed the hotels gesture. And for Grandma Abigaile, she felt like her journey to this big state was over.

She and her family were cutting their trip short. In two more days, they would be back on the road with many memories to reflect upon and share with their family members and friends. But before Grandma Abigaile left the ballroom, her very most favorite movie star, Dorothy Lamour, walked in.

Miss Lamour was interested in the story of Abigaile Amelie Hurley. During her stay there, their lives had over lapped. There was the possibility of making a movie about her. All Miss Lamour knew was that this lady was a legend in her own time. Moments frozen in time that could trans late onto the movie screen.

Everyone knew that in time of war, people needed to have faith in the recovery of a people and a nation. And it seemed like this aged piece of Southern gentleness could show this hurting nation that life is worth living and that hope was still alive.

As for Miss Dorothy Lamour, she could not let Abigaile Amelie Hurley leave the Baker without her phone number and address for further contact about the life and love of a Southern lady who had lived through wars and losses, only to live again, sort of like the story of Scarlett O'Hara and Rhett Butler in Gone with the Wind, but a true story of real people and real hope. That was the story she would pitch to her Hollywood producers.

As Abigaile Hurley spoke, Miss Lamour had already pictured in her mind the plantation and war and the summer of when the magnolias were in bloom.

In fact, that was the name of her new movie idea. Even though the time of Civil War was over and two other wars had erupted, a family could live, love, and hope.

Just like our country had survived before, we have to put the past behind us, or it could cost us the present and our future.

This was the cry of our country, to live for tomorrow, and this was what Abigaile Amelie Hurley had displayed.

Maybe not to the whole world just yet. But Dorothy Lamour was determined to tell her story, a story she knew would touch the American people.

Only two days left until the departure of four Southern ladies, back to their home state of Georgia.

Preparation for travel and the completion of a new venture for one who was chosen to be a new face, a new force of truth and victories for the Baker Hotel.

One last meeting with Miss Hollywood, Dorothy Lamour, and the great Baker Hotel.

A dinner to honor the new face of the Baker, and auto graphs to be acquired from Hollywood's favorites.

There was a surprise guest at the Baker. One who stood in the shadows. One who was looking and listening.

The author of a well-known literary work called The Maltese Falcon, Dashiell Hammett.

Rumor was going around that he was ready to venture away from his Sam Spade books to more home-grown stories of real American heroes. And by the look on his face and the notes he was jotting down, he might have found his next bestseller.

Only time would tell if Abigaile Amelie Hurley would allow her story to be revealed on screen or possibly in a book.

But no matter the possibilities, Grandma Abigaile knew that her life's story had already touched many in ways she knew about and some she would never know about.

She had entered this world in a gender time where women wore only dresses, and she had seen the popular ladieswear now included pants. That was something she just never got used to. And the swimwear of her time had gone from an all-over cover-up, to shoulders, arms, and legs all being exposed.

The Olympic pool at the Baker was an open parade of the current styles.

Grandma Abigaile had seen so much change in her years, but it still surprised her each time her more modest outlook was put to the test.

It had been a while since she wore her Southern belle costume, but she could still remember the only thing exposed on her person was her neck, shoulders, and her delicate small arms. Those areas were opened to be adorned with her princess emeralds and, of late, her Miss Matilda's opals.

But no matter the age or time she was in, Grandma Abigaile Amelie had tried to glean a new perspective on the new that seemed to invade her old way of thinking.

It was like what Miss Lamour had told Abigaile, "The differences in us all and our circumstances should be celebrated and not condemned."

This was going to be the way Miss Lamour was going to present her new movie idea to Hollywood about her new friend Miss Abigaile Amelie Hurley.

But she might just have a run for her money and her new idea because it might be a new book that Mr. Dashiell Hammett might be introducing as well. Of course, there would be only one real deciding factor in this bid for success. Grandma Abigaile Amelie Hurley would be the yes or maybe the no to everyone's idea of how to immortalize this great Southern lady of hundred-plus years.

But no decisions could be made until after these Southern belles returned home.

Just one more day, and off to Georgia. The car was ready, and the men back home were already counting the days and minutes until their darlings would be back home.

But before their departure, the Baker Hotel wanted one more interview and a short live radio spot.

Phone numbers and addresses were exchanged, and Grandma Abigaile's Hollywood contact and the author who was wanting to immortalize her life in book form were both were excited to have their futures include a part of the history of an American hero who had lived for a century and had more good to say about life than bad.

Perhaps this would be a sequel to the popular movie Gone with the Wind.

But again, only time would tell.

With clothes all packed and the car loaded, the move was on.

A basket of goodies from the Baker Hotel, memory towels, and pool spa bathrobes were given to the Southern ladies as a memento of their special time spent in Texas at the Baker Hotel. Grandma Abigaile had a purse full of money. She had almost as much as when she left Georgia. She was amazed, once again, how God had provided for her and her family.

Meanwhile, the time that was spent at the Baker Hotel had come and gone, and they were homeward bound.

The hours on the road passed quickly the first couple of days. Then it became tiresome, and little Sophie Grace was feeling the confinement, as all were. So, there was no stopping at sights, only for food and lodging.

One day closer, and the Hurley and Butler men were feeling like normal was just about ready to return.

A special homecoming meal was planned, and it was right around the corner. Hugs and kisses would be exchanged soon in a family reunion that would show each other that all were missed so very much.

Bertie Mae was beginning her last twenty miles of their four-week journey. She was so excited about being home she was going faster than the normal speed limit signs.

The last few miles seemed to fly by. The closer they got; they could feel the excitement mounting. The gates were visible, and little Sophie Grace stood up and began a song. No, you couldn't understand the words, but she was singing because she saw home. Or at least it was her second home. That of her Grandmother Bertie Mae and her Great-Great-Grandma Abigaile Amelie. She was just about two years old, but she knew where home was. They were all back in Georgia. Where the willow trees were waving in the Southern breeze, and the sweet smell of turned earth and the magnolias trees were beginning the summer bloom of snow-like flowers that perfumed the countryside where Willow Oaks and River Bend resided.

As the driveway and gates opened up, it said to the weary travelers, welcome home.

It was over, the long four-week trip to Texas was over. It couldn't have been more perfect.

From youngest to oldest, the time spent together was magical.

The time was late afternoon, and dinner was approaching. As they exited the car, they heard music and could smell the hint of barbecue cooking in the backyard. It was a taste of Texas right at home, but it had a sweet smell of sugar cane barbecue sauce. Bertie Mae had told her honey, Edward Darnell, that the taste was out of this world. As soon as the Southern belles stepped foot on the grounds of River Bend, they felt a peace of heaven had welcomed them. And the taste of Texas was about to say howdy to their hungry stomachs.

Everyone was extremely happy to be back home. The Hurley boys were back home for the week before their graduation from college. Of course they were put to work right away unloading Grandmas Cadillac. It was loaded to the brim with goodies from the Baker Hotel and souvenirs that were collected from the states these Southern ladies had passed through.

The Hurley men were like little ants. Back and forth, back and forth. They were busy little bees, and Mr. Buder was manning the barbecue pit. He had put chickens, steaks, and pork ribs on for the welcome-home dinner. There was early corn on the cob, and Bertie's honey had made a favorite of all, peach pie.

What these men had learned in one month of taking care of their homes and the food pantry was nothing short of a miracle. Bertie Mae was so impressed that she decided Edward Darnell could take over the kitchen at least once a week.

As soon as Sophie Grace saw her daddy, she began singing. No real words, but the melody was surely one of love and smiles. She ran to her daddy as fast as her tiny little legs would allow. It was a reunion of mega proportions. Mr. Harrison Butler never knew he could or would miss his two girls so much. But now, his family was complete, and he never wanted them to be gone that long again.

As for Grandma Abigaile Amelie, she too had made a decision. This long time away from home was fun, but she didn't want to venture out again anytime soon.

The car was unloaded, and suitcases went upstairs to Grandma's room and Bertie Mae's.

The dinner bell was ringing, and the welcome-home dinner was placed on top of the long mahogany table in the great hall dining room.

It was a display of a huge nature. Everything was in large containers and large platters.

Edward Darnell wanted everything to depict the big state of Texas, and that it did.

There was enough food left over for the next day and the next day. But instead of saving it for the Hurley house, it was packaged up for the next day's food pantry. It was a fully cooked meal that would bless those who were early comers to the food pantry.

The Hurley men gave the weary travelers a break for one week, and then they were asked to take over the regular routine again, house and food pantry.

With their goodies unloaded and their tummies full, the sun was setting, and the beds at Willow Oaks and River Bend were calling.

All the girls sank into their beds, and Mr. Sandman sent everyone fast asleep.

As for the next day's affair, the men had everything under control. The food pantry was top priority, and plantation business was second.

Grandma Abigaile was feeling her age. A short morning nap, another in the afternoon, and early to bed.

You might think she was taking advantage of her men folk, and you would be right. She was 103 years old and knew she should take advantage of every chance she could to feel special.

As for Bertie Mae and Abigaile Grace, they too were enjoying the stay-at-home vacation with all the benefits of the grand Baker Hotel. All their chores and meals were done for them. All they had to do was relax and show up for mealtime.

CHAPTER 16

Homeward Bound

YES, SOUTHERN BEAUTIES were back home, but the remembered times at the Baker Hotel was like a fresh dip in the waters of hospitality and sweet Southern love.

As the Hurley ladies gathered and the two Butler girls joined together for lunch at Willow Oaks, the topic of con versation was all about their girls' trip and the fabulous state of Texas. It was bigger and more welcoming than any other place they had ever visited. They all agreed it should be a place they should visit again. Abigaile Grace was particularly taken with it. It was not the Baker Hotel or the stars that were there, but the sleepy little town with hundreds of citizens with hearts of gold and down-home hospitality. As she was drawn to Mineral Wells and its people, she planned to tell Harrison of her feeling of belonging.

The week of rest and relaxation was almost over, and the reality of life on the plantation and the food pantry was facing all the travelers.

The time for fun and games were over, and the complimentary week off responsibilities at River Bend and Willow Oaks were at an end.

For the next day was food pantry day, and the men had gathered all donations to fulfill the next day's needs.

The morning came so quickly, and normal was in full swing.

The date was April 20, 1945, and all was well. The plantations were back to normal, and the food pantry in full swing. Donations for the food pantry were doubling. Everyone's gardens seemed to grow double the expected produce, and the livestock had double the amounts of offspring. Even the chickens were laying more eggs.

In Grandmas mind, it was just a sign of God's blessing on her heart's desire to help others in need, and she was, of course, His hand extended to His creation.

Little Sophie Grace was coming up on her second birthday, and Grandma Abigaile Amelie was wanting to plan an old-fashioned Southern birthday party for her dear one. Pony rides and everyone *dressed in Gone with the Wind costumes.* As for Grandma Abigaile Amelie, she would wear her own belle skirt and floppy hat that she had worn each time she had story time with her other dear ones just a few years back. She also wanted to bless Sophie with a special dress for the party. All in pink, Sophie Grace's favorite color.

Special invitations would be in pink, and the cake would be four tiers high with loads of pink flowers on it, and pink lemonade with strawberries and ice cream, pink of course.

But first getting back into the routine of life at River Bend and her pet project, the food pantry.

During Grandma's girls' trip, she had a revelation about kids, toys, and the military. She had talked to so many military GI's who couldn't be home for Christmas.

That was where her idea came from. There had to be some way, they as a grateful nation, could blessed the families of their military heroes.

All the way home, she had thoughts of food, Christmas decor, and clothing, but it could not compare to one very strong idea that kept surfacing. It was toys and children. She could remember all the Christmases past and her dear ones. The wide eyes of her dear ones on Christmas morning. The wishes of a child coming true.

Perhaps for the families of their brave heroes fighting for their country, the gift of hope and the dreams of little children could help make up for those who were not at home.

Grandma already knew that the party line she and God had shared over time was calling to her once again. There would be many hours of prayer and phone talks before this idea might come to be, but no matter how long it would take, Grandma she knew it was on the right road to bless America's heroes and their families.

As the week began and the food pantry duties began to call for these beauties, Sophie Grace became a little disagreeable terrible-two mess. She was all about the word no. There was no making this little mess happy. But when Grandma Abigaile Amelie came into Willow Oaks, the child that was not going anywhere all of a sudden wanted to go by.

You could tell that a special bond had been formed the same as her momma had with Grandma Abigaile.

The plan for the food pantry business proceeded as planned, and little Miss Sophie Grace was a picture of agreeable perfection. The day came off without a moment of disappointments.

And then April 25 rolled around.

Things had been going just peachy and everyone was filled to overflowing with joy, but no one could have guessed the events that were to come.

The plantations were running smoothly, and the food pantry was a home run. The crops were harvested, and new ones planted. The food pantry was overflowing with donations, and hungry families were being cared for.

What had started as an effort to meet the needs of the heroes' families turned out to help more of the hungry people in their area. No one was left out.

No one was ever turned away, and sometimes there was enough for the volunteers to have a take-home dinner as a reward for their love and support of others.

This was truly the heart of Grandma Abigaile Amelie Hurley. "Give and it will be given to you, pressed down, shaken, and running over, men will give to you." It was not the reason, but she was a giving person from the time she was a small child. All she wanted to do was help others and be a blessing.

Grandma drove home, and then she felt a touch faint. She had had a full day and had forgotten to eat. Bertie Mae and Edward Darnell immediately called the doctor, and a sense of fear gripped them all. As soon as the doctor arrived, Grandma was feeling better. She had let her blood sugar drop due to not eating. The doctor confirmed that Grandma had not kept up her blood sugar levels and made her promise to eat three squares a day from now on.

Bertie Mae was keeping a close eye on her and made sure the doctors' orders were followed to the letter.

Of course, a lady of 103 years of age was a miracle, but if she wanted to reach 104 plus, she would have to take better care of herself.

Another few days had passed, and Grandma was being a good patient, eating three squares and watching to make sure her level of activity was slowed down. Grandma knew that this would be good for her. She had a hard time turning over the reins to Bertie Mae, but it was necessary.

The date was April 30, 1945, and all was going great. The next day, they all got the news of a lifetime. The tyrant that had ruled a country and was the judge, jury, and executioner of the Jewish people had given up and committed suicide.

The news was a joyful one, knowing that the hatred and despised mentality of one man had ended. Everyone was shocked, yet joyful, but were wondering if the horrible actions of one were going to be passed down to another.

No one had ever prayed for the butcher of Germany to end this way, but for the families and friends who had fought so gallantly against hate and a people that targeted the Jewish nation, the reign of a mad man had ended.

Would this end World War II or would it continue? All of America was still on their knees praying. And so, the events of everyday life in America continued.

Plantation life was continuing, and the food pantry was showing no signs of slowing down. Even though it was apparent that Grandma Abigaile Amelie had some of her wind knocked out of her sails, she continued.

It seemed like the perfect time to complete her plans for little Miss Sophie Graces birthday party, the party in pink in and on everything. Grandma was turning 104, Sophie Grace was turning two, and her momma one year older as well.

She wanted everyone to dress in pink for the girls and any color for the boys. They would all be given pink bags with little pink balloons, pads and pencils and a pink Bible for the girls, and a blue Bible for all the little boys. There was a coloring book with pictures of Bible characters and bubble gum for all, and lots of crayons for all the little people who would be attending.

Grandma also ordered several dozen more so she could pass out a prize for the food pantry people. Summer was approaching, and school would be out. This could be a help for busy parents who were trying to make ends meet, and some small treats would help to make the time of war seem not so horrible.

This was indeed the cry of Grandmas heart. She wanted to be that hand extended, to help, to bless.

There was a new fire under Grandma. The idea of children and Christmas kept her mind all lit up. Now that the birthday party was underway, she had a meeting with the local recruiting office to inquire of the steps she would have to take to put her dream in motion.

The date was May 7, 1945, and everyone gathered around the dinner table. The radio was on, and then a silence filled the room. There was a radio test, and then a word that stunned everyone everywhere.

Germany had surrendered; the war was over. Americas boys would be coming home.

This was a news that no one had dreamed of but had prayed so diligently for since this war began.

Hands were joined around the table, and Grandma had a prayer of thanksgiving. The rest of the evening, a new hope had bloomed around the whole countryside.

Mrs. Abigaile Butler had called that night, and an expression of joy was evident. She said that God had answered her prayers.

In this great country, there were millions praying for the war to end, and now it was over. The war of a madman named Hitler had come to an end, and their boys would be coming home. Would this be the end of the food pantry, or would the efforts of one so loved continue?

It was like Grandma always said, "People will always need help, and I want to help those in need."

So, no matter the reason, the food pantry had begun. It was decided on this momentous day, May 7, 1945, that the food pantry would continue as long as the fields of Georgia would produce a crop of fruits and vegetables and the livestock would multiply. Grandma Abigaile Amelie and her family members, Bertie Mae and Abigaile Grace, were committed to helping. In fact, Grandma was so committed to the need that a portion of River Bends proceeds, 5 percent, were to be deposited in the bank to help cover the cost of running this blessing. A paper, a legal document, was drawn up and filed at the local courthouse. This document held River Bend responsible for the next ten years.

Grandma was sure that her dreams of helping hungry families could live on and was making sure of it before she was homeward bound to heaven. This made her a very happy little lady. From the days of having less during the days of the Civil War, she wanted her family and friends in Georgia to know God was always looking out for them.

The pink party of the century was just around the corner.

The Hurley boys were home, and college graduation had been accomplished.

Now that the war was over, the draft board was not as eager to recruit all the twentysomething young men.

It was as if the Hurley boys had dodged a bullet, but no matter the reason, the plantation was needing them to help carry on, and that was what happened.

And the Hurley family and their plantation had a future. Grandma Abigaile had made arrangements for her dear Abigaile Grace to be a silent partner with 10 percent of the profits, and the food pantry had a legal promise of 5 percent of the proceeds of River Bend for the next ten years.

One might think that Grandma Abigaile Amelie was putting her affairs in order. You might be correct, but she was simply wanting to bless others no matter how long she would be around, and later after she was gone.

After all, she was past the century age, so everything past those years was a gift from God, she always said, so try to make it count.

The pink party was just a few days away, and so many had RSVP'd.

Grandma Abigaile was also having a banner made to acknowledge the war being over.

Along with pink everywhere, red, white, and blue American flags were flying high, along with everyone's spirits.

It was truly a double-duty celebration, a birthday and a freedom of the land. Their boys were coming home.

But first the American heroes were helping to free the lost and imprisoned people of the concentration camps of Germany.

The focus of free America was to free those who were captured by terror and one man's crazy ideal and give those who fell prey to that horror a new hope and restoration.

Even though there were no concentration camps in America, there were so many who were captured by the hate of this one crazy person.

There were lives and a way of life that were lost. But today it felt like a new spring day where new life and hope was coming forth from a frozen and lifeless ground.

The hope of a nation had begun to be watered by the tears of joys that were shed during the last four years.

Even though the loss of brothers, husbands, sisters, and wives could not be replaced, America as a nation could rebuild their dreams, with the help of those who banded together in oneness and planted new seeds of hope. And the first sign of new life was a celebration of one little person born during this time in history when the free nation lent a helping hand to those in bondage.

So, for Grandma Abigaile, it was a show of life, liberty, and the pursuit of hope within the United States and her beloved Georgia.

She and her family were transplants from Europe and had planted themselves in Georgia and grew to be a blessing back then and now, to their new neighbors, an asset to their fellow man.

Grandma Abigaile Amelie knew that her life could not compare to others. The others of this world all had different crosses to bear. But no matter the task that she was given, she was determined to give it her all.

She would say that the events in our lives shape us, but it is our choices in life that define us.

The pink party plans were completed, and all the guests were arriving.

Bertie Mae was overwhelmed. Her granddaughter Sophie Grace came down the curved stairway on her own.

She was a big girl and wanted to do everything by herself. Her pink *Gone with the Wind dress* moved side to side each time she took one step and then another.

It was as if she was practicing for the entrances she would take in the years to come.

According to the Southern belles of Georgia, this was going to be the first of many parties and descents from the upstairs of River Bend to greet her party guests. Even at age two, she was being groomed for her entry into Georgie royalty.

The ponies were all dressed in pink bridles and pink headdresses. Pink feathers, of course, and pink saddle blankets.

The Hurley boys were the pony masters, ready to assist Sophie Graces party guests. The party games began, and Sophie Grace was singing with joy.

With ice cream, cake, candy, and pink lemonade, the sugar rush was beginning to show its effects, and the rush was soon to take a nosedive.

There were pallets set up for all the young ones, and moms and dads were going to talk business and family. The early summer breezes were giving the pink party a sweet magnolia scent, and the cool evening carried the fragrance of the magnolia forests and the sweet Texas barbecue that was roasting on the open pits. This was a treat for the adults, and little hot dogs were for the little people.

The balloons were held in a huge net waiting to be released soon after supper. The party bags were waiting on the entry table for all Sophie Graces guests to take home after supper, and a few more pony rides were waiting.

Even though it was a birthday party for three, only one was in the spotlight.

Sophie's mom had her focus on her daughter, and Grandma Abigaile Amelie was not focusing on her day but that of her little darling. Grandma was extremely happy to see her family grow and the age she had achieved. She had been through so much in her life and saw the pain and joys in her life help to propel her to her projects and redirect her thoughts to the needs of others more than herself. She was selfless. She never took credit for anything but would always say it was God directed.

The pink party was over, and the guests were all back home. Grandma Abigaile Amelie had one more year under her belt.

Her soft feather mattress was calling, and the ascent up the stairs seemed to take forever. As she dressed for bed, she remembered the birthdays she had celebrated with her love, Mr. Hurley, memories of walks on the grounds of River Bend when they first purchased their first acres.

A pride of ownership and the life they would carve out together, where the heavens touched the earth and waters of their new homeland met.

Together they were unstoppable. The children they shared and the gathering of her River Bend land was a joint effort, one that anyone could and should be proud of. For what was a dream so many years ago by two who loved each other had stood the test of three wars and trials of many kinds.

This was indeed something to be proud of, but pride never ruled the Hurley household. There was "love your neighbor as yourself" and "help those in need" as the mottoes of River Bend and the Hurley family.

Grandma Abigaile Amelie knew nothing stayed the same, but like the helpful new inventions of this century, she knew that her hopes for River Bend might change but would never change the blessing that it had been for so many.

Change is the essence of life, for if you live in the past, it will cost you your joy in the present. Life is about going forward, as her years had, and making the best of every opportunity and trying to avoid the mistakes of the past as to not repeat poor choices. We should celebrate our unique styles and qualities and not condemn those that are made different from ourselves.

As Grandma Abigaile Amelie readied herself for slumber, she peered out her bedroom window and remembered one of Mr. Hurleys sayings, "The only thing that is crowded in Georgia is the stars." For the stars lit up the night sky like the lights at the carnival. The moon was full, and the night was all aglow. The trees were waving in the soft gentle breeze, and the sweet flowers of the magnolia forest where whispering sweet loving memories of days gone by, and the times of love, laughter, and her dear Mr. Hurley.

Sometimes she thought of her life coming to an end, but each morning she would awake again, and God would give her another job to do. She longed for her dear Mr. Hurley, but her life burned with hope for the new day's arrival.

As she fell asleep, she prayed and asked for clear revelation for her tasks to come.

Grandma Abigaile had been on the party line already, and even though no words were exchanged she knew her directive.

It was the children and Christmas. With the war ending and the heroes coming home, there were still the men who were protecting the country who could not make it home for the holiday.

The armed forces were helping the country stay safe. The least we could do, Grandma said, was to make the gift of Christmas and the birth of Jesus call to each child, the love of the American people and their mom or dad who were not home.

It was like everything this little Southern lady touched was blessed. An ideal was planted in her heart with the idea and means to accomplish the blessing. She just knew it was right.

Her meeting with the local recruiter started the ball rolling. The news quickly spread to neighboring cities, and before the end of summer, Grandma was spearheading a new project. It was suggested that a sign be placed in all the businesses and grocery stores.

By the end of September, the stores had collected all sorts of toys. Things for children of all ages, boys and girls. There were even new baby beds and linens for those expecting new arrivals.

One of the barns was empty, so everything was stored there at River Bend with the excess, and there was some found storage at Willow Oaks.

Bertie Mae and Abigaile Grace were Grandmas elves. Grandma insisted that each package was catalogued, and large cardboard boxes were marked either boys or girls, along with ages.

It was the suggestion of the recruiter to bundle the toys in boxes so that the distribution would be easy. The food pantry was steadily growing, and more volunteers were showing up to assist with all facets of preparation and distribution. The food pantry was every Thursday, and the collection for the toys for the children's Christmas was every Wednesday from all the merchants. Therefore, the volunteers for food pantry could also help with collection and boxing of toys for the heroes' families, the love of a community coming together for the good of a people in need.

At some point in everyone's lives, we could all use a helping hand, and Grandma and her crew would be that hand extended for as long as there were hurting or hungry people.

Grandma Abigaile Amelie was not involved in the collection of toys or food but was heading up the organization of the home efforts in her hometown, a project she knew was not just a good idea but a God idea.

CHAPTER 17

Expressions of Hope and Dreams

WITH EACH PASSING DAY, the Christmas holiday was fast approaching.

The celebrations at River Bend had been quite elaborate in the years past. Grandma Abigaile had a detailed plan that started in the middle of summer. Her invitations for the annual River Bend Christmas celebration were back from the engravers by the first of October and addressed and ready to be mailed out shortly thereafter.

But it was the silver family ornaments that took the most time.

This year had to be something very special. The war was over, and this great land was beginning to show signs of hope and dreams for a future. The heroes were arriving home, and Grandmas toy project was in full swing.

The silversmith knew it was time, and Grandma was ready for her inspiration to come to life.

This year the family ornament was going to be a soldier holding a house inscribed with WWII.

For her it meant the heroes of the war were on the way home, a memory for each family member to recall how God ended a tragedy and loss, and new life was on the way.

Truly Thanksgiving was going to be a celebration of great magnitude.

297

In the Butler household, it meant that the two brothers Butler would also be coming home soon after their enlistment was over. And big brother Harrison had some new idea he wanted to discuss with them.

Since the time that Abigaile came back from the famed girls' trip, she had been filling Harrison's mind with a secret dream. A dream that she didn't even know was there until she arrived in a new state, a small town filled with people whose heart seemed as big as the state they lived in, Texas.

Harrison was so excited to see the dream that Abigaile talked about lighting up her eyes and her heart. For he too had a dream. One that he had kept hidden for many years. But for now, he was wanting to hear all about her dream.

She began with the people, the place, and then her idea of what it might be like to move to Texas and start anew, just like her parents and their parents and their parents before, from Europe to Georgia, and she was hoping Texas was a town of friendly people and an opportunity to make their mark in a new land and bring more of that Southern charm to a place that already had so much of its own.

Harrison did not want to steal Abigaile's thunder, so he waited until the time would be right to divulge his unspoken dream that had started small so many years when he saw his first glimpse of the horseless carriages his grandparents spoke of.

But for now, the focus was on Abigaile and the upcoming holidays.

The snow made its first appearance of winter, and the beauty wasn't surpassed by anything around inside or out. The Thanksgiving turkey and all its trimmings were set out on the long oak dining table at Willow Oaks. It was the first time Abigaile and Harrison hosted the family get-together.

Everyone from River Bend came, and they all joined together in a Thanksgiving dinner like no other. After prayers of thanksgiving for all their family blessings and before they all partook in the special dishes, there was a special prayer expressed by all for the war being over and the safe return of family and friends once again.

Who would have guessed that this was to be one of the last of three the family would share?

The Butler brothers had one more year at the military recruiter's office. Both had discussed the end of their tour of duty and decided that Willow Oaks was calling them home.

It was truly a God-directed idea because the secret that Harrison was just about ready to share with his Abigaile had to have certain things fall into place.

But Harrison was holding on to his secret dream for a little while longer. He was thinking of a trip to the little town of Mineral Wells, Texas, as a surprise for his sweetie pie as a Christmas gift.

She had talked so much about it that Harrison just wanted to see for himself.

Maybe the secret dream he was keeping might just come into the light when they went to Mineral Wells after the holiday was over. Perhaps for Valentine's.

But first things first. Christmas was coming, and the annual Christmas party at River Bend was needing everyone's attention.

Grandma Abigaile Amelie had ordered her family's special silver ornament and had the invitation for the annual Christmas printed. The special glass ornaments that she had always given out were not ordered so that something extra special would be offered to her parting guests.

Grandma Abigaile had penned a poem which she had engraved on special linen paper and had them placed inside a leather folder that was gold stamped on the outside with the words Hope Never Dies.

As the bookmaker marked and cut the red leather into the prescribed size, the pages were folded and glued and placed inside the smooth red leather cover. When the hundred books were completed, Grandma Abigaile began her annual gift-wrapping ritual. Each book was wrapped in gold paper with red velvet ribbon tied around each book.

A tag wishing everyone a Merry Christmas and blessings for the next year hung on each ribbon.

The prayers of a grateful nation had been answered, and the poem Grandma penned expressed that joy.

The Christmas tree graced the great hall and stood stately between the two walk-through windows that were dressed in cherry-red velvet drapes, trimmed with a beautiful golden silk fringe from top to bottom.

The ornaments, for the first time, were a combination of pink, blue, purple, red, and gold glass balls and long clear white icicles. A star glowed bright atop the massive blue spruce tree that almost touched the ceiling.

Grandma Abigaile picked up her family's silver ornaments and placed one in each member's room under their pillow.

As she placed the memento under each pillow, she saw the small tree that held each person's remembrances of the years past.

But there were none that held as many as her tree did. As she placed the last ornament, she told the Lord of her love for the people He had created, and the hopes and dreams she desired to complete. A feeling of peace and laughter began to explode. At her advanced age, she was planning as if she were seventy with decades in front of her.

She did not know the future of her days or weeks, months, or years, but had hoped for her dreams to not be lost but completed. She wanted to bless her fellow man and prayed she might have more time.

Grandmas new project was in full swing. The toys for the brave men's and women's children were ready for a round-up and distribution to the local recruiter's office. Then her job was almost over for the holiday.

The food bank had one more food handout, and then she was ready for her annual River Bend party.

She had been super organized about her needs for the party and almost had all her poems wrapped for the placement on the entry table.

A large seasonal floral arrangement was full of red poinsettias and white tulips. It was in a tall crystal vase, and the floral was nearing five feet tall.

All was set for the party; the food had been planned and was ready to serve many guests.

Grandma Abigaile read her poem to Bertie Mae and Miss Abigaile. Their eyes teared up.

The poem read true.

Hope Never Dies

The night encamped around the cities of a land far away
While daylight broke, the dark skies in other parts of the
land we love Some lulled to sleep by a day that had come
to a close
Yet others awakened by the dawn, the bright sun
All was not lost
More were the chances for redemption
No matter the problem No matter the cost Hope never
dies
To be born means life
And love gives light to the darkness of despair But those
who love never lose hope
We are a part of a whole Not just an island
We do not stand by ourself
Our hand extended to those in need No matter who
No matter where No matter when
We support our fellow man And ask no reward
We walk this earth Sometimes we are not seen A problem
Trouble follows Our choices are made
Hide or offer yourself up
Bridge the gap Help others to victory Our nation said yes
To help our brothers find freedom
In other lands not our own A struggle with great cost Our
lives go on
Hope never lost
But crushed temporarily Those who faced the enemy

And those who keep the home fires strong Hope never
left the hearts of men
For victory was in sight
The greatness of our Creator is bright And a strength that
wells up within We are proud to be an American
Love one another
For hope never dies in a grateful heart The war is over
cross the seas
And life moves on The war we face now Is here at home
Ourselves we charge Be great or fail
Be part of the journey
Don't wish or want For others' great fortunes
Or say, if only I had
But know that ups and downs Love and loss
Will always come A part of life
So, live your best Be ready to help Be ready to cry
Be ready to succeed For each day is new A time to hope
For hope never dies Within the heart of grateful men
Love never fails Look up, not down
Hand extended to help Smile and healing comes And life
goes on
We are proud to be an American

The three hostesses had to repair their tear-stained faces
and be ready to greet their guests. As they descended
the curved staircase, the doorbell began to chime, over
and over. The great door opened, and the guests were
welcomed.

As in the years past, the incoming guests could see the
parting gifts piled up upon the entry table, ready for each
family to take home the prize Grandma Abigaile had
fashioned just for them.

This was a gift from the heart of one who had seen much in her 104 years.

The evening was a delight. The food was beyond delicious. As the guests were ready to exit, one of the friends opened their prize. She began to read the beautiful poem that was surrounded by a ruby-red cover out loud.

She was a teacher, and the style of the poem called to her. She began as she would in a classroom. She said, "Listen up." And she began to read out loud. It made the group stand silent. Tears began to fill the eyes of those listening. It was as if someone had looked inside their heart and wrote the words to their feelings. Some were rejoicing for their loved ones were home, and others knew the pain of family lost. Still others had friends who were still helping the captives to be set free.

It touched all. For they had all been part of a war that seemed to never end.

This was a prize, a treasure, unlike any gift that had ever been given. This would grace the table or bookshelves of all and read many times over, again and again.

Grandma Abigaile Amelie had heard from the Lord. A word to instruct and a word to give hope. A gift of love that helped to expose the feelings of the heart.

Peace never felt so good. Grandma knew that she had listened to God. That party line had a lot of hours on it. Talking to God and God talking to His love, one Abigaile Amelie.

There was never a question in her heart that this poem would give joy to those who received it.

The night had come to a close, and only one ruby-red book was left on the table. This one was for the author. She had forgotten about herself.

She ascended the stairs and entered her room. The tree of family memories was lit, and it sparkled with mirror-like reflections.

So many were adorning the tree. But there was one that seemed to shine brighter than all the rest. It was a heart made in faceted lead crystal. The only one that was not silver. It was the last memory from her dear Mr. Hurley.

As the light danced about it, you could see a prism of light like that of a beautiful rainbow.

Her heart was filled with loving thoughts of her love and husband of so many years.

The feathered mattress called, and she joined her covers to dream new dreams of her love.

*****

The toy drive was a success. There was talk of making it an annual thing. But Grandma was not ready to make that commitment. She would get on her party line and ask for direction.

Christmas Day was here, and all the Hurley family were together to celebrate.

Gifts were exchanged, food enjoyed. And plans for the new year were discussed.

There were two new guests at the dinner table. Each of the Hurley boys had met the girl of their dreams. One of the girls was named Emily Mae, and the other was Addie

Paige. Both lovely young ladies, and it seemed like there might just be two more added to the Hurley family soon.

A fresh blanket of snow lay upon the ground. Even in the dark of night, it looked bright.

The moon was making the snow appear like light bulbs were turned on and daytime was there.

As the night light of the snow and moon joined together, it made sleeping difficult, but the day was long, and all just pulled the covers up over their heads and fell asleep.

Another day to come and new challenges to meet was their prayer.

The Christmas holidays were over, and the new year was knocking on their door.

The food pantry was starting again, and Grandma had turned her responsibilities over to Bertie Mae.

Grandma felt the need to slow down and turn over to a younger group of people the dreams that God had given her and helped bring to life.

Her focus was on a topic no one liked to talk about.

She knew her time was winding down. She was a planner, and she was going to have all her affairs in order. When her time came to meet her love, she was going to be sure that she left her family taken care of.

But no one knows when the end will come. She was going to be ready no matter what, when, or where.

CHAPTER 18
A Dream Revealed

WHEN ABIGAILE GRACE opened her Christmas gift from Harrison, her face had lit up like the Christmas tree.

The Willow Oaks plantation had one harvest behind them, and very soon the next three would be finished as well.

By the time Valentines would roll around, the hopes for the Texas trip could be realized.

As much talk about Mineral Wells was shared, Harrison was unusually excited. He had never been out of his home state of Georgia before except for his honeymoon trip. But never to the great state of Texas to visit a landmark known as the Baker Hotel.

Harrison had made arrangements for his mom and dad to fill in the gap and care for Sophie Grace. The trip might take a week or two, but they were up for the adventure.

It had been close to nine months since the girls' trip to Texas. Abigaile Grace had a deep longing to return to Texas; this was a great desire realized.

They would fly instead of drive as to spend more time at the Baker Hotel.

The hotel had been in contact on a regular basis because of their youngest visitor with the new oldest face of the Baker, hoping to lure them both back for another visit.

As the plane took off, hopes were high. The dream of Abigaile Grace was coming true.

Harrison had a fear of flying but buckled in like a trooper and tried to stay calm. He was like a chatterbox. Abigaile Grace had never seen or heard him like a windup toy. He just would not be still or quiet.

They landed, and he almost ran out of the plane and kissed the ground. He felt the earth beneath his feet and praised the Lord for his feet touching ground again.

Poor Abigaile didn't get a word in the whole way. Harrison was like a cat with a long tail in a room full of rocking chairs.

But for now, the reality of being on the ground made him as if a cat had gotten his tongue; he didn't have more than a dozen words to say while on the drive to the Baker.

As they approached the Baker driveway, Abigaile took Harrison's hand and told him she felt like she was home.

Harrison looked at her and saw a light from within that lit up her face. He was confused, but time would unveil the reason for her light. Harrison had won her heart, now he was going to know what it was to treasure it for the rest of his lifetime to come. Her hopes and dreams were going to meld with his unspoken ones. She didn't know his dream yet, but the Baker Hotel and the Texas town of Mineral Wells were about to be a part of the Butler family history in the making.

As they approached the entry to the hotel lobby, both Mr. and Mrs. Butler saw a group of militaries, and a few well-known movie stars. Harrison was taken aback. He had never seen a movie star in person.

Abigaile said, "Oh, that is Judy Garland." She was not name-dropping; it was simply an innocent comment. She had seen her the last time when the girls' trip had taken them to this place she wanted to call home.

After checking in, the Butlers were introduced to their room and the luxury of the five- star hotel. The management was waiting to invite them to a welcome-back dinner. The Baker Hotel was used to entertaining royalty and Hollywood stars, so to sit down with regular folks was a pure joy.

There was no need to put on airs or bend over backwards to impress a rather picky yet famous group of people.

With dinner plans in place, the Baker Hotel sent management up to the Butlers' room with a welcome basket of goodies and an invitation for a quiet dinner pool side.

Hoping to catch up with their poster child and the new face of the Baker Hotel, dinner was served.

Two days gone already, and a tour of the sleepy little town was planned.

The Baker Hotel was relatively close to town, so a short brisk walk was going to take place.

The noted general store was the first on their stop, known for the best milkshake this side of everywhere. Real ice cream was their secret. No artificial taste like in their signature treat.

After the afternoon delight, a stroll down the main street.

There were tiny dress stores, a jewelry store, and one very large grocery. Indeed, not a lot to look at. But what the tiny stores did not offer, the Poston's General Store did.

It took up a whopping three thousand square feet. Its main attraction was their soda fountain for the tons of visitors at the Baker, but it offered all the farmers and ranches within a hundred miles an assortment of tools and feeds for their equipment and animals of all sizes, from the chickens to the large beef cattle that became a part of the Baker Hotel gourmet menu.

Across the street from the Poston's General Store, there was a parcel of land that had no building on it. Just a huge, empty lot with a few trees, oaks and a couple of large weeping willows.

It looked like the entry to Willow Oaks Plantation. Harrison's heart stood still. He almost stopped breathing. He fell to his knees. He said out loud, "It's home."

Abigaile was so stunned with what she had seen and heard. What did this mean? Basking in the moment, Abigaile was too much in shock to ask her honey what he meant, so she simply stood silent.

The beauty of this piece of land was just breathtaking. Even though there were no leaves on the willows, the wind still waved their limbs and said welcome. The great oak trees of Texas were cloaked with evergreen leaves that provided an umbrella-like canopy from the intense sunlight of day, summer or winter.

It felt like they had never left their beloved Georgia. Peace was all around.

Lots of fabulous meals at the Baker, and the dreams of both that one day would come into the light.

Before the Butlers were ready to go home to Georgia, there were lots of walks, talks, and shopping. The list of movie stars they encountered were so many that the autograph book Abigaile had brought was completely filled.

One last walk to downtown Mineral Wells and one more vanilla milkshake from the famed Poston's General Store.

As they walked the same path they had taken for almost two weeks, there was one thing that had changed. Down Main Street, there was a sign with spear-like stakes that pierced the ground across from Poston's General Store. It was on the huge lot where the trees that looked like home were standing.

It was a for-sale sign. No price, just a phone number.

Harrison felt his heart begin to race. He began with, "Abigaile, when I was a boy, my grandfather took me and my brothers to town, and we came across a 'horseless carriage.' It was an automobile, but he insisted it was a horseless carriage. Well, ever since that time, I have had a fascination with the horseless carriage. When I was able to drive, I promised myself that one day I would own one of my own, a bright shiny car that could carry me anywhere I wanted to go. It came true. But that is not all. I have had a secret desire. I never talked to anyone about it. You are the first!"

Abigaile started to inquire when Hurley said, "No, I have to finish telling you, or I will chicken out. Here goes! I wanted a car, and I got one. I wanted you, and I was blessed with you as my wife, we got our darling Sophie Grace, and I felt as though my chest was going to explode, I was so happy. I never knew there could be anything that could top those experiences.

"But now I have found that, like the heavy cream in milk, it finds its way to the top. "My dream of something old has become something new.

"I did not know, before I saw that sign, that my boyhood fantasy could ever become a reality. I was given a third ownership in a family plantation that had been handed down since its beginning. A Butler family member has always been the caretaker of the family land we call Willow Oaks.

"I have never, until this moment seen a future anywhere else except at Willow Oaks. But then we came to Mineral Wells, Texas. The sign said that a part of Texas soil was ready for a new owner.

"It sat across from Poston's Store. The Main Street where those who came in or out drove past, the breeze blew through the trees just like at home. It whispered to me. This is home," Harrison said. "You told me many months ago about the peace you had here and the friendly people.

"I want to buy this land and start a car dealership, where cars of distinction can be purchased. Cars like Porsche and Mercedes-Benz, Rolls-Royce, Aston Martins, Jaguar, and the great American touring car, the Cadillac. It is so clear to me, this is truly my dream coming to life. I can see it all."

There was silence on the stroll back to the Baker. Abigaile was excited and fearful all at the same time. But no words were spoken.

Harrison held Abigaile's hand with the tenderness of a first date. He knew his heart, but he was unsure of how Abigaile felt.

The phone number on the for-sale sign was a local number. With Abigaile's approval, Harrison was going to make the inquiry. The phone rang two times, and there was a hello on the other end. He said, "My name is George. Who is this and can I help you?"

"Hi, hello. Hello, my name is Harrison Butler. I saw your sign."

"Yes, sir, I am George, and I own that piece of dirt. It is nearing three acres. Two across and one deep. Or I think that is the count. It is only for retail business. No home or pig farm or stockyard. Too close to people and other stores to be good business. So, what kind of business do you want to open?"

"Yes, I am interested, but first how much for the land?"

"Well, it depends! I would like to meet you first before I give you a price. I also have to access what kind of business and if it would be a good fit for my town. So, when can we meet?"

Harrison was so nervous. He told George they were staying at the Baker for one more day.

George interrupted. "How about now?

"Okay. Down by the pool in thirty minutes." "Yes, that will do. I live right down the way." "What do you look like?"

"You will know me. Everyone else does. I don't look like those movie star people, and I will have a pair of overalls on. I will put a red bandana in my front pocket."

There was just enough time for the Butlers to pray.

"Door open, Lord, or please close the door, and, Lord, we are ready whatever. Thank You."

Thirty minutes passed quickly. Just barely enough time to come downstairs and go to the pool on the other side of the lobby.

There he was! Overalls and a red bandana in his front pocket. That was George. He was clean-cut and looked like a worker from their plantation.

They exchanged greetings and got down to business. George was very direct. No mincing of words. "Son, what kind of business do you want to start in this my fair city? Is it food? We already have lots of food places. We don't have a movie theater. With all those movie people who are at the Baker, they probably would like to see themselves. Well, son, speak up."

"Mr. George, I am considering a beautiful place for people to come and buy cars of distinction. A place where people of all ages and financial means can buy the car of their dreams."

"Well, son, it sounds pretty interesting. When do you want to do this car thing?"

"I am not sure, Mr. George. I have to make plans. My family back in Georgia will have to take over my job there, and I would have to build a home here, as well as the special building that will hold these special and very distinctive automobiles. Now, Mr. George, how much is this land? I am sure you are excited about my plans. So how much? How much is the land?"

Abigaile was listening as if she were a silent partner. "Well, boy, sorry for that. I do like the idea, and it would be a nice addition to my town."

Abigaile was sipping on her iced tea and stopped for a moment. She had a couple of questions. "What is your full name, and what do you do here in this town?"

"Well, Missy! My name is George Barber. I am the owner of this piece of dirt, and I am the mayor of Mineral Wells. How did you come to know about our fair city?" George Barber was known for his very direct manner. It was as if a match was made in heaven.

There were no more inquiries. George Barber got right down to business.

It could not have been any better of a first meeting. He gave them a price. "I hope that it suits your pocketbook. I am ready right now to say yes, or do you want to haggle?" For Abigaile, it was a done deal, but Harrison wanted to haggle a bit.

Harrison asked for a few moments to talk it over with Abigaile.

Harrison wanted to offer less, but Abigaile said no. She said, "If this was yours, how would you like to be treated?"

Well, no more had to be said. Harrison agreed. His dream was just about ready to come true.

They met down at poolside, and with a short walk to the bank, Mr. and Mrs. Buder were just about to own a piece of Texas soil, but more important, the doors were opening for the hopes of a child to be the reality of a grown man.

The papers were signed, and the timing could not have been better. Tomorrow was the assigned time for their return trip back to Georgia.

Even the fear off lying Harrison had could not dampen his excitement. His dreams and belated hope were coming true.

The trip home to Georgia were filled with whats, whens, and wheres.

The purchase of Texas soil was to be kept a secret for a while. No one could know.

Meanwhile at River Bend, Grandma Abigaile Amelie was making sure all her affairs were in order.

It was only February, but Grandma felt the need to design the next years silver family ornament. The war was over, so what could be meaningful for her dear ones?

She remembered the times she gathered her dear ones together and began her stories with her signature phrase. "And the magnolias were in bloom." It was as if God had spoken to her. The silver treasure for the family was going to be a magnolia blossom.

It would take the silversmith some time because there was so much detail in this treasure.

It was a great idea to start early, because it was going to take some time.

There was another one of the Hurley family friends who had started the same tradition.

So Grandma had to jockey for the time for her creation.

With the arrival of the weary travelers, a special welcome dinner was planned.

Grandma was also digging around in her writing desk. She came across sayings and words of wisdom she had been collecting for many years.

She was planning a personal journal with all her collections for each of her family members and friends for the upcoming Christmas party months away, all gathered in a red leather book.

She Started out like this.

1. Your good is better, your better is blessed.
2. Get it into your spirit before you hold it in your hand.
3. I shall believe the report of the Lord.
4. When you pray for rain, you also have to deal with the mud.
5. Man gives information; God gives inspiration.
6. 'd rather be an optimist and a fool than be a pessimist and be right.
7. How come a bike can't stand on its own? Because it is tired.
8. Prayer does not change God, but it does change us.
9. You got married because you are in love; you stay married because you do love.
10. Sometimes people hear things and put meaning to them that were never intended.
11. Education gets you through this world; faith gets you into heaven.
12. If you need people and their approval, you are not leading the people; they are leading you.
13. Don't let the troubles of the past rob you of the joy ofthe future.
14. I just want to live a normal life without problems. There is no normal without problems. It is just life.

15. Better to let people think you are a fool, than to open your mouth and prove it. (Mark Twain).
16. God does not expect us to be beautiful, only faithful.
17. More being, less doing.
18. More understanding of others to be understood.
19. Crisis reveals character.
20. With great victory comes great sacrifices.
21. Make your home a reflection of you.
22. When you live in the past, you forfeit the present.
23. Great men do. Great men delegate.
24. Always keep your childhood innocence.
25. The most destructive force in our universe is regret.
26. Appearances are not all that count, but it is how we treasure each other each day.
27. When you are a hammer, everything and everyone looks like a nail.
28. Character does not build itself.
29. Regrets are a waste of time. They are the past crippling you in the future.
30. Mama always said, never be afraid to ask for a better price; all they can do is tell you no.
31. Don't spend your days as if it were your last, knowing you are going to die someday, but spend each day as if it were a gift.
32. Do what you love; love what you do.
33. Do something today that your future self will thank you for.
34. People are Gods hand to help.
35. I have been beaten up, but I am not beaten.
36. Why fit in when you were made to stand out?
37. Children are living messages that we send forth to a time that we will not see.

38. Without a vision, people perish.
39. Some of the greater lessons learned come with pain.
40. People matter more than things.
41. I have chosen to not be bitter, but better. It is my choice.
42. Be sincere in every word you speak.
43. I had a handle on life, but it broke.
44. Don't steal; life needs honesty.
45. You never know how strong you are until, like a tea bag, you are in hot water.
46. Death leaves a heartache that no one can heal; love leaves a memory no one can steal.
47. How can you tell if a politician is lying? His lips are moving.
48. Over the hill? I am not there yet. But I have a pretty good view from up here.
49. In a world full of problems, be the solution.
50. The best way to keep a secret is to keep it to yourself.
51. A cow is nothing but a lot of trouble tied up in a great leather handbag.
52. Do more of what you are born to do.
53. People always say, wait for the good things to come. You are the good thing.
54. You don't know how vulnerable you are until you fail.
55. NEWS: North, East, West, Sout
56. Nothing of value comes without effort.
57. Hating is easy, forgiveness is hard.
58. My anything says the River Bend is my everything.
59. Forgiveness is a sign of strength, not weakness.
60. Doing good for selfish reasons does not make you good; it just makes you good at being selfish.
61. When God guides you, He provides.

62. People fail, God rescues.
63. The most destructive force in the universe is gossip.
64. Never desire to be like someone else. That would be a copy, and an original is always better.
65. The mighty oak of today is yesterday's nut that stood its ground.
66. You can change the world one act of kindness at a time.
67. ARK: act of random kindness.
68. You live in hopes of becoming someone's memory.
69. These pants are too big. Clothes are like family. You have to live in them a while to get the perfect fit.
70. It is not a perfect life, but sometimes the fleas come with the dog.
71. Love is a two-way street.
72. Mexican Phone Co.: Taco Bell.
73. If someone prays for patience, do you think God gives him patience, or does God give us an opportunity to be patient?
74. Stars cannot shine without the darkness.
75. Every problem has a solution.
76. We do our best; that is all we have.
77. Tough times don't last. Tough men do.
78. Jesus says, "Luck will run out on you, but I will never run out on you."
79. All that is necessary for evil to succeed is for good men to do nothing.
80. We cannot gather knowledge about everything
81. We cannot experience someone else's pain, but we can forgive and assist others in their trials and joys.

82. A traveling salesman said, "If I knock on every door, I might make a sale now and then, but If I never knock on any door, I will never make a sale." Don't give up.

83. The troubles of the past can meet the reality of the future if you let it.

84. Everything in life is a work in progress, including friendship. It requires an effort in understanding others and their gifts, and blessing those who are different.

85. When you lose someone or something, don't let it dictate a path of destruction but instead a road to victories.

86. Let your faith be bigger than your fear.

87. There is no making friends with pain. Just walk through it with Jesus.

88. It is something to know everything about yourself, a whole other thing to know what to do with the information you have.

89. If God had intended us to have a permissive society, He would not have given us the Ten Commandments but the Ten Suggestions

90. Fear is a thief; it steals all you todays by making you dread tomorrow, but today is all you have. So, what are you going to do?

91. Hatred in a man's heart makes its way to the words of his mouth, and vile works follow from his hand.

92. The sign of a beautiful person is that they always see the beauty in others.

93. Educating the mind without educating the heart is no education at all.

94. Story of Easter: Death came on Friday, life on Sunday, but there was a very hard day in between.

95. Story of Easter: Death came on Friday, life on Sunday, but there was a very hard day in between.
96. Love is a choice
97. You can't do everything all the time, so do one thing great each time.
98. Life is full of Nevers.
99. She traded the power of love for the love of power.
100. Responsibility is not a burden but a privilege
101. Everybody fails sometimes.
102. Peace is a virtue; virtue is a grace. Put them together; it makes a happy face.
103. Forgiveness is not a sign of weakness, but one of strength.
104. Hating is easy, forgiveness is hard
105. Your heart and your soul are like a river; it can be poisoned very easily if you are not careful.
106. A world of hate begins with a room full of anger that starts with one single thought.
107. There can be no buts when you ask for forgive ness; no conditions.
108. It is not a sin to be a survivor but a gift.
109. The color of racism is fear.
110. Stand and risk rejection.
111. Don't stop trying, do keep loving.
112. For every time you are hurt, there is a choice. Stay or walk away.
113. We are love or hate in action.

This were some of Grandma Abigaile Amelies pearls of wisdom.

She told the story of a pearl. The oyster is in a large body of water. It swallows a small grain of sand. He does not feel comfortable with the foreign substance. It has invaded his home. He begins by covering the sand grain with a lubricant.

It is not a comfortable situation for the oyster. So, what does he do? Well, he continues to cover the grain of sand with the shiny lubricant. Each time he covers the grain of sand, it hardens, and the size of the sand grain grows with layers of an iridescent milky covering, making a luster that not even a rainbow after a rain could rival. In fact, it looks like the colors of pastel everything.

The oyster never expels the lustrous sand grain. It keeps layering it year after year.

When it is found by a pearl diver and he opens it, it reveals a gem of such beauty that the Bible says they are in the gates of heaven.

But you have to know, that beautiful gem would have never gotten that way unless it encountered a problem.

We are like that oyster. We can produce a gem of beauty for all to see if we keep on trying, no matter how hard things might be. For in time everything changes.

CHAPTER 19

Lasting Impressions Forever Memories

GRANDMA ABIGAILE AMELIE was a lady a lady with great skills and organizational ability.

The toys were being collected and stored at River Bend.

The second year of her dream of giving to the children of Americas military heroes was underway.

The lady who had always made the invitations for the annual Hurley Christmas party was commissioned for the "words of wisdom" book that Grandma had gathered for her party parting gift at the annual Hurley Christmas party. She was almost finished. Just a few more to go, then they would be carried to the bookmaker and placed inside the red leather cover Grandma had picked out once again.

The silversmith was also completing the masterpieces that Grandma Abigaile designed, the magnolia.

With so many books to wrap and toys to organize, Grandma had her hands full.

Bertie Mae had taken over the food pantry chores. But wrapping a hundred books and the silver memories for her family was going to keep her pretty busy.

In the meantime, the secret that Abigaile Grace and Harrison were keeping just about leaked out to Grandma Abigaile.

After the month of October, Thanksgiving was in sight. The table would be holding two more place settings.

Edward and Carter were about to be married to their loves. Addie Paige was Edward's sweetie pie, and Emily Mae was Carters honey.

This was truly going to be a very busy end of the year. Weddings were planned one week before the Hurley Christmas party and one week after.

So, there was Thanksgiving, wedding party, wedding, and Christmas. All within four weeks of each other.

So, wrapping paper and tape were bought in huge supply. Grandma Abigaile made one slight change-up in her parting party gifts. She was going to place a golden bow around each of the hundred books and make the red leather and gold ribbons be the front-table decor that encircled the tall floral that would show off the flowers of Christmas, and the color of love, red, in loads of shades, from a pinkish red to a lipstick red. A truly magnificent welcoming feast for the eyes and all the guests that would grace the grand old halls of River Bend.

The long mahogany table was dressed in Miss Matilda's green China, and the silver trays of history were removed from the silver closet. The holiday feast was placed inside each bowl and on each platter.

A turkey and duck were cooked to perfection, golden brown. Sweet potatoes and regular mashed potatoes were overflowing; beets and cranberries were surrounding the tender, golden-brown turkey and duck. A duck pate was laid upon a bed of lettuce, pomegranates were halved, and small round red droplets of fruit fell upon the slices of fresh oranges; there was a boat of gravy that would sink a battle ship, pickles, homemade bread and butter, sweets, and the family's favorite dill. And of course, dressing and homemade rolls.

Emily Mae and Addie Paige were taking in all the festivities. Knowing that soon they were going to be part of this family made them excited for the day when their last name would be Hurley.

Thanksgiving was the same everywhere. Everyone ate too much.

That was the case again this year at River Bend. Leftovers would be shared with those coming to the food pantry. Again, the blessings of bounty were on display.

Grandma Abigaile had filled her petite frame with more food than she normally ate in two days. She was stuffed just like the turkey. She asked her dear namesake to assist her to her bedroom upstairs.

This might be the perfect time for Abigaile Grace to share her secret with Grandma Abigaile.

As they approached the landing upstairs, Grandma said, "I want to talk to you, my sweet." My darling, my dear, I have lived many years here on this earth. I have seen our family tree increase.

I have loved and lost. My dreams of love when I was young kept me hopeful, then I met my Mr. Hurley. An older gentleman.

The lessons my parents taught me I still today practice. My love for people has given me many friends. But when the war, the Civil War, erupted, River Bend was under attack.

The silver and China we have used for years was hidden from the enemy. Thus, we were able to preserve our treasures for our family.

Even in the midst of this adversity, we tried to treat others like we would want to be treated.

Then I raised my children and worked very hard. We, Mr. Hurley, and I continued to purchase acres of land to build up what you know as River Bend.

We worked really hard, and God blessed us. Our crops were increasing each year in production. The acres just seem to bring in more and more. Mr. Hurley and I knew it was the Lord who was multiplying our bounty. We had only Him to say thank you to.

We put money aside for rainy days, and it grew each year.

The Depression hit, and the rainy-day funds came in handy. We got through those hard times, then Mr. Hurley died, and my world became a routine where I woke up and performed my duties like a robot. I went to church, but I didn't know what the pages of my red leather Bible said on how to survive loss.

Then the preacher challenged everyone. I still didn't listen, but sometime after that, I actually opened the Bible, and it was like the sweet tooth I have. I had a little and wanted more. Then I was not able to go a day without my sugar fix. The Bible.

For so many years now, it has been my road map. My phone line to God has had many hours logged in.

Now I want to tell you about you and how you made me look at life differently. Your momma and daddy blessed me so, when they chose to name you Abigaile. You lived in a home with family members who were as old as River Bend.

I welcomed your mom and dad to my home, and it made my home alive again. My Mr. Hurley had built this home to be a blessing for his family. Here you are, and you are a part of his legacy. It is because of that fact that I have made special arrangements for you, your mom and dad, and your two brothers. You are married now, no longer living here, but you are a Hurley. You are therefore a part owner in River Bend.

You no longer assist in day-to-day running of the plantation, but I have divided my ownership into four portions. Ninety percent is divided three ways, forty percent to your mom and dad, and twenty-five to each of your brothers. You will retain ten percent of the ownership and ten percent of all profit from the moment I met Mr. Hurley. But before I do, I have a little something from me to you, my namesake. I put this back for you since you were very young. In my day, they called it a dowry. I have done the same for each of your brothers.

You can collect it at the bank when you want. My gift to you from Grandpa Hurley.

Now, darling, what do you need to tell me?

*****

A knock on the door, but Grandma said, "Not now."

"Grandma, do you remember our girls' trip? You became the new faces of the Baker Hotel, and Sophie Grace was the youngest visitor to the Mineral Springs? Harrison took me to that piece of heaven last February. I fell in love again with the people and the town of Mineral Wells, Texas. Harrison was taken with it just like I was.

"We stayed at the Baker Hotel and walked to town every day. On the last day before we were due to come back home, we stopped and had a milkshake at the Poston's General Store. As we were on our way out of the store, right across the street, we saw a sign. On the sign were the words Tor Sale.' It was not there before. It was like it appeared right before our eyes. Harrison stopped and looked like a marble statue, his eyes glazed over.

"He was holding on to a secret, but I had no idea. We sat on the park bench and then walked back to the hotel. On our way back, he shared his dream of years ago."

"His dream! What is his dream, darling?"

"Grandma, he loves cars. Beautiful cars. He wants to order and sell cars in Mineral Wells, Texas. He wants to start small, used cars first and then some European cars.

"The property across from Poston's General Store had willow trees and oaks on it. It was the one that had the for sale sign on it. We bought it. We are now owners of part of Texas soil. That is where Harrison wants to do his car dealership."

"Well, my sweet Abigaile, that is lots to take in. When?"

"Grandma, it will not be for a while. Harrison's brothers are back at Willow Oaks. They have been learning the ins and outs of Willow Oaks since they have been gone. Harrison wants to turn over part of his ownership of Willow Oaks. His brothers want to live there at Willow Oaks and raise families there. Harrison has not told them yet, but he knows in time it will come up.

"We have to build a house and the dealership first. It will take nearly two years to accomplish.

"You are the only one who knows. We haven't told anyone else yet. We are talking to God about the plans, and we will know sooner or later when it should be."

As Grandma was listening to her dear one, she noticed a gleam appear and a tear fall from Abigaile's eyes.

Grandma knew the sign. This was going to be a reality. Her namesake was going to move to Texas. It was Grandma Abigaile who knew things were changing, but this news took her by surprise.

The feather mattress was calling, and as both Abigaile's had shared their hearts, a calm covered them, and they both fell asleep.

A short two-hour nap, and both awoke with smiles on their face.

They joined the rest of the family, and all began the stories of what they were thankful for.

Addie Paige and Emily Mae had a feeling of belonging. The Hurley family was growing, and Grandma found true joy that her babies' babies had found love.

A trip home for the Butlers, and the end of a day of revelation and truth, first impressions, and lasting love memories were shared.

Now young Abigaile Grace's heart had a secret. When would she tell Harrison about the big dowry? It would be soon, because she didn't keep anything from him.

Grandma Abigaile Amelie had one more thing to cross off her list. Her mission was to get all her affairs in order, and the list had two less things on it. Now she was looking for her dear Bertie Mae.

Everybody had recovered from Thanksgiving and two weddings, a Christmas party, kid's toys, and the food pantry were all coming up.

So much in such a short time. But it was like Miss Matilda, Grandma's friend, always said, how do you eat an elephant? She would answer herself and begin to dance. You eat an elephant one bite at a time!

This would always make her laugh, and then things didn't seem so bad.

That is exactly how things would be handled. One bite at a time. Besides, nothing was on the same day, so it definitely was something that could be done.

Bertie Mae was arranging volunteers for food pantry duty for the month of December. Grandma Abigaile and Abigaile Grace were searching for people to help wrap and catalog the toys for the military heroes' children.

The red leather books of Grandmas sayings were already tied with the gold ribbon and ready for placement on the entry table for the big Hurley Christmas party.

Things were very busy for everyone. But one thing that was in the Hurleys' favor was that the weddings and receptions were not at River Bend.

Grandma was still waiting for her special time with Bertie Mae, then out of nowhere, a lull in all the goings-on.

Bertie Mae and Grandma took a seat in the grand hall. With a glass of iced tea in hand, Grandma began.

"I have wanted to tell you long ago, and I just kept putting it off.

"When you came to River Bend, I found a hole in my heart began to fill. I have lived a long time. I have seen many changes in our land. But I never knew that the change I needed to experience was you. You were the daughter I never had. A friendship that I never knew I was longing for. When you and Edward named your daughter after me, I came alive again. You gave me hope and a love that I never knew.

"I know you are not my daughter, but I could never have asked, wished, or wanted anyone more perfect. It has been my honor and privilege to have you, Bertie Mae, in my family. Thank you for loving me as you have. You have filled the gap, and made me a very happy little old Southern lady.

"My darling, you have been a light in my life that makes me shine brighter each day that I am here.

"Before we end this talk, hold out your hand. I am giving you a ring that my Mr. Hurley gave me many years ago."

Bertie Mae looked down as Grandma Abigaile Amelie placed a ring of gold with ruby and seed pearls onto her hand. It fit like a glove. Tears fell down Bertie Mae's face, and each were speechless.

The hug was so precious, but the grooms-to-be interrupted the moment.

No words were left to be spoken, just a never-ending smile that was evident to the ladies of River Bend.

Bertie Mae always loved Abigaile Amelie, but now a depth of respect and love was more evident than ever before.

As all were ready for the first wedding celebration, Bertie Mae grabbed her new old ruby ring, and it completed her dress for the wedding.

Edward saw the ring and asked about the gift. Tears began to trickle down Bertie Mae's face as she shared about the exchange. "It was a love gift from my new mom! I really never knew how she felt about me because I married into the Hurley family. You know the in-law thing, but I can tell you I have always loved Grandma Abigaile Amelie, my new mom, ever since we have lived here."

The wedding came off in great fashion, and the Hurley family had a new member.

Grandma was blessed to see her family growing. Her name was Addie Paige Hurley.

One wedding down, and the next week the annual Hurley Christmas party.

The time seemed to fly by. The Hurley party was one day away. The flowers were set atop the entry table and the red leather books encircled the lead crystal vase. Red flowers and red leather books welcomed the party guests, along with a table of delicacies to please every palate. The tree decorations were glistening and drew each guest into the great hall. The fire was glowing, and the warmth invited the guests to come closer. A good time was enjoyed by all. There was music, friends, food, and a goodie to take home.

The guests were the same as in the years past. Again, just like last year, there was one guest who just couldn't wait to see what was inside the red leather book. She opened it and began to read. At first, she read silently. Then she began to laugh. This was just like last year. All stopped and stood quietly and listened with an anticipation of what was going to be read next.

Unlike last year, with the poem Grandma Abigaile had written, this year's offering was more on the lighter side, from serious to joyful laughter. It was another book that would grace the bookcases and end tables of the party guests for years to come, a feather in Grandma's cap. It was a winner! A book of memories and words of wisdom one could take home and live by and laugh with.

Some asked Grandma if she had ever thought of being a writer. No was her answer. That was not her calling. This book was a one- or two-time effort, probably no more, unless God inspired her again.

Guests were leaving River Bend, and the snow began to fall. By the time the last of the party guests had left, there was a blanket of white. So much had fallen that you could not see anything except the gleaming white blanket of sparkling snow. It was like a clean load of bleached white laundry everywhere. The moonlight seemed to light up the snow like the chandeliers did inside. A pale shade of colors like a rainbow after a rain was all across the lawn and atop all the trees that surrounded this home of history and love.

Leftovers were saved for sharing at the food pantry.

Before the second wedding was going to take place, the toy drive had to be completed. One more food pantry distribution, and the family silver memento had to be placed under the pillows of each Hurley member.

Again, Grandma had left a memory for each of her dear ones. Another trip down memory lane each would take for years to come.

Grandma had made one extra silver magnolia and placed it under her namesake's pillow. When Abigaile Grace found the two magnolias, she knew Grandma Abigaile Amelie had been on the phone party line with God again. She was going to be a momma again. She had not told anyone. Harrison and Abigaile wanted to announce the blessing at the family Christmas Day dinner.

Grandma Abigaile was on point, and she didn't even know about the news the Butlers were going to share, but then again, this was not the first time she had talked or listened to God. She had an impressive track record, but Grandma Abigaile, just like her namesake, couldn't stand the secret she was keeping. So, the phone call to her dear one, Abigaile Grace, was placed.

From the moment Mrs. Butler answered the phone, a shout of great tidings came forth from Grandma Abigaile. "You are going to have a baby! God told me. That's true, yes?

"Yes, Grandma. It is true."

"And God said, Abigaile Grace, it is a little girl!"

"She is due in May. We have already picked out her name, Kaity Cory Butler."

"God told me she would have dark hair and blue eyes. She would be a spitting image of her daddy."

Well, this would be another member added to the Hurley clan. What a blessing!

Emily Mae was due to become a Hurley family member in two days.

Everyone was ready for the celebration. Her flowers were white for her bouquet, and she had ten bridesmaids. Her attendants all wore rich amethyst purple and dresses with collars of white fur.

Instead of a huge bouquet, Emily Mae chose a white fur muff made of the same fur as the collars on her bridesmaids' dresses. Emily Mae was not traditional, so everything about her wedding was very unique.

Emily Mae had a fan. Grandma Abigaile was just like her. Unique, different, and unpredictable. She was going to fit well into this, her new family, Grandma Abigaile could bet on it.

Another Hurley added to the family tree, and Emily Mae was her name. Carter and Emily would wait to honeymoon until after Christmas Day. Carter knew it may be his last Christmas with his Grandma Abigaile. After all, she was getting up there, and those are memories you cannot regain.

Grandma Abigaile was not surprised. Carter was a very sensitive young man, and they had shared many special moments together.

With all the hubbub over, the week of Christmas was a moment for peace and quiet. Grandma Abigaile had surprise after surprise this year, and for the first time, she was ready to sit out everything for a while.

Bertie Mae had the food pantry under control, the toy drive was over, and the two weddings were behind them. The family Hurley Christmas party was a no-brainer. It had been a staple for so many years. It practically arranged itself.

With particular things crossed off the list Grandma Abigaile had made, she felt a real sense of accomplishment. A few more trips to the lawyer, and her list would be complete.

Rest was on everyone's list; no parties to attend, and no more weddings to plan or attend.

Just Christmas Day dinner, and the news the Butlers would get to surprise the family with.

The table was set with Miss Matilda's green China and the ruby-red stemware, and once again the Civil War silver graced the table.

Another opportunity for God to show off. It was snowing again, the fire was burning inside in each room downstairs. The warmth beckoned all to relax.

Thanks to all the busy weeks that December, everyone had dressed in their comfy clothes. The Christmas feast was ready to enjoy. It looked very similar to the Thanksgiving feast, with one exception. A small suckling pig baked and presented with a red apple in its mouth.

Could anyone complain about the cold weather outside? There was no mention of that at all. Just joyful hearts and plenty of blessings for the year to come and the birth of Jesus. The reason for the season, after all.

Grandma was helped upstairs, and she realized that she had not told everyone how much she loved them. She had always thanked God for them all but was not that good at thanking each for their love and sharing their whole life with a century-old Southern lady.

First thing in the morning, she knew she had to con vey her feelings, more now because that was her directive from God.

Each new day that Grandma met reminded her that no one knows when their time on earth is over. A bounty frill of blessings and praise were on Grandmas lips. Every time she blessed her family, she felt sunshine and hope enter her heart.

With Abigaile and Harrison expecting again, Grandma was noticing the changes in her namesake's little tummy. She was showing the gift of life that was growing inside of her.

Grandma would touch her tummy and pray blessings over her little Kaity Cory, the newest family member with the last name Hurley-Butler.

The Texas dream was moving ahead. Some plans for the car dealership were being prepared. The house plans were beginning to show promise. Abigaile was set on a plantation- style house located in town and close to the Baker Hotel and their new business. They had secured the land across from Poston's for the dealership but nothing yet for their home. Mr. Barber, the mayor, was on the lookout and had two possibilities. One was outside of town; they turned it down rather quickly. The second was close to the Baker and a walking distance to the dealership.

Mr. Barber had never been to Georgia, so he decided to take a trip and bring all the information to his new friends the Butlers. If they were going to buy, he had everything in hand to make the sale and present a deed of ownership to them.

Mr. Barber was a huge supporter of the Butlers' new venture. He was willing to promote his town in any way he could, so the trip to Georgia was a town expense.

The pictures and the location were just what they wanted. With the dowry Grandma Abigaile had blessed them with, they paid cash. Now they were true Texas land owners, and the move was on for sure. Leftover dowry money would build their home. The snow was covering all Georgia. It was a blanket of purity covering all the high ways and byways. Mr. Barber was amazed; the beauty was breathtaking. On his way back to Texas, he knew this couple would become a part of Mineral Wells history.

Carter and Edward were returning home from their honeymoons, and business at River Bend was in full swing.

Grandma finished her business at the lawyers, and now all things on her list were crossed off. Abigaile Grace was doing well with her pregnancy. Harrisons brothers were back at Willow Oaks and were teaching lessons every day on the new crops and times for harvest. Aaron and Jeffery were relearning plantation life. Their times in the military taught them more discipline and attention to detail. But the plantation had gone through some changes.

Harrison was training his replacements. His brothers had no idea. The plan for now, was to be still and prepare the Buder brothers for the rules of new plantation life. Also, little baby Kaity Cory needed to be born and have a chance to know her four uncles and Bertie Mae and Edward Darnell, her grandparents.

There were only four months left until Kaity Cory would say hello to the world.

It was February, and the weather was changing. The snow had stopped falling, and the spring buds were trying to emerge.

Valentines just two weeks away. Harrison told Abigaile Grace the future home site (land) was their Valentines gift to each other. She agreed.

There was no argument. The upcoming move had to be kept quiet. Things were just not ready yet to inform every one of the changes of address, but like everything, the time would reveal itself in time.

Grandma Abigaile was preparing her Valentine gifts for her dear family.

Grandma remembered the handmade cards her Mr. Hurley had given her each year since they met. This was going to be what she would do for her dear ones.

A trip to the store and a list of craft items she would need to complete her cards. But when she arrived, she found she was missing the one thing she wanted to complete her gift. She ran out of the store. Well, ran was not the term for a lady of her age. It was more like a slow, slow giddy-up. Grandma Abigaile Amelie had forgotten the silver hearts. As she hurried, she knew.

It was truly a gift from God because as she entered the silversmith workshop, he was in a mode of nothing to do. His worktable was empty. No jobs to start or finish. It was the most perfect timing.

Grandma Abigaile had been a customer for so many years, he knew she had another project for him.

She said, "You have to help! I forgot the hearts!"

"What?" he said.

"I forgot my hearts!"

"Calm down, my dear. How big? How many? When?" Grandma took a breath and knew he had her back.

"Well, I need one for each of my family, plus one. My namesake is expecting."

"When?"

"Can you do it for me in one week?" "How big?"

"Between three and four inches."

"Yes, can do. One week from today, they will be Grandma said, "Remember to put a hole in the top so it can be hung on the family memory trees."

Back to the store and the supplies for Grandmas homemade valentines. She also picked up some linen stationery paper. Grandma had a special saying from a playwright of long ago.

Thornton Wilder wrote, "Money is like manure. It is not worth a thing unless it is spread around encouraging young things to grow."

She was going to hand-write this saying on each of her valentines. Along with a check for each of her family members. Except for Abigaile Grace. She got hers already.

For Bertie Mae and Edward Darnell, there was a double portion. They had been such a huge help just when Grandma needed it the most. After Mr. Hurley had passed, she was alone.

And a woman with such a large responsibility needed a man's help. So, Grandma wanted to bless her deliverers doubly.

Hours alone in her room produced the most amazingly beautiful handmade Valentines. The insert was hand written and showed the aging hands penmanship. A little shaky and sometimes a double line, but all would be able to read it clearly enough to get the gist. After all, whose hand is as steady at 105 as when they were twenty? But Grandma knew this was her swan song. She wanted everything to be perfect. All she needed now was the silver hearts. But they would not be ready for another four days. Grandma just wanted everything to be perfect for this Valentines.

Grandma Abigaile Amelie wanted her days, no matter how many she had left, to be filled with purpose and blessings.

As for the Butlers, great news, the plan was going to be revealed Valentines Day. The move to Texas was going to take place, and Willow Oaks was going to be in good hands.

Aaron and Jeffery Buder were picking up the job as if no time had passed. All that Harrison had to do was okay the plans for the dealership building, and Abigaile Grace the home plans for the plantation-style home that she grew up in. She wanted a picture-perfect replica of River Bend. Big and white, walk-through windows, fireplaces, and a beautiful curved stairway. Oh, and a bathroom and closets for each bedroom. As the wishes and wants for the River Bend replica were added up, the squared footage came to 6,500 square feet.

Grandma Abigaile forgot one thing. She called up the silversmith and asked if he could engrave "I love you" on the hearts. It was not a problem, but he told Abigail it would add another day to her completed order. She agreed; now it would be five days until the hearts would be completed.

One more day closer, and now it was four more days before her hearts would be ready. But Grandma had to make another change. She called the silversmith and asked for the engraving to say, "From my heart to yours. Love, Grandma Abigaile, 1947."

"No problem! But it will add another day to your order, okay?" "No problem."

Now it was back to five more days, but Grandma felt that would not pose an issue.

The days passed rather quickly. Grandma had her handwritten notes all done. Another trip to the store to pick up the heart-shaped boxes she would place her love gifts in. As she walked in, she immediately saw the heart box display. She did her slow, slow giddy-up run toward the prize. She asked for one to assist her because as she counted, she found she couldn't hold that many by herself. As she counted the ruby-red heart-shaped boxes, she began to panic. "I am down to the last boxes! Oh no. Is there enough?" She took a breath and recounted. "Wonderful. Thank You, Lord. There was just enough and one left over."

Grandma noticed the lady behind her pacing up and down. She looked like a nervous cat in a cage. The lady asked, abruptly, "Are you finished?"

"Yes, dear. How many do you need?" Grandma was always noticing others and wanted to help.

The lady was embarrassed and said quietly, "One, just one."

"Wonderful," Grandma said. "God saved one just for you." They walked out with what they came for, both happy.

With the days passing and all the preparations, Grandmas Valentines was ready. The silver hearts were ready to be picked up, and the bank drafts were being completed.

Grandma had eight days left to finish the assembly of her Valentine gifts for her dear ones.

Grandma Abigaile was planning a noontime dinner for all her family. She wanted there to be red heart decorations everywhere. The long mahogany dining table was going to be dressed in the fine linen, the dishes would be ruby-red China, and the stemware the same color. The silver serving dishes were coming out of the silver cabinet once again, with lots of red roses and their sweet smells.

This was going to be an explosion of red and hearts everywhere, to remind everyone of love and family.

Grandma had two more days before her Valentines extravaganza was to take place.

She had taken a short stroll up to the family cemetery where her boys were laid to rest with their daddy, Mr. Hurley, Grandmas great love.

There seemed to be worry and joy expressed on Abigaile Amelies face. Smiles, laughter, and tears. Not a word was spoken. It was quiet; you could hear a pin drop.

Grandmas' thoughts were not spoken, but anyone could see she longed to see her God and Mr. Hurley, her first and only love once again.

Little did anyone know about when time is up, but it looked like she had a clue. At any rate, once again, time would tell.

On her walk back to the house, she noticed that the magnolia trees were beginning to show signs of budding. It would not be long before there would be the sweet smell of magnolias to perfume the Southern air. Something to look forward to. It was one of Mr. Hurleys favorite times of the year.

The feather mattress called to Grandma a little bit early. Yet it was just in time. Grandma was tired.

One day until the party. Abigaile Grace arrived at River Bend to do a short visit with Bertie Mae and Grandma Abigaile.

The time was exciting; the baby, Kaity Cory, was moving a lot and loved the music that Grandma Abigaile was playing. Litle bumps and movement were already showing off the musical talent they knew she would have, for she, Kaity Cory, would only move that way when music was playing.

Everyone was excited about Grandmas party. All would show up the next day right on time, as Grandmas requested, noon.

The mattress filled with feathers called out to Grandma once again. She laid her little body down and fell fast asleep.

She had slept through the night without awakening once. Breakfast was ready, and everyone arrived downstairs.

No decorations had been put out yet, and no one could have had a clue as to the upcoming festivities. It was going to be a surprise, orchestrated by one cunning little Southern lady who had lived through three wars and a love that was lost; she could not have been more excited to share her love for her family once again.

As all went about their chores and duties. Grandma requested all to stay away until noon.

Bertie Mae was a little suspicious. Yet she respected her Abigaile Amelie, so she didn't dare ask.

With everyone out of the house, the party decorations were revealed, hearts, flowers, linens, and China; the silver cabinet was opened and the silver serving bowls and platters were hauled out in multiples. Everything sparkled like a beautiful diamond. The roses were not in vases but laid blossom to blossom, the length of the grand dining table.

Grandma did her slow giddy-up run upstairs and retrieved her valentine boxes. She had also made name cards for each place, a place card with hearts and flowers and each person's name handwritten by Grandma Abigaile herself.

The time was coming close to noon, and Grandma had just one more thing to do. She went back upstairs and changed into a dress that was the color of love, red. This dress was a belle skirt with a drop-shouldered bodice. It was one she had made for this special occasion.

Grandma was setting the mood for old Southern dress and hospitality.

No one else would be dressed this way, but this was her party, her way, for her family, one she knew they would all remember.

The time had come. The party guests were all arriving.

The clock chimed twelve times, and the entire family was present as Grandma Abigaile had requested.

The hostess greeted each person and thanked them for being on time but most of all for being her family.

Each person was escorted to the great dining hall. As they entered, they saw love all around, not just in the table settings and decor but in the faces of each Hurley member's face.

Grandma had captured a moment in time that would never be forgotten by her family. Stuffed chickens and dumplings were the main course, with wine rice, green tomatoes, string beans, and collard greens; these were Grandmas favorite.

It was like when the loves of history said I love you, this was Grandma Abigaile Amelies way, in word and action and food.

There was no pomp, just a desire to bless those closest to her.

With tummies full, Grandma Abigaile offered another prayer and wanted her valentines to be opened. There was a count to three, and everyone dove in. The room was silent. The first thing each member saw was the silver heart. Each person held a piece of Grandma Abigaile s love. They read the inscription. Tears began to fall. Emily Mae and Addie Paige were completely taken aback; neither one had known this type of love.

Yes, their parents loved them, but this was a type of love that made their hearts melt. Grandma was God's love, and it was felt by the two newest members of the Hurley clan.

The rest of the valentine gift was visible as soon as the hearts were removed.

The room stood still and silent again.

Grandma stood up and began to speak. "Now, I want everyone to know that it is my pleasure to bless you. When Mr. Hurley and I started River Bend, we knew our days would come to an end. We wanted to bless our family. So, this part of the blessing, the money, is for you to start something of your choosing.

"But remember to be wise in your decisions. Also, there are legal documents that the lawyers will read to you after I am no more.

"River Bend was started by a Hurley, and the hope is it will be a Hurley plantation forever." The party was coming to an end; dessert was still to be served. A five-layer red velvet cake with a luscious cream cheese frosting was presented to each Hurley member on a ruby-red crystal cake plate. A little extra for the sweet tooth, that each had inherited from Grandma Abigaile.

An afternoon nap was calling Grandma Abigaile. As she ascended the stairs, her heart skipped a beat. She was full of joy knowing she had completed her chores and her love party. But she was just pooped, more than usual. A short nap for all was in order.

All joined together for the evening meal. Leftovers were served. It was a Valentines feast all over.

Grandma was filled twice in one day with her favorite foods, a treat that pleased her vision and her tummy twice. Who could complain

From the time Grandma had begun her love Valentine's party, the buds on the magnolias were growing, and it would not be long before the sweet smell and large white blooms would be covering the Georgia countryside.

This was a time when Grandma Abigaile and her love would walk the grounds of River Bend. Plans were made for the future and their love would bloom fresh for another year.

This was when Grandmas signature phrase came into her life. "And the magnolias were in bloom."

This was how she began her life with Mr. Hurley and her stories with her dear ones, with that saying. It could not have been more appropriate for this Southern belle.

Like all of us, we have seasons of sweet blooming blossoms, and other seasons are like the cold harsh winter that hides the signs of life. These are rough times.

But even the harsh days of winter when her life seemed empty and without purpose, God had a plan, and the magnolias would bloom again for Grandma.

The soft feather bed that Grandma had slept in for years and years called once again. It called soft and sweet, come join me.

After all the thank-you and I love you, all retreated to their bedrooms.

Everyone couldn't stop talking about the party.

Grandma Abigaile Amelie placed her Valentine s dress upon a hanger and put her nightie on. The stiff crinoline petticoat hung on another hanger next to the red beauty. The look on Grandmas face was priceless. Joy flooded her every wrinkle and tears of peace, joy, and exhaustion dripped from her eyes.

As she looked around her room, she saw the picture of love where she and Mr. Hurley shared their life together.

She lay in bed and prayed for her family to be safe. She prayed that Kaity Cory would be that special blessing to all who would know her. Emily Mae and Addie Paige were remembered also.

As she drifted off to sleep, if you were a fly on the wall, you could see a smile that shone all the way up to heaven. She had met her Mr. Hurley and her Creator during the night. Her time was over.

This was a true joy realized by a dear sweet Southern belle who had lived for a century plus, a lady who left a legacy, not one of money but love and family.

She had finished her work on earth. The food pantry was going to live on, and the toy drive would find a purpose that would carry on for a long time to come.

The life and legacy of the Hurley family continue.

The plantation, River Bend, is retained by Hurley descendants, and the crops of yesterday's past still grow and are harvested to bless our country.

The Butler brothers ran Willow Oaks and handed down their legacy to the next generations, one after the other.

Harrison and Abigaile Grace had two daughters when they moved to Mineral Wells, Texas. Harrison opened his car dealership and sold automobiles of distinction to the farmers, ranchers, and Hollywood stars.

Abigaile Grace raised her girls, and offered to her friends and her family words of wisdom, saying there was always time for Jesus. This was her signature saying.

Grandma Abigaile would have been proud.

Memories are what ties a family together down throughout the generations, and memories are the greatest gift a mom and dad can give to their children.

THE END

HURLEY FAMILY TREE

1) Katherine Ottile Schrade
   m. Jeffery Harper Koenig
   a) Ottile Amelie Koenig
   m. Edward Charles Brandt

1) Floyd Everett Brand
   m. Caryn Camille Carter
  a) Abigaile Amelie Brandt
   m. Abner Darnell Hurley

1)Carter Jefferson Beauregard Hurley

2)Edward Harper Oakley Hurley
   m. Sophie Elizabeth Schrade
  a) Edward Darnell Hurley
   m. Bertie Mae Harpe

1)Carter Jefferson Beauregard Hurley
   m. Emily Mae Fuller

2)Edward Darnell Oakley Hurley
   m. Addie Page Ebrom

3)Abigaile Grace Hurley
   m. Harrison Darcey Butler
   a)Sophie Grace Buder
   b)Kaity Cory Bude

BUTLER FAMILY TREE

1)Genell Elizabeth San Roman
   m. Samuel Clayton Ten Boom
   a)Lexie Kenna Ten Boom
   m. Everett Edwin James

1) Douglas Charles Ten Boom James
   m. Priscilla Marie Lyn Lazlow
   a) Josephine Janet James
   m. Gregory Patrick Butler

1) Arron Jeffery Poe Buder
   m. Delila Grace Willingham
   a) Lawrence Alexander Butler
   m. Temperance Star Goodso

1) Thomas Joseph Buder
   m. Rebecca Ann Riley
   a) Harrison Darcey Buder
   m. Abigaile Grace Hurley

1)Sophie Grace Buder

2)Kaity Cory Buder
   b)Arron Lazlow Buder
   c)Jeffey James Butle

ABOUT THE AUTHOR

With words and a very vivid imagination, Tela Dawson can transport you into a world of yesteryear, where you become a part of living history, living as they did, always seeing the glass half full, never half empty.

Her hopes and dreams have become entangled with the characters of this must-read novel.

She can compel you to read page after page, and then another.

She was educated in private schools, but it is the school of this world that has given her memories to share in story form.

Blessed to awake each day and proclaim life again, she works with integrity, strength, and character.

She blesses her family and reaches out to others with a desire to give and give again. She is blessed with family and friends and offers smiles and prayers for all.

Maturity is her great teacher, and wisdom she holds in great esteem.

9 798889 639 3887